THE SNO

THE SNOW CRYSTALS

KENDRA HALE

Publishing
Covers & Formatting

http://paradoxbooktrailerproductions.blogspot.com.au

DEDICATION

To Marie (1915-2005), a sorely missed, dearly loved friend, mentor, author and never-ending inspiration.

CONTENTS

THIS BOOK WAS WRITTEN WITH THE INTENTION OF SHOWCASING BRITAIN AND LIFE IN THE COTSWOLDS TO THE BEST OF THE AUTHOR'S ABILITIES. PLEASE REFER TO THE SHORT COMPENDIUM OF TERMS BELOW FOR ANY COLLOQUIALISMS OR TYPICAL BRITISH TERMS YOU MAY FIND DIFFICULT TO UNDERSTAND.

The Cotswolds - The rolling hills and farmland of the Cotswolds was designated an Area of Outstanding Natural Beauty in 1966. The area constitutes a range of hills in Southwestern and West-Central England, 25 miles across and 90 miles long, lies mainly in the counties of Gloucestershire and Oxfordshire, and extends into parts of Somerset, Warwickshire, Wiltshire and Worcestershire. The area is characterised by charming small towns and picture-postcard villages, with many houses built in Cotswolds stone, a yellow oolitic limestone limestone. The wool trade made the area prosperous in the Middle Ages, and to this day, the area remains affluent and attracts the well-to-do and wealthy.

In The Snow Crystals, the market town of Combe-Norton, and the villages of South Woodside and Thatch Hall are entirely fictional.

A&E - the Accident and Emergency department in
hospitals

AGA - a cast iron heat storage stove and range cooker,
which is very popular especially in rural/countryside
homes.

amidst - among

bin - garbage can

Blackpool - a very popular seaside town in the North
East of England, amongst others famous for its rather
excessive illuminations.

bloody - a British slang intensifier; for instance: bloody
good, bloody idiot

(car) boot/carboot sales - a much loved, - often, too,
year round - British Sunday past-time as many load up
their cars and vans to sell their unwanted items or
wares in designated areas, be it a farmer's field, a
marketplace, or a town's or city's car park. And many,
many more descend on the carboot sales in search of
treasures.

Canary Wharf - one of London's two main financial
centres, which is tailor-made for careerists, offers every
conceivable convenience, but mainly excels in business.

chap - man, fellow

The Snow Crystals

cheque - check

chip shop - a shop selling fried fish in batter and chips or French fries. There is barely a town or village in the UK without at least one, if not several, chip shops, and while the range of foods offered has increased over the years, 'fish and chips' as sold by chip shops is a tradition, a countrywide living national legend.

chips - French Fries

chocolate-box cottage - originally used to refer to art on chocolate box covers. Now, for instance, a chocolate-box cottage refers to very pretty and idealised "roses-around-the-door" properties.

cinema - movie theatre

crisps - potato chips

chockers - like in chockabloc... full.

daft - silly

Del Boy - the main character in the popular 1980s BBC TV series Only Fools And Horses, about the roguish yet lovable wheeler-dealer trader Del Boy, his brother, his granddad, his uncle, and friends.

estate (car) - stationwagon

fag - cigarette

flat - apartment

gormless - a bit stupid, simple.

GP - General Practitioner/ doctor

Grade restrictions - were introduced by English Heritage in 1950 to preserve Britain's heritage. When a building - be it a castle of international stature and importance (Grade I), or an old cottage (Grade II) of special interest - is listed, it means amongst others that any changes/renovations/alterations to either the inside or the outside, require careful consideration by English Heritage.

HGV - stands for heavy goods vehicle, which is a stonking huge truck

hitherto - until now or until the point in time under discussion

hoover and hoovering - vacuum cleaning. Hoover is/was the brand name of a popular upright vacuum cleaner. So, to hoover meant to vacuum clean, and now, decades later, whether one uses a Hoover or a vacuum cleaner by any other make, be it an upright or a pull along one, we continue to "hoover".

lass - girl

lorry - truck

mad - crazy

The Snow Crystals

me old fruit - a jocular term of endearment mostly used
between male friends.

Men Behaving Badly - a 1990s BBC TV series about two
men friends sharing a flat, and all the crazy things they
get up to, often with their girlfriends, all the while
blissfully living in a state of absolute chaos and disarray.

nab/s - grab/s, or even steal/s. Usually without
knowledge of the owner.

perfect nick - good/excellent condition

petrol - gasoline, fuel

pillock - another word for idiot or fool

Ploughman's - bread, butter, cheese and
chutney/pickles. Typical pub food.

power failure - electricity failure

pub/local - formerly a public house, it's a drinking
establishment that is fundamental to British culture,
and often the focal point of the community. Many pubs
also serve lunch and dinner.

quid - one, two, three - or any amount - quid. A
regularly used term for the British Sterling Pound or
currency.

removers/removals van - the men who help people
move. And the removals van is the truck they use.

roundabout - in the USA, a traffic rotary.

rubbish - junk. Or someone can react with "Rubbish!" to something which is unbelieveable, is a lie/a fib or nonsense.

Sainsbury's - one of the UK's largest supermarket chains.

specs - glasses

tea cosy - a padded cover used to keep a teapot warm. The author has called Aidan's cats tea cosies, having fashioned his two British Shorthair cats after her own Tommy, who indeed resembles a tea cosy.

the green (in a village) - a plot of grassy land for recreational purposes

threw a sizable paddy - more often than not a child's temper tantrum

tizzwazz - stressed, worried, a state of confusion.

twee - cute

up the duff - one of a variety of British slang terms for being pregnant.

Victorian terrace or a terraced house - terraced houses are residential properties which are attached to each other on either side, and which are also identical on both the inside and the outside. They can equally be

The Snow Crystals

grand like the famous Georgian terraced residences on the Royal Crescent in Bath, or small and basic, as built in the 2nd half of the 19th century for factory workers/labourers. They can also be 20th century or even contemporary, but Victorian terraces are the most prolific type of accommodation in the UK.

wally - an idiot, a fool

ACKNOWLEDGMENTS

A very special thanks to Ella, editor and my dearly loved and much appreciated friend, in both the calm and the stormy seas leading to the publication of this book. Your knowledge and advice have made this an amazing journey. And I am looking forward to our future journeys. I love you! At a difficult time last winter, an insightful Facebook post by Lavinia was the nudge I sought, and this book is, amongst others, the result of that much appreciated post. Thank you, Lavinia. It was love at first sight, when Patti sent me the cover she'd designed for The Snow Crystals. It couldn't be more perfect, as she got the essence and atmosphere of the story and the Cotswolds, in one go. She's not merely the much appreciated cover artist, but I am infinitely grateful for her help in formatting this book for both e-book and print, and for helping me through the jungle of bringing this book to the market. Thank you, hun. And last but certainly not least, a special thanks to Lavinia, Bev, Tina and Ellena for beta-reading this book and their helpful comments and observations.

.

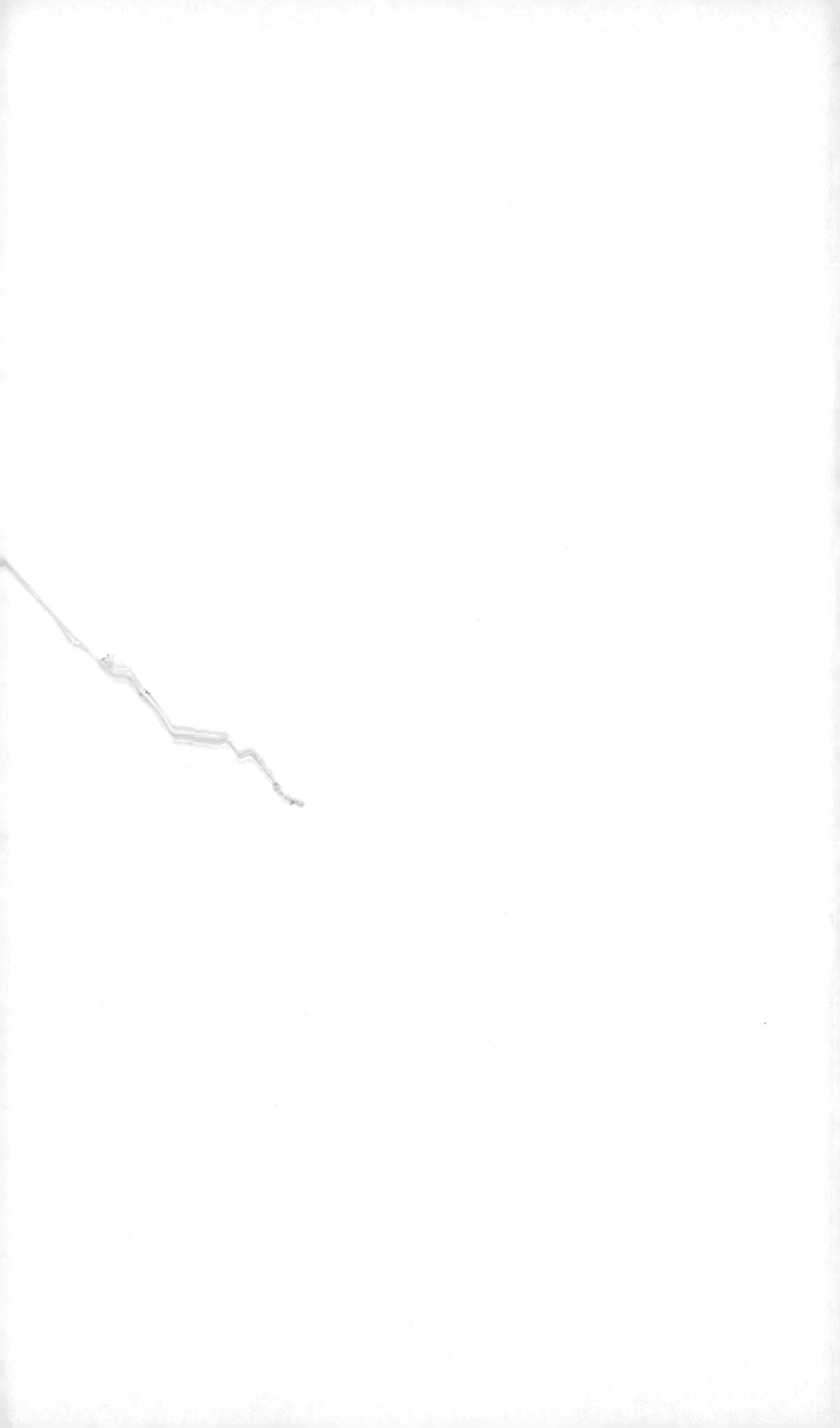

CHAPTER ONE

Twenty six Days to Christmas

Full moon.

Wistfully, Aidan glanced up at the pearly orb which had just, but only just, scaled the black skeletal fingers of the wintry trees grouped beyond the parking lot.

As a small child he'd been fascinated by the moon, and often held lengthy one-way discourses with that all-elusive and always silent Man in the Moon.

"At least I never believed the moon was made of cheese." Out loud, he chuckled at the memory.

Full moon.

The chuckle died away, and other memories and thoughts and worries of a more current nature drove away the peace that had surrounded him.

The memories were poignant and no amount of time would ever erase that ever-hovering dull ache.

Although the wounds had long healed, as scars are wont to, under certain circumstances, they still smarted. And tonight the full moon peacefully rising amongst the scattering of glittering stars, on her night time journey across the velvety black sky, brought it all back.

Looking up into the icy white calm of Luna, his memory resurrected the physical, unceasing and immovable gut-wrenching stabbing pain that had accompanied him throughout those first days, those first weeks.

Had his childhood friend, the Man in the Moon, looked on helplessly that night? Or even cared?

Aidan shivered. The moon blurred and swam before his eyes.

It was just over six years ago, on an October full moon evening, in this very place, that his father had breathed his last breaths, with only the full moon for company.

So much had changed that evening.

He'd not only lost his beloved father, but a dear friend. A worldly wise and mature friend who'd always been an ever-present beacon in both the calm, as well as the stormy seas of his life, as he grew up from child to adolescent, to a mature man. As much as his cousin Donald was his stalwart and life-long best friend, his father had always been the safe harbour enveloping him with parental love and understanding.

But from one minute to the next, he'd lost his guiding beacon. His hero. His inspiration. His father!

And with it, on that October full moon evening, in this very place, the directorship of his father's company befell him.

As the moon waned on its path to a New Moon, so

did the initial excruciating physical pain which held him in its grip.

How symbolic... It had been a Saturday evening, and a New Moon when, days after the funeral, he chose to set foot in the building and his father's offices, as its new director. He'd chosen a late Saturday to wander about his father's stronghold, alone, unhampered and undisturbed... He sat at his father's desk and on his chair... all the while aware of his fragile emotions. Aware of his father's essence... his presence in the very fibre of the building.

Six years on, Aidan knew his father would be proud of him and his achievements. Life was good. The company was thriving. And his grief had long since dulled, replaced by a constant memory of deep love and affection. He was his father's son, and Aidan was immensely proud of that!

In the silence of the moonlit car park, with only the moon and its twinkling guides for company, Aidan could almost hear his father's voice caressing him as it was carried on the gentle breeze.

Aidan looked away from the - by now - severely blurred moon and stars, and his mother sprung to mind.

Six years ago, from one minute to the next, his mother, a devoted and contented wife and housewife, had become a widow, and her world fell apart.

Six years on, grief continued to be his mother's near-on-constant companion, as every step forward was undone by two or three steps backwards.

Her previous interest in the company waned into non-existence, as she adamantly refused to share in any of Aidan's business-related successes, no matter how minute or how large. She did not wish to be reminded...

And tomorrow, as promised and planned, Aidan

was taking his mother shopping before her departure for Cornwall.

Of course he loved her. Dearly! But going by the last six years, Aidan knew that tomorrow would be heavy going. Added to which, his mum's relentless, persistent and insistent matchmaking attempts dominated each and every outing, ad nauseam.

Of course he loved his mother. But... *"Mother, please, desist! Enough already!"*

All because love continued to elude him. His mother just could not understand that he just had not met the woman of his dreams yet. "You're such a good-looking man, darling. That cannot be it! And you're a successful businessman..."

"Yeah, yeah, Mum! Please let it rest!"

Women-wise, his cousin, Donald was not much better off. And Aidan wondered how Donald's date was going...

"Hey! Wake up, boss!"

Lost in his own tumultuous little world, Aidan turned around in shock. "Oh! Hi, Gary... I... I was looking at the moon."

The young man smiled at him. "Spectacular, isn't it? Off home. Mum'll have dinner ready." He dashed off, waving. "Enjoy your evening."

A moment later his little old car chugged out of the parking lot, and quiet descended once again around Aidan.

The moon had risen out of the reach of the grasping, tangled, barren branches, and now hovered freely surrounded by a myriad of twinkling stars.

Suddenly, Aidan became aware of a sound. Was it the breeze picking up and rustling through the trees? Or was it some noise carried over on the gentle breeze from the centre of town? He couldn't place or recognise it. He looked around him. Nothing. Everything was as it had been minutes earlier.

From the corner of his eye, he caught sight of something. Like the enigmatic sound, he couldn't place it either. And then it was gone, before he could even attempt to identify it.

Baffled, he stood in the middle of the parking lot and did a three hundred and sixty degrees turn. Nothing. But there had been something; of that he was sure.

He looked up at the moon, which still appeared hazy and blurred. "What is happening? Is it you... or... Dad? Is it you, Dad?" Hot tears burned and spilled down his cheeks. He had not wept since that October, six years ago. "Life is really good, Dad." He turned and pointed at the building that housed Galbraith's. "Look, Dad. Still the same. But greater, even more successful. We've gone global..." The building disappeared into a liquefied blur. "I've worked so hard, Dad."

"So hard, that more often than not I forgot my own life... I forgot to live."

"But life is really good, Dad!"

"Is it?" Was this a thought of his own fabrication, or had it been planted there by his father? With difficulty, he swallowed a sob. Why weep now? After all these years...

The moon had risen higher. Aidan realised he'd lost all sense of time.

Home. High time he got home. Tom and Tessa, his two cats, would be waiting for him.

Sniffling, and inelegantly wiping his nose with his gloved hand, he walked the short distance to his car. The same spot where his father had always parked his car.

The sound whispered around him again, and he stopped in his tracks and looked around him. Once again, he noticed something out of the corner of his eye, and whipped round before the apparition could disappear.

They glittered and sparkled in the soft white light of the full moon. They came slowly at first, then built up momentum. Like confetti tossed over a bride and groom at a wedding, the most perfect snow crystals fluttered and danced on the gentle breeze and descended on and around him.

In surprise, he watched the snow crystals come to rest in his outstretched hands. Some were minute, while others were quite sizable. All were exquisitely beautiful and perfect.

Aidan didn't dare move, lest he'd step on any of the diamanté-like creations.

It was a perfectly clear November evening, to which the full moon and the stars-strewn sky were testament, but snow crystals had come fluttering down from somewhere.

He took his gloves off, and ever so gently picked up one of the crystals. The warmth of his fingers did not melt the delicate lace-like beauty. In fact, the crystal felt quite solid. Icily cold, but as light as a whisper. He gathered up more of the crystals, which all remained intact.

"What is this? What's going on?"

He placed the snow crystals safely in a paper handkerchief he'd dug out of a pocket.

As he bent down to pick up more, the peculiar gentle sound rang in his ears again, and the last of the crystals swirled around him before they disappeared into the winter's night.

To ensure he had not been dreaming, Aidan cautiously pushed aside an edge of the tissue, and breathed a sigh of relief to find the crystals trapped protectively within. He had not been dreaming! They were for real!

As he reverently folded the tissue paper around the crystals, he realised that he was standing on the exact same spot where his father had died. The snow crystals dancing into his life, and on this fateful spot, had to mean something. Didn't it?

Trembling, he got behind the wheel of his car and switched on the engine. He was cold, as was the car. He waited a while before he put the car into first gear to drive away. But before he did so, with his foot on the brake, he had one more peek at the mysterious and magical contents in the glove compartment... Still very much intact! Still very much present!

Instinctively, Aidan knew that something magical had happened tonight.

CHAPTER TWO

Twenty five Days to Christmas

Aidan pushed through the front door of the pub. The frown hadn't left his face all day, it seemed. It was high time he found a way to lose it, or he would end up with premature wrinkles. The thought amused him enough to break through his gloom. His gaze fell on Donald, his cousin and best friend. He was already propping up the bar, his two King Charles Spaniels woven around his ankles.

"Hello, my gorgeous girls!" Aidan deliberately ignored the human and hugged the canine duo. They wagged their tails endearingly, and went mad over their "uncle". Untangling himself from the besotted welcome, Aidan grinned at Donald. "You want to be hugged and kissed, too?"

"I thought you'd never ask! I feel hurt and neglected." Donald simpered, then pushed a pint towards Aidan, then added in his normal voice. "I already ordered for you."

Aidan picked up his glass. "Cheers." He took several sips. "I needed that."

"As bad as that, eh? Was it today you were supposed to see your mother? How is she?"

"Back in a dip." Aidan took another swallow. "Look, I understand that she misses Dad. As do I. But after six years, you'd think that she'd have moved on some. I am worried about her. She just does not want to listen when she gets like that. I was trying to tell her something tonight, and she accuses me of drunkenness."

Donald shook his head understandingly. "Drunk? You? Hah! Your last hangover was when the so-called Lovely Lucy turned out to be only interested in your bank balance."

Aidan nodded agreement. They both drank in silence for a moment.

"Glad I escaped that one in time. At dinner, Mum raised the subject once again, and kept it up as I was driving her home. Oh, help! First Nancy, then Anne, and some minor, not worth remembering, love interests."

"Sex interests!"

"OK, sex interests! But always with that elusive hope of love..." Aidan shrugged, defeated. "I have accepted the fact that I am singularly unlucky when it comes to love. At least you got married..."

"Come on, disastrously so!" Donald cut in. "You know divorce was the best thing that could've happened to me. Aidan, me mate, one day you'll strike gold. You have so much going for you. You're a good looking bloke with a great personality, a successful businessman, and a house to die for."

"Aw, you say the nicest things."

"I'm serious. Anyway, you're a great guy, Aidan, and one day, you'll find the right woman. Someone genuine. And don't listen to your mother. I think the world of my aunt, but do not listen to her. Women and love, and forever afters, those are things solely for you to decide on."

"Aye, aye, Sir." Aidan chuckled. "Talking women, how did your date last night with... with, what's her name, go?"

"What's her name's name is Diane. It didn't. Turns out she doesn't like dogs. Doesn't like animals, period. It was over before we ordered dinner! She spotted some dog hairs on my coat..."

"A pet owner's occupational hazard."

"... and commented on it. So, I told her about my ladies. Aidan," Donald was laughing heartily now, "you should have seen her face. I really rubbed it in. She finished her Martini, stated coldly we had nothing in common, and left."

"Sounds like a lucky escape."

"She was a real looker. Imagine I'd been head over heels, and had brought her home..." Donald burst out laughing. "The potential hysterics I escaped! There is a God after all!"

They drank in amicable and comfortably at ease silence for a while, as only the best of friends can. It was Donald who broke the silence.

"I'm off to have a very early Christmas dinner with my parents Wednesday. Be back Thursday morning. It's official, they're off to Boston on Friday." His good-natured face turned dark. "Mom tried her darnest to get me to consider joining them for a family Christmas. I don't mind Christmas dinner at my parents, but I damn well am not going to play happy families with my sanctimonious sister and her even worse sanctimoniously lost-up-himself husband. And pay return airfare, and be forced to buy gifts for those rabbits, for the privilege. She used to be a nice kid, till she met that chap... From thereon it was downhill all the way."

"Looks like we're on our own, then, this festive season." Aidan put down his empty glass. "Another?"

Donald nodded, and Aidan reordered.

"Mom's leaving for Mrs. Becket's first thing tomorrow. Got young Gary to drive her down."

"You're thirty two, Aidan. Not ninety two! Young Gary... honestly!" Donald laughed.

Aidan laughed, too. "Yes, OK, you're right. Gary's twenty, but at least he is a responsible, trustworthy and sensible chap. Glad of the extra income, too. Mum really likes him."

"You and me this Christmas. Two pathetic bachelors who just have no luck with women."

Aidan shrugged. "I think we should make the best of it, mate. I'm off to get me some decorations tomorrow. Need some outdoor lights and a door wreath. Think I will also indulge in some new decorations for indoors, too. The ones I have are rather past their sell-by date."

"That's the understatement of the year! I'll join you. Make sure you'll buy tasteful and listed-cottage-and-protected-village-suitable decorations. I'll even help you put them up. When you going?"

"Earliest possible. Don't you trust me? I'm not going to get a plastic, singing and dancing snowman or a plastic prancing reindeer. Honest! I do have a semblance of good taste."

Donald peered at his friend over his specs. "Not going by the rubbish you put up for years on end. They're going to be binned, burned, destroyed, rendered totally unusable tomorrow, no arguments."

"Not even bag them off to a charity shop?"

"That would be an insult to any charity shop!"

The Snow Crystals

Donald rolled his eyes.

Aidan raised his hands in defeat. "OK. OK. I got the message!" Chuckling, he emptied his glass. "Shall I pick you up? Want to be at the garden centre at nine."

"Sounds good to me." Donald put down his empty glass.

"Oh yeah, something I wanted to tell you. As I said, I tried to tell Mum but she chided me like a fanciful child. It happened last night. Dark, of course, when I left work. You probably will pronounce me totally mad, but as I made my way to my car I saw..."

Aidan's next words were drowned out by the raucous laughter from a nearby table. Donald listened intently and wondered whether he had heard correctly. The laughter died down, and he just wanted to ask Aidan to repeat himself, when Aidan added. "... and I have proof at home. I'll show you tomorrow."

Donald decided to leave it for the next day. If he had heard correctly, no wonder his aunt had told her son to grow up. Yet strange things did happen. He'd witnessed a few himself, and Aidan had never mocked him. Just accepted it at face value. They were both down-to-earth men, who simply accepted that there were mysterious forces at work in the universe. Whatever Aidan had proof of, Donald would see tomorrow.

Leaving the pub, Aidan bent down to stroke the two dogs, and bid Donald good night. They each went in opposite directions.

The smile which had lit up Aidan's face and helped lift some of his gloom slid away and was replaced by his earlier worried frown. With thoughts about his mother swirling around in his mind, he walked home on automatic pilot. He was infinitely relieved that she was leaving for her dear friend tomorrow, and spending Christmas and New Year in Cornwall. She always perked up when she was with Mrs. Becket.

"I'm home, darlings," Aidan called out as he closed the door to the porch behind him, and walked from the hallway into the kitchen. As was to be expected, his two gormless-looking British Shorthair cats lay lazily curled up and entwined in their capacious bed next to the warm AGA.

Large orange-eyed, blue and white Tom yawned, stretched and jumped onto the table and, purring loudly, head-butted Aidan lovingly. "Hello, my gorgeous tea-cosy."

Smaller, but equally chunky Tessa blinked her golden eyes, and she, too, yawned. Elegantly, the all-blue girl also jumped onto the table, and vied for Aidan's attention. "Hello, sweetness."

The twosome always brought a smile to his face. "We're off to bed in a moment," he chatted as the two watched his every move, as he went about the usual pre-bed ablutions.

Before heading upstairs, he went into his office and

The Snow Crystals

retrieved a small box from a desk drawer. Near-on-reverently, he opened the box, unfolded the white tissue paper, and stared down at the strange contents.

Gently, he picked up one of the bewitchingly beautiful crystals. As before, it still felt icily cold. But despite the warmth of the room, it remained in perfect condition. Precision-perfect snow crystals of varying sizes. They sparkled like a myriad of diamonds. Perfect snow crystals, yet neither made of snow, nor ice, nor glass. They were soft to the touch, too. Velvety... Colder than ice, yet they didn't burn as ice would. They were delicate, and as fragile as the finest lace, yet they were indestructible. They were unbendable, unbreakable, and thoroughly solid. They didn't stick together, or to his hands like an ice cube would have done. They just lay there, cradled in his hands, works of sheer perfection.

"They're real, Mum! I wasn't drunk! I didn't dream it! They're real!"

CHAPTER THREE

Twenty four days to Christmas

At 8:30 Aidan arrived at Donald's house, and unceremoniously banged on the door. The two ladies barked their welcome. A barely audible holler of "the door's open" reached him. Stepping into the hallway he was enveloped in doggy love.

"Want a coffee?" Donald yelled above the fracas.

"Yes," Aidan yelled back. He noted a large tartan blanket lying on the trunk in the hallway. The ladies would be joining them.

As he walked into Donald's amazingly cosy country kitchen, a mug of coffee was shoved into his hands.

"We need to stop for some shopping at Sainsbury's." Seeing Aidan's puzzled reaction, Donald grinned. "We'll need lunch. You're feeding me."

"We can go to the pub..."

The Snow Crystals

"No, we are not. Pub dinner is an option, but not lunch. If you want to uphold and further nurture your respectable reputation in the village, I am going to ensure that your first Christmas here will be a decorative success."

"Do rub it in that you are the artistic and creative one, and I am crap at it."

"Yes, Sir, I am! And yes, Sir, you are!"

Aidan shook his head and chuckled. There was no denying that Donald MacIntosh was gifted. His father came from a long line of known and respected artists and writers. He employed Donald's talents gratefully and with great success in his own business.

"C'mon, me old fruit, drink up. Let's get there before the hordes hit."

Before Aidan could fully empty the mug, Donald snatched it out of his hands, emptied the last bit in the sink, together with the contents of his own mug. He meticulously rinsed out the sink, and placed the mugs in the dishwasher. Donald's bohemian dress sense was in stark contrast to his near-on-obsessive neatness and cleanliness.

Away from his former professional London city life, Aidan had reverted to his old habits and dress style, and all too often he and Donald were mistaken for brothers. Whilst Donald was compulsively organised and neat in his home and life, Aidan regularly felt guilty about being the exact opposite. Except for his work and business, where he practiced meticulous precision, Aidan was a self confessed slob.

Donald shrugged into his coat, draped a lengthy knit wool scarf several times around his neck, and placed a wide brimmed hat on his profuse pony-tailed mane. "C'mon, me mate. Let's go and cause brash havoc amidst the gentility of the garden centre." With his canine companions on their leads, he went out. "Close the door behind you," he ordered Aidan.

"Park right by the entrance, so I can easily check up on the girls."

Aidan did as told. The thought flashed through Aidan's mind, as it had numerous times before, that going by Donald's love and care for his dogs, he would undoubtedly make a great dad. But with their continued amorous misfortunes, he was starting to have serious doubts of that ever happening.

"What are you looking so gloomy about?" Donald asked. "Afraid of spending money?"

"Was I? No, just thought about how rubbishy our love lives are. And no, not afraid of spending money. On the contrary. All but raring to go."

"Let's forget women for now, and go spend some serious money!" Uttering sweet nothings to his two ladies, Donald got out of the car. Before entering the garden centre, he turned around and waved at the twosome.

Shaking his head, and chuckling, Aidan took Donald's arm, and marched him into the festively decorated centre.

"You'll need a trolley," Donald announced, and removed the basket from Aidan's hand.

"A trolley?" Aidan asked in amazement.

"We'll need it! You'll see! In fact, more than likely, we'll need two."

The Snow Crystals

Good humouredly and obediently, Aidan did as bid and followed his friend.

"You need a Christmas tree, indoor and outdoor lights, decorations, some wreaths. And new mugs!"

"Whatever do I need new mugs for? I've got mugs."

"We're going to sling those, too. Their ancientness is not the point, it is their cracked and chipped state that is an affront."

"Oh… OK…" was all Aidan could think of answering. He saw a sign for Christmas trees, and made for the doors out. Donald yanked him back before he got too far.

"I love real trees too, mate. But, believe me, with that allergy of yours to pine needles, you'll be better off with a really nice fake one. If you get a good quality one, it'll last you for years! Also, you have to think of your cats. Besides, consider it your environmentally friendly seasonal contribution." Donald pointed at a lusciously impressive 7 foot tree on display. "That one!"

"Why not that one?" Aidan asked, in turn pointing at a charmingly decorated 5 foot tree, perched on a low round table.

"Too small. Believe me, the 7 foot one is it."

Aidan appraised the tree. It was rather splendid, and impressively life-like, too. "You're right, Donald. Must admit, I like it. Lots."

The boxed tree dwarfed Aidan's trolley. "I'll go and pay for the thing, and stash it in the car. Save me lugging it about."

"Good thinking. Give the girls a cuddle for me, will you?"

When Aidan rejoined Donald, his friend was studying lights.

"Wow, the selection!"

"Where have you been hiding all these years?" Donald asked.

Aidan had barely picked up a box with multi-coloured lights, before they were whipped from his hands and replaced on the shelf.

"White lights for indoors. It's classy and elegant, and makes the decorations sparkle," Donald announced.

Sparkle... the word immediately turned Aidan's thoughts to the strangely beautiful sparkling crystals resting in a box at home. He imagined a tree full of similar exquisite snow crystals. Yes, that would be it! He smiled to himself.

Aidan, with his thoughts on the enigmatic crystals, paid little to no attention to Donald and the boxes which were deposited in his trolley.

"Some white and blue ones for outside. It'll look magical," Donald said and placed some more boxes in Aidan's trolley. "And now decorations."

"Snow crystals," Aidan mused.

"What?"

"Snow crystals. I want snow crystals in the tree. Glittery snow crystals."

"Hallelujah! The Lord be praised!" Donald threw his arms exaggeratedly wide, and dropped to his knees. "Hallelujah! Miracles do happen!"

"You daft pillock!" Aidan sniggered.

Carole studied the decorations and sighed. "So bloody expensive." With no answer forthcoming, she looked around for her friend. "Kristie? Where are you?"

The Snow Crystals

"Over here," came the answer from behind a stand. "Found something that won't bankrupt us."

"Tell me about it. Who nowadays can afford that extortionate crap?" Grumbling to herself, Carole joined her friend. "Oh, not bad. They're bright and cheerful."

"And on special!"

"Getting better all the time. Let's get some of these then, and see if we can find a tree to go with 'em."

"Real or fake?" Kristie asked. "I rather fancy a real tree," she added hopefully.

Carole ignored Kristie's question, and said, "We don't want to waste our money on Christmas decorations alone, do we?"

Obediently, Kristie nodded agreement, and then spotted tinsel. "The tinsel's only a quid each."

"I like tinsel." Carole remembered her childhood Christmas trees full of sweets, and both home-made and a few much-loved old and faded decorations which had belonged to her grandmother. There had always been lots of tinsel, too, sparkling by the light of the one multi- coloured thread.

They were quite poor back then. Every year the same ever-scraggier fake tree was put up and decorated. For years the little tree had appeared magical, but then Carole had discovered that there were other kids who were far better off than she was. Kids whose parents owned their houses. Kids whose parents owned cars. Kids whose parents sent them to private schools. Kids whose parents could afford large Christmas trees weighed down by extravagant decorations, and lit by hundreds of lights. Parents who could afford to buy their offspring whatever they desired from that fictional red-suited man. And with this, Carole discovered jealousy.

Kristie had been Carole's schoolmate, and lived next door. They'd both married, with Kristie marrying Carole's brother, and they'd been divorced within months of each other. Neither had had children. For many years, they shared a small three-bed Victorian terrace in a somewhat rundown area of town. Their work was a short walk from home. They owned a small old car between them. Their social life was limited to the pub, and an occasional weekend visit to a club or the cinema. With due care, they managed to live reasonably well.

In their early fifties, they were aware of their unfulfilled lives, and unceasingly on the outlook for that special man. A man with money. Carole had never admitted, let stand confided in Kristie, her envy of the more fortunate.

With it being their last Saturday off before Christmas, and elated by a recent and immensely satisfying win in the lottery, which they'd shared fifty-fifty, they had found their way to the garden centre. They were treating themselves to some new decorations, and would enjoy some coffee and cake at the restaurant to round off a - for them - near-on-perfect morning.

"Which colour tinsel shall we get, Carole?" Kristie broke into her friend's musings.

"Oh... er... gold, I suppose?"

"Yeah, gold. Goes with all colours."

"We could do with some new lights, too," Carole said.

Kristie nodded. "Before we get the lights, shall we have a look at trees? I do love the smell of a real tree..."

"Ugh, all those needles! Besides, a fake is more economical."

"Perhaps some real branches which we can put up?"

"We'll see," Carole said dismissively.

After changing their minds several times over, Carole suddenly spied a lonely pink tree in a far-off corner, reduced to rock bottom price.

"That's it! I love it!" Carole whispered. "We can make it look like a fairy tale. It's magical!"

Looking at the contents of their basket, Kristie shook her head. Pink was Carole's favourite colour. "Back to the drawing board. These decorations do not go with a pink tree."

Kristie would have preferred a real life tree, with traditional red, green and gold decorations, but didn't dare say so.

Carole's eyes sparkled. "It's so cheap, that we can get some of those expensive baubles without wrecking our Christmas budget."

Bravely, Kristie smiled. "Yes. If they've got 'em, I suppose you'll want some pink lights and tinsel?"

"Perfect!"

The respected Combe-Norton Garden and Home Centre was the Forbes' family's pride and joy. With her much-loved, imperious father-in-law swaying the sceptre over the whole, Susan ran the home section while her husband, Mike, was the perfect choice to run the garden and plant section.

Susan was well-educated, elegant, sophisticated, and a local. And unlike her predecessor, Floyd, whose cosmopolitan, avant-garde London style didn't win him any favours, Susan knew what the customers wanted. Where possible, she favoured Cotswolds-based businesses, products, artists, and craftsmen. Galbraith's products were especially popular, and she always ensured that the centre had plenty on offer.

With Floyd storming off in a huff back to London - and what he called "civilisation" - several years ago, Susan had taken over at the helm. It had befallen Susan to sweep the home section with a giant broom, and oust all of Floyd's faux pas during some carefully timed sales. Everyone sighed a sigh of relief when the last of Floyd's blunders had sold for rock bottom prices this past spring.

But yesterday, like a bad smell that stubbornly refused to go away, a straggler had been discovered in a forgotten corner of the stockroom. It was an ultra pink and ultra fake looking six foot tree. Susan had seen to it that it had been put out for sale, and reduced to a give away price. She hoped she'd be seeing the back of it sooner rather than later.

Although it was still early, the centre was already filling up nicely. Susan made a habit of walking around several times a day, noting clients' reactions to products. Sometimes she even asked them why they liked a certain item. This was her first walk-about of the day. She loved the Christmas season. She loved every item on sale.

There were several people buying trees, and suddenly Susan spotted two women oh-ing and ah-ing over the despicable pink tree. Her heart all but leapt for joy. Could this be the swan song of Floyd's legacy? She hastened to them. As she drew nearer, she noted that the two women and the tree were a match made in heaven.

"Are you interested in buying this tree?" She masked her eagerness with friendly professionalism.

The Snow Crystals

"Oh yes, it's gorgeous!" the shorter of the two women said. Her companion nodded vigorously, seemingly enthusiastic, but Susan noted that her eyes conveyed anything but.

"There's a box with it." Susan looked around for one of the sales personnel. Then she remembered something else. "I believe that there were also some decorations to go with this tree." She spotted the eagerness in the smaller woman's eyes.

There were decorations to go with the pink tree, but the temporary Christmas staff must have forgotten to put them out. On a whim of the moment, to clear out the last of Floyd's legacy, she decided that, if the decorations could be found, with certainly one of the women clearly besotted with the pink atrocity, they could have the lot for five quid. And good riddance.

The tree might have been pretty enough new, but had become a bit soiled and tired with having been a display model. It was clear that the shorter woman did not notice or care about this. She'd fallen in love, and saw the pink tree through rose-tinted specs.

"I'll be back in a moment."

Susan went in search for one of the staff. Several minutes later, she rejoined the women, followed by a young girl carrying a box.

"Found them!" She smiled, and opened the box to show the contents to the two women. "It's your lucky day. Decorations, lights, the lot for five pounds. Old stock which has to go."

With sparkling eyes, the shorter woman looked at her. "Do the lights work? I mean, if they don't, then we'll have to buy lights."

The girl plugged the lights into a nearby socket. A hundred white fairy lights twinkled on.

The women thanked Susan several times over, and, in an elated state, they made for the cashier. Susan looked at the two as they walked away. The shorter woman's eager delight had been obvious. She wondered about the taller woman's dull, clearly faked pleasure, then decided it wasn't any of her business, and dismissed them from her mind.

She continued her walk around the ever-busier centre. Business was good. She'd bought wisely.

Passing the cards and books department, she spotted two familiar faces.

"Aidan! Donald!" They exchanged kisses and hugs. "So lovely to see you." Donald was looking at some greeting cards. "Charming, aren't they? They are selling like hotcakes. By a very well-known, gifted Cotswolds artist." She grinned. "Ever heard of him?"

"Stop teasing. You're making me blush, girl," Donald chided. "So my designs are selling well?"

"Oh yes!" Susan nodded. She turned to the other man, "Aidan, at the rate they're disappearing, we may well run out of them. Can we get some more?"

Aidan looked both pleased and stumped. "That was a helluva big order, Susan. I'll see what I can do… Please send an email listing what you want, but I cannot promise anything."

"That's alright, honey. I understand. Just trying." She turned back to Donald. "Did you get my email? Sent it yesterday afternoon."

Donald shook his head. "Haven't been online since yesterday early morning."

"Typical, that, for our Donald." Aidan sniggered.

"We sold two watercolours and five prints."

Donald punched the air. "Yes! That'll keep my bread buttered the coming weeks or so."

Susan had to continue her walk about and they said their goodbyes.

She liked them both a lot. They were great to do business with, and were wonderful friends. She checked her watch. Not even ten o'clock yet. She could feel that it was going to be a good day for the centre. The sale of that pink thing had to be the highlight.

Carole and Kristie paid five pounds and took their treasures to the car. With veneration, Carole looked at their purchases.

"It will be so beautiful, Kristie. It will be the best ever."

"Yes, I am sure it will. " Kristie couldn't share in Carole's enthusiasm.

"Let's see if we can get some pink lights. And some branches. Maybe they have some reusable fake ones."

Acknowledging that her envisioned Christmas hopes and dreams were once again dashed, Kristie bravely said, "Coffee, cake, and some more decorations. Shall we give the old ones to the charity shop? Or do you want to keep them, Carole?"

"Nah, fresh start, eh? Maybe our luck will continue and we might even find our Prince Charming."

Placing her arm through Kristie's, Carole walked them back into the centre, and headed for the decorations.

CHAPTER FOUR

Aidan wandered off to the book section, leaving Donald browsing the many seasonal and other cards with professional interest.

A book about decorating the home for Christmas caught Aidan's eye. There were some more on general home decoration, and on gardening.

Leafing through the books, it dawned on him that he did not like his interior at all, as it totally lacked the personal touch. With this revelation came the understanding of what Donald had been on about since Aidan had moved into the pretty thatch. His home needed personalising. It needed cosying up.

Donald's home, on the other hand, was cosy and personal. Which needn't mean feminine and frilly! The idea of a Men Behaving Badly interior rather appalled him. It was bad enough that he was prone to sloppiness. He knew that he really should take a leaf out of Donald's book. He wasn't quite sure how to go about it, but with these books and Donald's help, he hoped he'd get there.

It hardly was the decorator's fault, as Aidan had stressed that he wanted an easy-to-maintain, contemporary, utilitarian, and above all masculine, environment. And thus he'd ended up with an interior befitting a minimalist Canary Wharf flat, or even an office, and not to a Cotswolds thatched cottage. With a busy life, it had initially suited him well enough, but it always lacked something. Why ever had he not realised this before?

Donald had been at him often enough about it, but he'd just never gotten it. And now, in the middle of a garden centre, he'd seen the light.

He loved being at Donald's. The kitchen was a comfortable haven to lunch or dine in. The sitting room was one of those rooms where you could get enveloped by the sofa or one of the wingback chairs, prop a cushion in your back, and put your feet up, as you sat drinking a coffee, or sipping a glass of wine or whiskey by the roaring fire on a winter's day. The whole house was welcoming. Even the garden was a haven of delight on a hot summer's evening.

Donald had that special touch. It had to be the artist in him.

Aidan was eager to learn. For it was warmth that his home sorely lacked.

Leafing through the books, Aidan decided to buy them all. Between Donald and these books, he might finally get what he really wanted and needed. Besides, he loved books. A few more were always welcome. Thus, his to-read pile remained more or less constant as he read and then added more on a regular basis. He chuckled under his breath, acknowledging he was a bookaholic.

He spotted another book he could use. Cookery made easy. He'd passed the burning water stage years ago, but continued to hover nearer the hopeless than the less than basic cook level, more often than not relying on ready meals and takeaways. Not that Donald didn't resort to these luxuries when he was busy or working against a deadline. But Donald was quite capable of rustling up a delicious meal consisting of two, three or more courses.

Aidan greatly admired his cousin's talents, and wished his mother, or even Mrs. Becket, had seen to teaching him some basics. But both had been of the old school belief that women took care of their men. Which was one reason his mother was forever onto him to get married, so that a woman would take care of him, and run his house for him. Bless her! If that was the case, he might as well hire a housekeeper.

When Mary Jennings had started cleaning for him, she had praised Donald's good taste, and how much she enjoyed working in such a beautifully decorated home. The only comment she had made about Aidan's place had been "You must like grey".

No, he did not like grey!

Thankfully, he had insisted on keeping the walls a creamy white, otherwise these, too, might have ended up in one of a variation of greys. But he was stuck with a very modern leather anthracite grey suite, positioned around a large shaggy pale grey rug. He liked the large dresser against one wall, but the decorator had insisted on it being grey, too. And that was just part of his sitting room. With the grey theme running throughout his house, he was all but drowning in a sea of grey.

"And not to forget those occasional black accents,"

The Snow Crystals

Aidan thought with a cringing sinking feeling. *"I really hate it! All of it!"*

The enigmatic sparkly snow crystals sprang to mind, and the Christmas tree he and Donald would be decorating later on. He envisioned a tree glistening with snow crystals. He considered for a moment hanging the mysterious crystals in the tree, or placing them somewhere on display. But following his experience with his mother, he doubted the wisdom of that, unless it were somewhere safe. In all, he was rather reluctant to share his secret with anyone save Donald.

The snow crystals were something precious and personal, but he could share them with Donald. And as he thought about the beautiful crystals, he could feel their feather-light non-weight in his hand.

It struck Aidan that those snow crystals had really affected him! Stranger yet, they had started to impact his life, lifestyle, but more so his mindset since he had found them. Since their discovery Thursday night, he had started to re-evaluate and analyse not merely his life but that of those around him, too. Slowly, this need for change had been seeping into him. Changes and improvements which had to be made.

His life was good. Certainly, where it concerned his business. Since his father's death, together with his devoted employees, he'd made an even greater success of an already much-respected company. The Galbraith name and brand stood for quality, class and originality. Aidan decided that, besides the yearly company Christmas dinner and party, he'd have to conjure up something else for his employees, to thank them and show his continued appreciation.

But it was his own life that needed changing primarily. Love might continue to elude him, but he sought something that warmed him. Something that would give him the same sense of homecoming as Donald's home. All those greys predominating in his life and home were chilling him.

His ponderings and wanderings had brought him into the home-wares department of the centre. Especially here, Susan's superb taste and know-how of her wider clientele was evident.

"Oh yes!" he mumbled excitedly as he looked around him.

Aidan was considering buying a dinner set decorated with trailing ivy, when Donald sidled up to him.

"Nice, that! Very nice, actually."

Aidan held up a plate. "A set of six or eight? What do you think?"

"You're planning on entertaining..."

"You and me, our lady friends..."

"Chance would be a fine thing!"

"... some other friends."

"Eight," Donald said.

"OK, eight it is. Do you like it?"

"Yes! Very much so. And it sure beats that bloody grey," Donald sniggered.

"Ah, it bothers you, too?"

"It's your home, mate, and you do in your home whatever you want, but... let's just say that... What's this about bothering me, too? The emphasis being on too. And incidentally, I hate all that grey, but as I said..."

"Yeah, I know, it is my home." Aidan looked apologetic and downcast. "I am just very sorry I spent money on fifty shades of grey."

"Minus the kinky sex."

"Yeah, minus the kinky sex." A wistful smile came

and went. "I so want rid of it! The grey, not the sex."

"Sex... can hardly remember what it is all about."

"Let me remind you. It goes like th..." Spotting some people eyeing him and Donald with interest, Aidan decided against making some lewd movements. Instead, he jokingly said, "I'll lend you one of my porn books."

"Only one?"

"OK, all three of them. Happy now?"

"Ecstatic. Back to the dinner service. I really like this. With the right table decorations, it is Christmassy enough for the festive season." Donald pointed at a festively decorated table laid out with the service. Aidan nodded agreement. "It is the perfect autumn and winter service."

"Which means I need to get another one for the spring and summer?"

"You know I have two different sets. Plus one for outdoor entertaining."

"You do? Oh... yes, you do. You're a right prima donna, you are." Aidan laughed. "I'll get the hang of this. I really want to get the hang of this. Donald, you have no idea how sick to barfing I am of all that bloody grey! I'm selling the lot! Putting it on eBay, or if need be, giving it away! As long as it is out of my home and life. Rather today than tomorrow!"

"What brought this change of heart?"

"It must have been there all along, but it just hit me. Will you help me?"

"Need you ask? Of course I'll help you! Let's get this dinner service sorted first, and some individual mugs, too. I'll accord you the honour later on of smashing the old ones up in the bin."

"It'll be my pleasure!"

Carole and Kristie, having found their desired pink lights, had seen the sign to the home-wares department and couldn't resist the temptation to go there before selecting some more decorations.

"Maybe we can pick up some ideas, if nothing else," Kristie said.

Carole sighed. "We need men with some serious money to their name. These prices are totally out of our league."

"Most prices, even the cheapest, are out of our league," Kristie stated and added sadly, "Even in the sales, these things are out of our league."

With Carole grumbling over the price of some seasonal kitchen towels, Kristie spied two men buying a dinner service. "Oooh ar!" She poked her friend. "Did you see those two hunky specimens?"

"Yeah, just saw them. Oooh ar, indeed!"

The women moved closer by, and caught some of the conversation.

"So tell me about this eureka moment of yours," the ponytailed man said.

Carole rather took a fancy to him. She hadn't a clue what eureka meant, though. There was something about him. Tall, well built, a handsome face with lively, very blue eyes, and she quite liked the wild and wavy chestnut mane tied with a leather string. Although casually dressed, his clothes and boots were of an obviously excellent quality. The sort of quality that could only be equated with money.

"I'll tell you later, over a caffeine shot. But first I really want to have a look around. If I see something..."

the other man answered.

Carole smiled. The considerable dinner service piled up in his trolley, together with some other things, was all she needed to surmise that this man, too, beyond a shadow of a doubt, was more than likely loaded. And he was awfully cute. Much dressed like the ponytailed man. Equally tall, and handsome. Longish, curly mahogany brown hair brushing his collar. And he had gorgeous hazel eyes.

The two men moved off, looking at the wares on offer, stopping here, then there. Sometimes picking up an item to look at it closer.

"Let's follow them," Carole whispered.

"But not too closely. Let's do as they're doing. Window shopping."

Carole caught sight of herself in a nearby mirror, and smiled with satisfaction. "Glad we did our hair the other day, and that we're wearing all our slap today." She poked lightly at her excessively bleached blonde hair.

"Yeah." Kristie glanced at herself in the same mirror, as she stood next to Carole. Except for wearing clothes of a different colour, with Carole loving pink and Kristie red, they looked like clones.

"I hope you're not going for the ponytail..." Carole said.

"He's gorgeous. But I do prefer the other one."

"Oh, good."

Carole's elation was contagious, and Kristie mindlessly followed suit. Slowly, they moved forward, trying to stay within earshot of the men's conversation. They caught the occasional word.

Their morning was turning out better than they could have dreamt of.

"I really like the creamy white kitchen units, and the tiles in various shades of yellow. But all those damn grey accessories, and that grey dresser in the kitchen, make the white and especially the yellow look so damned bilious," Aidan said.

"A variation on a theme of naval grey."

"So, not sex then?"

"I'd never get it up in your place."

"I'd not particularly fancy you screwing on my hearth rug."

"Your GREY hearth rug."

"Whatever." Aidan chuckled. "You can screw in your own home."

"We're a sorry lot, aren't we? Before you know it, we'll be scuttling off into some sleazy establishment for a leg over…"

"Or order a blow-up doll online…"

With scenes from television's much loved rogue wheeler-dealer Del-Boy springing to mind, aided on by his own vivid imagination, Donald burst out laughing. "One of those blow-up dolls of Del-Boy's? Oh God, can you imagine one of those?"

Aidan was leaning on his trolley, all but crying with laughter.

Several people looked up from their shopping to stare at the two men. Carole and Kristie stopped in their tracks and stared, too.

"I wonder what's so funny," Carole said.

"I'd love to know." Kristie pretended great interest in an - in her opinion - extortionately expensive coffee table.

The Snow Crystals

Carole moved a bit closer to them. Their laughter was dying down. Before they moved on to the next display, she noted that neither wore a ring on their left hand. This did not necessarily mean that they were available, but it sure increased the chances that they were.

Kristie had joined her.

"We're going in for the kill," Carole stated. "At the right moment, we're going in for the kill."

"Going by what mine said, it looks like they're going for coffee, just like us."

"So we'll follow them," Carole said.

Both women were already totally proprietorial of their quarry.

CHAPTER FIVE

Neither Aidan nor Donald were ready to leave for the restaurant yet. They were totally unaware of the two women who zigzagged steadily after them. But then no one would have thought anything of it. To any onlooker, the four appeared to be interested and eager shoppers.

A traditionally styled suite, upholstered in a light contemporary fabric, took Aidan's fancy. He inspected it from various angles. "I really like this." Then he looked at the price ticket. "I can live with the price, but I want it now. Not in the spring."

"It will need ordering, bro. It'll be the same everywhere. Unless you go for a vintage or an antique. Or even a second-hand. You have to wait for a new one."

"I could try to sweet-talk Susan..."

Donald chuckled. "You could try... but don't bank on it."

Casting the suite one last longing look, Aidan

moved away.

Next, he spotted a large rug. "I like!"

"And I agree. I like it, too. But don't buy the scarf before the suit and overcoat."

"Eh?"

"What I mean is, get the main pieces of furniture, like a suite, a dining set, and such first, after which you can buy a suitable rug. Capisci?"

"Oh... yeah... OK." His face brightened. "This dinner service would really go well with that suite. As well as the rug."

They looked around for several more minutes, as they slowly made their way out of the home-wares department. The Christmas department lay invitingly to their right. "Let's see if we can find some of those snow crystals you envision, my boy."

Stealthily, Carole and Kristie followed their quarry through the festively decorated archway into the Christmas department. Although the department was already quite busy, they were close enough to catch some of the men's conversation, as they'd stopped to look around them, taking in woodland-inspired decorations.

Ponytail said, "Remember, it is a big tree, which needs lots of decorations. Do you know where you're going to put it?"

"The bay," Hazel Eyes answered.

Ponytail nodded sagely. "Yes... perfect. You're lucky that bay extension was done before the grade restrictions came into force.

"I know. It's one of the quirks I love about that house."

Carole cast Kristie a meaningful glance. More than likely, Hazel Eyes had his own house. More than likely then, that Ponytail did, too.

The men moved on from the woodland section, and much to Carole's regret, hastened through a pastel pink, lilac, and purple-themed area.

"We must come back here," Carole whispered.

The men did not glance at the traditional red, green and gold decorations either, which rather saddened Kristie, for they had spotted the next area full of mirrored, crystal, silver and white decorations.

"If anywhere, we should hopefully find your desired snow crystals here," Ponytail said.

"Look." Hazel Eyes pointed to a stylish and elegantly decorated tree. "They've got 'em."

"Got what," went through the two women's minds. Both found the decorations beautiful, but Carole was firmly embedded in her pink dream while, deep down, Kristie favoured traditionalism.

"Can I pop 'em in your trolley?" Hazel Eyes asked Ponytail.

"Why do you think I insisted on two trolleys?"

Carole heaved a longing sigh when she saw how charming his smile was.

Kristie felt her knees buckle at Hazel Eyes' dimpled smile.

As the men were selecting the decorations, Carole saw their chance, and firmly grabbing Kristie's arm, approached.

Loud enough so she'd be heard, Carole exclaimed, "This is Christmas decoration heaven."

Kristie, taking her cue, said equally loudly, "It's all so beautiful. If I'd known, I'd have brought my camera."

Carole leaned across the display, and supposedly suddenly spotted the man across from her. She cast him a wide smile. "Such lovely decorations, don't you think?"

Ponytail looked up. "Sorry, are you talking to me?"

Once again, Carole flashed what she assumed was a seductive smile. "No... yes... beautiful, aren't they?"

Ponytail smiled politely. "Yes, they are." And he returned to the task in hand.

"You must have a very large tree which needs lots of decorations," Carole persisted.

Once again, Ponytail smiled politely. "They're for my friend's tree." He nodded in the direction of Hazel Eyes, who was now intent on another display.

Kristie decided it was time to join the conversation. "Your wives are very lucky to have husbands with such excellent taste." She smiled brightly.

"No lucky wives..." Both women missed the hint of a snigger to his words.

"Hey, bro, come and have a look at these. What do you think?" Hazel Eyes called out and, without another glance at the two women, Ponytail turned away.

"No lucky wives..." Carole whispered excitedly. "Which means they are single."

"Do you think it is enough for that giant of a tree?" Aidan asked.

Donald shrugged. "We'll put the thing up, and if you need more, we can easily come back. The centre's open tomorrow."

Side by side, each pushing a laden trolley, the men left Christmasville through another sparkly decorated archway.

Unbeknownst to them, the two women followed at a reasonable and unobtrusive distance. They arrived in a huge, enclosed, greenhouse area.

The women just caught the words, "They've got wreaths over there."

Two sizable, fully decorated wreaths were selected, as well as several table pieces.

"Coffee!" Aidan announced. He and Donald headed for the restaurant.

Carole looked at her watch. It was almost 10:30. Yes, she, too, was ready for a coffee, as would be Kristie. At a safe distance, and moving casually, knowing that they'd not lose their quarry, the women ambled along from display to display. A Santa and a Snowman, both on special, found their way into the women's basket.

Jealousy surged through Carole as the niftily dressed woman who'd sold them the pink tree stopped to talk with the two men. The three laughed and talked for a moment, and then parted. Bristling, Carole dragged Kristie with her.

On entering the restaurant, they noticed quite a few tables were already taken. But they spotted the men immediately. They were at a table for four. They'd left their trolleys in a designated area, amongst other laden trolleys.

"You get the coffee and cake, and I'll grab a table near them, before someone else nabs it," Carole ordered her friend.

On joining Carole, Kristie was immediately struck by Carole's furious expression. "What's wrong?" She handed Carole her coffee and cake, and sat down.

"Someone's joining them. There's a third coffee. Bet it's that posh tart."

No sooner had she uttered these angry words,

than said woman joined the men. She was quite pretty, with dark blonde, casually upswept hair, and elegantly but conservatively dressed in a dark suit.

"She looks and dresses like a wrinkly old bat of a nun," Carole observed, enviously bitter. The smoker's lines around her mouth became even more evident, as it puckered in jealous disapproval. "I could do with a fag now," Carole pouted.

"Blame Brussels," Kristie said.

"No respect for us smokers." Carole was on a roll.

No matter how much the women strained their ears, they could not catch a word of the conversation between the threesome at the nearby table. The hum of voices, paired with seasonal background music, as well as the typical sounds of a busy restaurant, left them none the wiser.

Despite the rising frustration, both agreed that the coffee was delicious, and the cake to die for.

Amazed, Susan countered, "You are really getting rid of all that horrid grey? Wow! Call the press! Aidan, darling, hadn't you ever noticed that it just did not go with the cottage?"

Aidan shrugged. "No. I just wanted something easy, functional... masculine... modern... I..." He shrugged again. "Maybe deep down I knew it didn't go, but it never hit home. Not until now."

"I'll see what I can do, but I am not promising anything. I'll get onto it immediately," Susan grinned. "Like I know you will do your best to supply me with..."

"Are you blackmailing me, Susan Forbes?" Aidan gasped in feigned horror.

"Who? Me?" Susan reposted. "Never! Seriously,

though. Aidan, the Galbraith products are very popular. I'm delighted for both of us, but it's a popularity I just had not foreseen." She smiled apologetically. "My bad. Anyway, I've already had a list of all we'd like, if possible, post haste emailed to your office."

"Monday first thing OK?"

"Perfect, thank you. I'll phone you as soon as I know the deal on that suite and the rug."

Aidan smiled gratefully. "Susan, whatever the outcome, I appreciate your trying."

She touched his hand. "I'll do my best. By the way, there is a new shop... not that new... it opened last year. And shop is a bit of a wrong word, really... it is an antiques and vintage emporium, with a gift shop and a delightful tearoom attached. Located on the marketplace. Go and have a look there. They have some lovely stuff."

"I know where it is," Donald said. "You palming us off on the competition, Susan?"

She grinned. "Hardly! It's a delightful treasure trove, and a totally different kettle of fish from ours."

"Thanks for the tip, Susan."

"I'm sure you'll find quite a bit at..." Her phone lying before her on the table buzzed. "Oh, gonna love ya and leave ya." They exchanged quick kisses and she sped off.

CHAPTER SIX

With their coffee drunk and cake eaten, the two got up.

"We're done here... I think," Aidan said. "You wanted to get something for lunch at Sainsbury's..."

"Forget Sainsbury's. Earlier on I took a detour through the food department. It's a foodie's culinary dream come true."

"OK, and then en route home we'll stop off at that emporium."

"It has a crazy yet delightful name. The Trivia of Cabbages and Roses."

"OW!" Aidan yelped. He bumped into Donald, who in turn stumbled into a table and came close to falling. "Jesus! That hurts!"

Aidan bent down to rub his bruised ankle, and saw the cause of this torture... cheap, shiny, black, fake patent leather knee-high boots, armed with killer heels. He looked up along tight red jeans, an equally tight black jacket with a fake fur collar, all revealing too much of its owner's bony feminine assets. It was all topped off by a lived-in and overly made-up face of a leering woman whose shoulder length hair was bleached palest blonde to within an inch of its life. The smell of cheap perfume fought for recognition alongside the stench of ingrained nicotine. Aidan straightened up.

Her bony hand, with long, blood-red lacquered nails, clamped onto his arm. "Oh, I am so sorry! Did I hurt you, lover?" she asked beguilingly in her smoky voice.

Aidan drew back in revulsion from the mixture of smells invading his nostrils. Her breath was testament not only to the coffee she'd just drank, but also her smoking, and carried a sour hint of alcohol.

"Sit down. Let me have a look at your foot. I am so sorry."

Her hand was still clamped onto his arm. Aidan could feel her strength and determination through the layers of his clothes.

Donald, who'd bumped into a table causing some coffee to spill, said apologetically, "Sorry folks. Let me get you new coffees."

The young couple shook their heads. "No worries, mate. We're all but done. Not your fault. I bet anything those tarts did it on purpose. They had their beady eyes on your table the whole time. Better rescue your friend before those two swallow him whole."

"Those two?" Donald turned and groaned. "Oh God! No."

"Escape while you still can," the young man advised Donald, grinning.

"We must stop meeting like this, handsome, or people will talk." It was the husky croon of the bleached blonde parody who had hit on him earlier. A vice-like

The Snow Crystals

claw with long, brashly pink lacquered talons clutched his arm. "You alright, lovey? You could have hurt yourself." Her sigh emitted a nauseating mixture of coffee, cigarettes and old booze. "Might as well get to know each other now, as we keep meeting up." What she supposed was a sexy laugh was in fact a farcical throaty cackle. "My name is Carole. And that is my friend Kristie. What are your names? I take it that you're local?"

Intent on making a hasty retreat, well away from these hags, both men purposefully blanked out the women's utterances.

"Excuse us, but we have to go," Aidan stated with a calmness he was not feeling. He found the women disturbingly terrifying. He looked at Donald, who had been hit on by a shorter version of his assailant. "We have to go now!" he said through clenched teeth, and yanked his arm out of the woman's powerful grasp.

"But I am so worried I hurt you. I just want to help. Make sure you are alright."

"Yeah, that's what friends do..." The shorter of the two, having released her grasp on Donald, reached for Aidan's arm but failed as he recoiled from her.

"Let's get the fuck out of here!" Aidan grumbled at Donald, relieved at having managed to extract himself.

They sped towards the food department and selected some items for their lunch, then made their way to the cashier. With growing impatience, they waited as their wares were safely wrapped in tissue paper.

"What the hell was that all about?" Aidan asked.

"The couple whose table I almost toppled said those tarts probably did it on purpose."

"Yeah, I can actually believe that. It was too bloody

well timed. Look at me! How can you miss a 6'2" man? I'm hardly a hobbit."

"The shorter of the two hit on me when we were buying decorations. Trying to chat me up."

Aidan groaned in sympathy. "There's something desperate about them. Creepy."

Their purchases safely packed, they beat a hasty retreat. They were not aware of the two women in the old dark blue car which followed them out of the car park at an inconspicuous distance.

The obvious rejection had not put the women off, least of all Carole. In fact, it had merely strengthened her resolve. She was on a mission. Silently, she swore that she'd make sure she'd get her man.

"I know I'll have a stinker of a bruise. My foot and ankle really hurt!" Aidan grumbled. "Bloody stupid woman! Did it on purpose, you said?"

"So it seemed."

"Stupid tarts!"

Neither man said anything further. Best to forget the two hags. They had better things to do and think about. The drive into the centre of town did not take long, and they found a parking place off the market. Aidan accompanied Donald as he gave his two ladies a short trot around, then saw to it that they were cosily resettled in the car, in their warm blanket.

They did not notice the old small dark blue car which had entered the parking lot and found a place a short distance from theirs.

"I'm surprised you never heard of or went to that shop," Donald said.

"Well, you know me. Between you, the business and Mum, and not to forget the occasional disastrous female encounter, I keep quite busy. I am just glad to get home and put my feet up."

"You so need to get a life, Aidan. All that grey has had a detrimental effect on your brain cells."

"Which are grey to start with."

"Yeah, too much grey, mate. Too much grey."

"I noticed a grey hair the other day. I pulled it out and had a good look at it. Definitely grey!"

"So the degenerative process has started, eh?"

In answer, Aidan gave Donald a shove. Both were laughing as they entered The Trivia of Cabbages and Roses.

Aidan glanced around him appreciatively. "Nice! Very nice indeed."

They wandered around the displays and cabinets, pointing out things they liked to each other. All the while blissfully unaware that they were being watched... and followed...

Aidan stopped in his tracks and called Donald back. "Look at what I found." His eyes were sparkling. He pointed at two beautifully upholstered wingback chairs. "Aren't they perfect?"" Donald nodded agreement. "And the price is just... wow! I want them."

As Aidan guarded his trophies, Donald went in search of a salesperson.

Suddenly, Aidan noticed a movement out of the corner of his eye. No, it couldn't be! He had to be imagining things. Those two hags had really gotten to him. They couldn't be here. They wouldn't be here, now, would they? That would be too much of a coincidence. But the movement he had caught, only just, had consisted of black and red and topped off by a hay bale concoction. The thought made him feel slightly ill. Cautiously and casually, he once again glanced in the direction of the hideous apparition, supposedly on the outlook for his friend and some sales assistance. It was gone. Seeing Donald approach with an older man, Aidan could breathe easily again.

The man introduced himself as Peter, and this was his stand. "Only brought in the chairs this morning. They are in perfect nick. There's a big footstool to go with 'em. Same upholstery. It's still in the van. Been busy this morning, and haven't had a chance to put it out yet."

Aidan confirmed that he would more than likely be interested in the footstool. "I'm definitely having the chairs!"

Peter's eyes twinkled with pleasure. His day was going well. "Have you tried the chairs?"

"Actually, no," Aidan confessed.

He sat down. It was like snuggling up in one of Donald's cosy wingback chairs. Just the right amount of softness paired with the right amount of support. Aidan closed his eyes for a moment and imagined himself by the fire, glass of wine in hand. His two beloved felines curled up in the other chair, or on his lap. The tree all beautiful and sparkly in the bay. Seasonal music playing... *"You're turning into a soppy git,"* Aidan thought with amusement. But at the same time it felt so right. And he loved that feeling.

"And? What do you think?" Donald broke into his reverie.

Aidan's eyes snapped open. "Perfect!" He smiled.

Peter tore off the tickets, slapped sold stickers on the chairs, and ushered Aidan and Donald to the back of the shop, and out to his van.

As he pulled the footstool forward, the blankets

fell away from two beautiful round mahogany side tables.

"Are those for sale?" Aidan asked.

"Didn't manage to get those in either, yet," Peter replied. He told Aidan the price. "Can do a special price for chairs, footstool and those two tables." He named a figure. "And I'll be happy to deliver them."

"You're on," Aidan said, quite elated, and shook hands on it. "I live at The Cottage, Old Orchard Lane, South Woodside".

Peter smiled broadly. "I know you! You're Aidan Galbraith. My cousin and her son work for you."

"Not Mrs. Jennings and Gary."

"The very same. Mary and Gary." Peter laughed. " He turned to Donald. "And you're the artist, Donald MacIntosh, who also lives in South Woodside. Mary also cleans for you. My Mrs. bought one of your prints the other day, as well as your Christmas cards. We both love your work. Recognise you from the folder the Mrs. got with the picture."

"Thank you for the compliment," Donald replied. "Wow, it's a small world."

Peter looked at Aidan and asked cheekily, hiding a grin, "Will those chairs go with all that grey?"

Donald burst out laughing, as Aidan groaned. "I'm getting rid of the lot," Aidan said.

"Mary will be delighted. By the way, if you are interested, I have more where this lot came from, back at my shop in Thatch Hall." Peter whipped out his phone and fiddled around with it, and showed Aidan several pictures.

Donald looked over his friend's shoulder. "This could be the answer to your prayers, me mate."

"When can we come and have a look? If some of

the furniture in these photos is as nice in reality, I think I could well be interested in several more pieces."

"You won't be disappointed. How about mid-afternoon? I'll make sure I'll be there. I will load up these things, and if you want more, it'll all go on the lorry. And make it a nice round price. How's that?

"Will a cheque be OK?" Aidan asked.

Cheque, cash, whatever suits you."

"What are you going to do with those fifty shades of grey? Store them in the garage till you sell them?" Donald asked Aidan.

"Yeah, they'll have to go..."

"If you want, I'll buy them off you. I know some people who will be interested in... in grey."

"Don't know about you, but I need a caffeine boost," Donald said. He thrived on coffee. "My treat."

The three men walked back into the centre, talking and laughing like old friends.

As they made their way into the tearoom, they were watched by two women hiding behind a display.

CHAPTER SEVEN

Carole and Kristie had watched Peter Sullivan usher the two men out the back. They'd been able to keep an eye on their quarry from a suitable vantage point, a window at the back of the shop, right near their friend Doris' stand.

Doris, who'd been busy with a client, joined them and handed them a big bag with books. She was always glad to offload any romantic M&B novels on the two women. It saved her traipsing with them to the charity shop. This time the bag was bigger and heavier than usual. The twosome chortled with delight.

"Doris, honey, would you by any chance have some binoculars for sale? Or would you know who had some for sale? " Carole asked in her sweetest voice. She knew for a fact there were some binoculars for sale around the centre. She'd seen some recently, lying forgotten in a cabinet. They'd been there for months.

Doris eyed Carole. "I know you, missy! You

probably have your eye on a pair. What do you need them for anyway? It won't be for bird watching."

Carole smirked. Kristie just looked puzzled.

"Well, you see, it is like this, Doris... Kristie and I have met our Prince Charmings. And we want to get a better look at them."

"That makes sense." Doris was not adverse to some subterfuge. "Where did you see the goggles?"

"Old fart-face Bellamy's cabinet. Bottom right. As you walk into his stand, on the left."

"You've got it all figured out, haven't you? " Doris shook her head. "Come with me."

"No, we're staying here. Must keep an eye on them."

"They're here?"

The women nodded.

"OK, I'll be back in a moment." She was as good as her word. She turned her back to the aisle and showed the binoculars to her friends. "Bellamy got twenty six quid on them, but the ticket's so old, it means they've been there a long time. How did you know they were there?"

Carole shrugged. "I was looking at a brooch which I rather liked but found too expensive. That is when I spotted 'em."

Doris moved to the back of her stand... a moment later she was back. "Six quid OK?"

"How did you manage that?" Kristie asked.

"You know I've been over twenty-five years in the trade, girls." She tapped the side of her nose. "So, six quid?"

Before either Carole or Kristie could answer, they saw Peter and the two men walking by in the next aisle. They were totally wrapped up in conversation.

"That's them!" Kristie exclaimed in an excited but suitably hushed tone.

"Nice! Very, very nice!" Doris pushed the binoculars into a bag. "Six quid, please." She accompanied them to the cashier, and took the money off Carole. "Have fun, girls. And good luck! Let me know how it goes."

"If you can get anything out of old Peter... or hear something else..."

"Stop fussing, Carole. Of course. I, too, am rather curious now."

They exchanged goodbyes, and Doris went back to her stand, where a client was waiting.

A row of glass cabinets between two pillars offered perfect protection as they eyed the men. The tearoom was filling up for lunch. But it appeared that the men were only interested in coffee. They watched Hazel Eyes answering his phone; less than a minute later he pocketed it.

Peter had taken his phone out, and passed it on to Hazel Eyes.

"What are they doing?" Kristie wondered.

"Peter always photographs his stock."

"That must be it."

Having pretended to study the cabinets' contents a few minutes more, they beat a hasty retreat back to the car.

"Let's hope they return to the car when they've finished their coffee. I'm not going to waste petrol just to keep warm," Carole grumbled, taking a cigarette and lighting it. "You want one?"

Kristie accepted the offered packet.

Silently, they sat side by side, their eyes focussed on the lane leading to the market, waiting for the men to appear. Both lit a second cigarette.

"There they are!" Carole couldn't control her excitement. She emitted an orgasmic groan. "Oh... I can feel him. I want him! I need him!"

Carole did not see the glance Kristie cast her. "Oh, really?"

"Oh yes, really. We'll get them. They're ours."

They watched Hazel Eyes toss the car keys to Ponytail, who made for the driver's seat. Hazel Eyes appeared to be limping. Without haste, they left the parking lot. Several other cars were arriving and leaving simultaneously, and this gave Carole the chance to keep a safe distance. The men wouldn't know they were being followed.

"We have to find out where they live." Carole held her hand out for another cigarette.

Even though there were several cars between them, the large 4x4 was easy to follow.

As they approached the outskirts of town, a gleaming maroon estate drove out of a gated property, and joined the queue behind the 4x4. Carole smiled to herself. They couldn't be more inconspicuous in this Saturday traffic.

Carole's phone shrilled. "Get that, will ya," she ordered Kristie.

"Oh, hiya, Doris." Kristie was silent for a moment. "Oh, really?" She listened some more. "Thanks, hon." She snapped the phone shut. "Good old Doris! You know what she is like..."

"Well, out with it!"

Kristie chortled. "She went up to Peter. That it was turning into a good day. Peter agreed. She heard him talking to Andrew, that he would be leaving after lunch. Two gents, who'd bought some furniture off him this morning, were coming to his place to look at some more."

"His home?"

"Nah. His shop in Thatch Hall. Doris will text us the address."

"Oh, goody! They're in our grasp," Carole squealed. "Well... they will be shortly."

Except for the white van and the maroon estate, no other cars were between them and the 4x4. They noticed that they were on the road to South Woodside. Barely ten minutes later, the white van turned off to the right to a farm, and a mile farther on they entered the beautiful village of South Woodside. The small dark car and the estate were still trailing the 4x4. There was nothing suspicious about this Saturday traffic.

"Pretty village! Look at those cottages!" Kristie exclaimed, waving her cigarette at some chocolate-box stone thatched cottages.

Carole grunted disinterestedly, keeping her eyes firmly on the cars in front of her.

"Imagine living here," Kristie voiced dreamily.

The estate slowed down, as the 4x4 turned to the left, off the village green, up a short dead end lane. The estate continued. Carole slowly drove the car past the lane. The 4x4 had stopped behind a removals van.

A burly man in a dust coat bearing the removal firm's logo rushed out of the neighbouring cottage. "Sorry, Sir, hope we are not blocking you or your drive."

Aidan got out of the car, and winced. Damn foot! "No, no problem at all. Have to go out again after lunch. So, I am finally getting some new neighbours, then?"

"Two lovely ladies. They'll be arriving later this

afternoon." The man smiled. "You are sure, Sir?"

"All we have to do is unload the car."

"Since we are blocking your drive, let us please help you unload. Besides which, you're limping."

"He got accosted by some woman in killer heels," Donald said as he got out of the car.

"Ouch!"

The man and his two assistants, together with Donald, took the boxes and packages from the car. They followed Aidan, who opened the door.

"Thank you for your help. Can we make you some coffee, tea, lunch?"

"So kind of you, Sir. We have everything, but a coffee would go down well."

Donald filled the kettle with water and flicked it on. "Aidan, you park your butt, and I'll unpack those dishes for you and pop them in the dishwasher."

Aidan sucked in a sharp breath as he managed just, but only just, to get his shoe off. Pulling his sock down, he angrily exclaimed, "The bloody tart! Look at my foot!"

"Frozen peas," the burly remover said.

"Yeah, that should help," Donald agreed, and headed for the freezer in the utility room. "A bag of ice cubes. Even better than peas."

As Aidan sat nursing his bruised foot, topped by a bag of ice cubes, Donald made coffee for the men, and a pot of tea for him and Aidan. Then, without ado, he started to unpack the boxes with dishes. "Now that you have these, are you going to let Peter take that atrocious white and grey dinner service?"

"Yes! All the grey's going." He turned to the removers. "So, my new neighbours are two ladies?"

"Sisters. Lovely ladies. I am sure that you will like

58

them." They put down their empty mugs. "Thank you for the coffee. We have to get cracking, as we have some unpacking to do, too. Once the van is empty, we'll move it so that your drive is free again."

Aidan thanked them, and Donald let them out.

Walking back into the kitchen, Donald said. "Two ladies. Young? Old? In between? I wonder... The house has been in the Moreton family, as far as I know, since the 17th century, so I doubt the old lady would have sold it. She may have rented it out."

"Possible. It's been empty for as long as I've lived here. But, someone's obviously been tending and maintaining the house and gardens."

"I have to admit that I am curious. Two ladies..." Donald put out plates, mugs and cutlery, and unpacked their lunch.

"Looks good," Aidan said.

They ate in amicable silence, clearly enjoying the food.

"Do you have Arnica in the house?" Donald asked as he cleared away the empty plates and placed the leftovers in the fridge.

"Eh?"

"For your foot." With Aidan shaking his head, Donald continued. "The girls need a stroll. I have a tube at home." He called his ladies, and shrugged into his coat. "We'll take my car this afternoon."

Aidan wasn't arguing about that. "Thanks. Much appreciated."

CHAPTER EIGHT

With the pain in his foot and especially his ankle growing worse, Aidan wondered what shoes to put on. They would have to be soft and well worn... he knew he had some old footwear hiding in a corner of his dressing room.

Aidan hobbled into his sitting room, where the two cats were busy investigating the still-packed Christmas decorations. "Don't exert yourselves, darlings." He laughed. "Save your strength for later on. You'll need it." Two broad, sweet faces looked up adoringly at him.

As he glanced around the room, the chill it emitted hit him hard. Why hadn't he noticed before? Donald was right, he needed to get a life. He'd all but fallen in love with this old cottage. It was everything and more than he wanted and had ever dreamt of. But from there on it had gone pear shaped. Like the love of a woman continued to elude him, so did the love he should be feeling for this place.

"That this place is a symphony in grey is entirely my own fault." The cats cast him quizzical glances. "But for the life of me, my disastrous love life cannot be my fault. Or is it?" He looked at the cats. "Is it my fault that I am such a lousy, sad failure?" Purring profusely, the twosome wove around his legs and feet. "You two love me. And I love you, too." He sat down and they immediately jumped on his lap, vying for attention. "What would you two do? Hm?" He cuddled them for a moment, then got up and went upstairs to search for some suitable footwear.

He found what he wanted, and gently eased his right foot into the well-worn runner. Bearable and tolerable, but only just.

He still had not gotten round to showing Donald the enigmatic crystals. Were they still cradled in their box and intact? Or had it all been a dream?

At least the box was in the desk drawer where he had placed it the other evening. That part was real.

He peeled away the tissue paper and smiled.

They were still there. Still perfectly intact. Sparkling. Glittering.

A sudden break in the cloud cover brought a weak, wintry shaft of sunlight creeping over his desk and the crystals, which enhanced their radiant beauty even more. Aidan imagined how exquisite they would be in full sunlight, or by flickering candlelight.

A thought struck him, and he took the box into the shadowy hallway. The crystals continued to sparkle. He took it one step further, and went into the hall closet and closed the door.

"I must be losing it," Aidan muttered to himself.

On touch alone, he reopened the box, and the extremity of the light that came from within the crystals almost blinded him. "Whoah!" While they'd sparkled and glittered before in both day- and lamplight, this was a near-on-unearthly revelation. "Oh my God!" With trembling fingers, he closed the lid, and velvety darkness settled around him again, save for a shaft of light seeping from beneath the lid. What were they? Where did they come from?

Scratching and meowing at the closet door brought him back to reality, and he opened the door. Satisfied that their human was still there and had not disappeared, the two cats casually ambled off to the kitchen and their AGA-side bed.

Shaking his head at the antics of his cats, Aidan went back to his study and replaced the box in his desk.

The earlier hint of sun which had warmed and softened the contemporary decorated study had disappeared. Despite the cosy warmth of the house, Aidan shivered involuntarily. That chill he had become acutely aware of the other day fingered him annoyingly like a persistently itchy, icy rash. Wherever he went in the house, that chill followed him around like a shadow. He accepted that it was of no one's but his own making.

He thought back to January, when Donald had excitedly phoned him about a cottage for sale in his village. Donald had sold some paintings to the owners, and he'd occasionally socialised with them in the pub. "It's about time you get a home of your own, mate. A little treasure is coming onto the market, and you have first pickings. A short walk from the pub, so not far from me, either. If you'll like it, pestering each other will become a regular feature."

Donald had all but dragged him to view the property. A chocolate-box thatch with roses around the door. But not on that cold late January morning. The hefty powdery dash of snow had transformed the cottage and surroundings into a Christmas postcard scene. Despite the cold grey day, the honey-coloured Cotswold stone facade had radiated warmth and a friendly welcome. A heavily set, centuries-old door led into a porch, and from there on into a small hallway, with a large sitting room, a dining room or study opposite, by the front door. At the back lay a large dining kitchen, and utility room. Upstairs, three bedrooms.

Upon entering the cottage, Aidan had been engulfed by an excessiveness of twee. The blessedly simple chalk white walls had been undone by a riot of flowery ruffled and swagged curtains. And the floweriness continued on in the upholstery, and the innumerable cushions.

Decorative items abounded, and an empty spot came at a premium. Photos of smiling brides, cutesy babies, and imposing gowned young women and men proudly clutching their degrees, as well as large family groups, covered every surface and wall space. And that was merely the large sitting room.

The colourful frilly cacophony continued throughout the ground floor, and carried on up the stairs. The bedrooms had wall to wall flowered Axminster carpets. Aidan had barely been able to see through the flouncy, frilly, floral extremes. It was all too much. Amidst all this, Aidan had hardly been able to find Donald's paintings.

But he had to agree with Donald, the couple were delightful. They'd been generous with coffee and cake.

The coffee cups and cake plates, too, were awash with flowers. The cake lay lost amidst flowers. Aidan loved flowers and plants, and with a horticulturally inclined mother, he had learned his fair share since earliest childhood. But this was overkill.

The doting owners had presented him with a comprehensive file on the property, set up by an estate agent. Aidan was pleased to find floor plans, plus every possible detail necessary for an interested buyer.

As Donald and the couple had chatted, Aidan had

concentrated on the document, then commenced wandering about the house on his own. Under all that clutter, he had barely been able to appreciate the room sizes. The saving grace were the simple white walls. Thankfully, the contemporary country chic kitchen was comparatively new, and he liked the fresh white and sunny yellow of the space, which overlooked a large walled garden.

As he had concluded his solo tour, he cast a last glance over the document, and decided that the house had everything he wanted, and more. The vendors would empty the house of their much-adored floral madness, and happily create a cluttered floral clone of this one in their new home.

For the first time that morning, Aidan could imagine the peace that would settle over this house, once it was empty. After another floral coffee, and a piece of cake playing hide and seek amidst blowsy roses, having made up his mind, he'd invited them to lunch at the pub. Over heartily warming cottage pies, the deal had been settled. And two months later, the simply named The Cottage had become his.

Once empty of all the clutter, the size of the cottage had come as a phenomenal surprise. It was large without losing its country cottage charm and loveliness. With spring blooming and blossoming, Aidan had moved into his dream cottage at the end of April.

He had let a decorator loose on the place. She'd

done some work on his offices, which had improved them and their workability no end. He had all but cajoled her into doing his home. "I do offices, Aidan, not homes. I can recommend a more suitable decorator."

But he had been insistent. He'd taken the easy option. Someone he knew who had done a good job. Someone who would get on with it, and not bother him with every detail and every step of the way.

"It's a cottage, Aidan!" she'd exclaimed.

But he remained adamant. Remembering the cluttered, floral excessiveness and exuberance, he had merely re-enforced his demand... He wanted masculine, contemporary, easy to manage... Stubbornly, he'd stood in front of her, ticking off his demands and wishes on his fingers. He was moving out of his rental flat, and he wanted something that would give him no grief. Life was busy enough as it was, without contributing more work to it.

What a fool he'd been!

Shuffling from study to kitchen to living room, looking around him, he shrugged to himself in utter defeat. "I cannot blame anyone but myself! This is all of my own making! But why, WHY, didn't I twig sooner? Why now?" In the farthest reaches of his mind, a tiny voice piped up, "It's the snow crystals, Aidan! They woke you up."

Aidan dropped down onto the sofa. Why hadn't he twigged before how uncomfortable the thing was in reality? There was no comparison, when he considered the cosily comfortable chairs he had bought earlier on, and the stark rigidity of this designer contraption, trying to pass for a sofa.

A wild sense of satisfaction overcame him. By tonight, this accursed thing would he history. If Peter would not buy all this stuff off him, it would be condemned to the garage for now. He wanted rid of. It was a need that hurt. The worst pain he had ever felt was upon his father's death, and quite incomparable. This was another kind of pain. A nagging hurt. It was paired with a chill. Aidan knew that by ridding himself of this pain, the chill, too, would go.

"Here. Catch."

Aidan had not heard Donald enter. His head snapped up in shock. He'd been miles away. He missed catching the box Donald threw at him, and it fell into the dense grey profusion at his feet. "Oh. Hi. Sorry."

"Not your coherent, with-it, self, are you, mate?" Donald picked up the box with Arnica, and placed it in Aidan's hand. "Smear it liberally over the affected area, and let the skin absorb it before putting your sock back on." He perched himself on the edge of the sofa and eyed Aidan. "Earth calling Aidan. Anyone there? Over."

"I'm here. Over." Aidan smiled. He took the trainer and the sock off, and did as Donald ordered. "I was thinking..."

"No! You could've fooled me. You were miles

away."

Aidan did as Donald advised, and winced. He could see where the killer heel had done the worst damage. His ankle throbbed, and the bruising was spreading fast up his leg and down into his foot. Morosely, he sat back, staring off into space. "I was thinking back to that day you brought me here the first time, and the floral nightmare that hit me smack in the gob."

Donald sniggered. "It was rather OTT, wasn't it? But they were, and are, a delightful couple, even though slightly excessive in their tastes. But look who's talking! You've done the exact same thing, only in the other direction. From one extreme to the next. A bit like the pot calling the kettle black. Despite the heating, snow and ice would keep in this room... this house."

Aidan looked up sharply. No, this would be too crazy. Were the snow crystals still intact... because...? No, totally crazy, that idea. Now would be a good time to see what Donald thought of the crystals, now that he was sitting here with his foot basting in Arnica. "I've been meaning to..."

A crash outside sent Donald rushing to the window. "Oh shit! Poor guys. Better go help." As he rushed out, he ordered Aidan to stay put. "You're not going to be any use. Stay."

"Woof!"

Aidan hobbled over to the window, and saw the removers struggling with a large dresser. He should be there helping them. But too much pressure on his foot reminded him that he would not be much use for a day or two. Out loud, he let out a string of profanities. It didn't make him feel any better. Seeing that the four men were righting the problem, Aidan returned, defeated, to the sofa. The moment had passed. He'd try talking to Donald later on. Once again, he shivered involuntarily.

CHAPTER NINE

Carole manoeuvred the car slowly around the green, and found a narrow, densely-foliaged lane. There were no houses on this lane which led out of the village. She found a spot where she could easily turn the car so that it faced Old Orchard Lane, giving them a good view of the cottages.

"I'm gagging for a fag." Carole reached for her handbag on the floor behind her.

Kristie removed the binoculars from the bag, and aimed them at their quarry.

"It looks like someone is moving into the cottage next door. Ponytail parked behind the van, and they are getting help from the removers unloading the car. Oh, the poor darling, he's limping!"

"Ponytail?" With the cigarette glued to her lips, she cursed under her breath, unable to find the lighter.

"No, Hazel Eyes." That it was due to her, and more so their crass and desperate behaviour, did not enter her mind. "Oh, he is opening the door. He's got the keys. Must be his house. Looks really nice from here."

Carole found the lighter and lit the cigarette. She snatched the binoculars from Kristie's hands. "Let me have a look." She raised them to her eyes. "Damn! Can't see a thing. It's all blurred."

"They were OK when I looked through them. When you grabbed them, you must have changed the setting."

During the mere seconds that they didn't have the binoculars trained on the men, they missed seeing Ponytail entering the cottage with his two dogs.

Having found the correct setting, Carole sighed with satisfaction. "They're really good, these goggles." She took a deep drag of her cigarette. "Looks like they're inside. Let's wait a bit longer and see what happens."

Five, then ten minutes passed, and all stayed quiet in the lane. Eagerly, Carole had lit yet another cigarette.

Kristie's phone rang. "It's Doris! Hi, hon. Oh, OK, hang on." She put the speaker on.

Doris' metallic voice invaded the car's fuggy space. "Have some news for you!" She sounded excited. "Peter being Peter, the king of integrity, of course did not share anything with me, but he did with his pal, Tony." She giggled. "I did what we dealers tend to do. I was very interested in the contents of some cabinets near where they were talking. I couldn't catch it all, but still got quite a bit." She took a deep breath. "Tony complimented Peter on a good morning's work. Peter said that he knows his clients indirectly, through his cousin and her son. Tony asked if they were a gay couple. Laughing, Peter denied it. So, that is good news. That they lived in South Woodside."

"Yes," Carole piped up. "We know. We are here

now, not far from their house, and been watching them with the binoculars."

"Glad they're useful. Anyway, Peter is picking up a rug for one of them, and they'll meet him at his shop around three. And before you ask, I'm texting the address in a moment! Couldn't catch the name, but one of the two was after some more furniture. Peter asked Tony to look after his stand, and that he doubted he'd be back that afternoon. Oh, and I forgot to add, I caught Peter saying something about his cousin being very fond of them both. And Tony asked to say hello to this cousin. So they know each other... somehow."

"Peter and Tony are as thick as thieves," Carole said scathingly.

"Yeah, they are," Doris agreed. "And elusive towards the rest of us. So, what are you going to do now?"

Carole and Kristie looked at each other. "I saw a pub nearby," Carole said.

"Shall we get a snack there, and then drive to... You won't forget to text us the shop address, will you, Doris?" Kristie asked expectantly.

"Of course I'm not forgetting, you daft bird. But I was busy playing Powroot." She pronounced Poirot as Powroot.

"And we're very grateful to you." Carole took a cigarette and shoved the packet in Kristie's waiting hand. "Yeah, we'll grab a ploughman's or such, and follow them." Carole cast Kristie a meaningful glance. "They're not getting away!"

"Texting you the address. And have customers waiting."

"Thanks, Doris. You're a right mate, you are." Carole started the car. "Let's get to that pub. Might as

The Snow Crystals

well get some lunch while we're at it."

The texted address appeared on the phone's digital display. Kristie showed it to Carole, who nodded. "That'll be easy to find."

"Wonder what our men are eating," Kristie said dreamily.

Christmas had arrived at the pub. Gold lights sparkled in a large tree, and amidst the low evergreen shrubbery surrounding the building. The whole radiated tastefully refined festiveness, sparking a sense of cosiness and warmth in the ever-greying early afternoon light.

"Do you see those cars? Oh my God! A Roller, and a Porsche..."

"... and a Jaguar over there," Kristie gasped.

"They must be loaded here."

"Then our boys must be, too." Thoughtlessly, Kristie dropped her cigarette end and left it. Carole did likewise.

Low-beamed, elegant yet cosy, the pub was testament to traditional old world charm. A tree with more gold lights and a traditional mixture of gold, red and green decorations held pride of place near a cheerfully roaring open fire. Other decorations were dotted around. Nothing ostentatious. All quietly radiating class.

"Our pub wouldn't palm us off with this." Carole snorted, disdainfully looking around her. "Andy's a proper publican. He knows what's right."

Hesitantly, Kristie agreed. "Pretty but a bit underwhelming!" By the triumphant look on Carole's face, she knew she'd given the right answer.

Oblivious to both the amused as well as

disbelieving glances cast in their direction, the two teetered to the bar on their impractically high heels.

A young barmaid dressed in a non-revealing, simple black outfit, with a gold scarf artistically draped around her black gamine-cut hair, eyed them questioningly. Not her usual kind of clientele.

"Do you do bar lunches?" Carole asked.

"Certainly, madam. We also do à la carte in the dining room." With the women's blank stares speaking volumes, she took out the bar menu, and handed it to them.

Carole and Kristie glanced over the menu, their faces displaying shocked surprise and dismay.

"There has to be something cheaper. Something we can afford," Kristie groaned.

"Patience! Before you know it..."

"Yes, but we need to eat something now. Me throat feels like it's been cut off at me belly."

"We saved lots of money by getting that gorgeous pink tree. We can afford this little luxury. And it is for a good cause. Ours!"

Resigned, Kristie sighed. "Oh, alright."

"I could murder a pint, but I will not be caught behind the wheel..."

"You have the pint, and I'll drive," Kristie offered.

"Oh, no!" Carole exclaimed. "I do the driving. We'll have coffee, and... what do you fancy?"

"A ploughman's, but look at the price! Andy does them for less than half that."

"We're going for it," Carole decided, and placed her order.

They hung expectantly around the bar for a moment, till they were told politely but firmly by the barmaid to find a seat. Coffee and lunch would be brought to them.

"I feel a bit like a fish out of water," Kristie confessed. They found a corner table, near a window, with partial view of the car park.

"Wonder who that Roller belongs to." Kristie pointed at the prestigious, shiny maroon car.

"Bound to be some top brass, a wealthy pimp, or..." with her mind in exaggerated overdrive Carole added, "some successful gangster."

"Could be some celeb, too." Kristie looked around her.

"Don't see any celeb types here. Hey, do you see that scruff over there?"

Kristie followed Carole's gaze, and her eyes came to rest on a tall man with a wild shock of dark curls on which a flat cap was balanced. The women did not recognise his faded and well-worn coat for a Barbour. Some straw clung to a long knitted scarf well beyond its glory days. Well-fitting rust-coloured corduroy slacks were shoved down mucky green wellies.

"Andy wouldn't stand for a tramp in his pub," Carole sneered.

Their ordered lunch was placed before them.

"Oh!" Kristie looked up in surprise at the waitress. "We ordered a simple ploughman's..." She pointed at the pot. "And coffee."

"That's right, madam. This is a ploughman's. The only one on the menu. And that is a pot of coffee, so you can pour yourself a second cup."

"Blimey," Carole mumbled. "They're weird here."

"Didn't you want to get used to this?" Kristie reminded her. With Carole giving her a withering glance, Kristie quickly changed the subject. "This is bloody good, by the way." Ill-mannered, she waved her fork around.

Carole finished her meal first. "Could do with a fag now. And more coffee."

"There's still coffee in the pot."

With their lunch eaten, and plans for the afternoon laid, they glanced around at the pub's clientele. Two men similarly dressed to the scruff walked into the pub, waved hello at their look-alike, and joined him.

"Lots of old farts and scruffs," Carole said derisively. "Do you suppose that our two know this lot?"

Kristie shrugged. "They live here, so they'll drink here. Looks like it is the only pub in the village, too."

"I am going to miss our local." Carole sighed nostalgically. She sure would miss it. Miss the regular as clockwork greeting by the pub's landlord "There we have our Christmas carolers! What can I get my karaoke warblers? Your regular, girls?"

"Yes, I suppose so." Kristie got up. "Better go pee before we leave."

"I'll go after you. I'll pay."

As Carole waited at the bar clutching her precious banknotes, she glanced over at the three scruffs. They were laughing and talking quietly. She couldn't make out a word. One of the two newer arrivals called the barmaid over. Carole was quite taken aback by his posh speech, which did not go with the clothes. It looked like they were ordering lunch.

A moment later, the gold-scarved barmaid faced Carole, and gave her the bill. With pain in her heart, Carole handed over the hard-grafted-for cash. It may have been the best ploughman's ever, it still rankled her.

As the barmaid turned away to the cash machine, the original scruff slapped the newer arrivals on the back, called out a cheerful cheerio to the barmaid and left. A moment later, she saw him turn off into the road, sitting behind the wheel of the Roller.

Aghast, she blurted out to the barmaid. "That scruffy bloke... he... he... He nicked that Roller! He drove off in that Roller! Call the cops!"

The barmaid cast her a pitying look. The two leftover scruffs laughed heartily, as did several others within earshot of her too-loud voice.

A rotund elderly tweedy gent and his equally rotund elderly tweedy lady, wiped away tears of laughter. "Oh, that is a good one! Must tell his Lordship... "Listen up, George, dear chap, you must stop stealing your own Rolls. It's rather confusing." Once again, he and his wife descended into peals of laughter. "Haven't laughed so much in a long time. Thank you, my dear."

"Lordship?" Carole whispered.

"Yes, Lordship," the barmaid stated coolly. "I would have thought Lord Mayhew was well enough known around the Cotswolds and beyond." She rolled her eyes, sighed empathically, and returned to her business.

Kristie materialised at her friend's side. "That's me done. Now you go. Shall I get the car?"

"OK, but I am driving!" Carole hurried off. A Lord! She might have served lords and ladies in the shop for all she knew, but this was the first time that she'd seen a real-life lord. She was not impressed. She filed away his name in her memory. Later on, back at home, she'd have a look on Google. See if a Lord George Mayhew popped up.

CHAPTER TEN

Kristie drove the car away from the car park and waited for Carole by the pub's entrance. The weather was turning. The earlier, short-lived, watery sun had been pushed away by grey clouds.

As pretty as the village was, she missed the lights, and the hustle and bustle of town. On the one hand, she'd have loved to fit into this chocolate box village. If she were to believe Carole's fantasy, then she'd have to. As would Carole.

On the other hand, maybe they could tempt the men to town or even city life. Both she and Carole had lived in the city till they married. Totally loved up back then, they would have moved to the moon and beyond for their husbands, and that's how they ended up in a Cotswolds market town. Years later, and both divorced, they were still in the same town. Their erstwhile husbands had long since moved away. With no kids in the equation, the divorces had been final. Any and all contact had been lost.

The two women had adapted to their life and the lively market town well enough. Kristie had become quite fond of Combe-Norton. Doris had, of course, been their life saver. Cunning, wily, sly Doris. She'd taught them a lot. And she'd let them move into one of her terraces. She'd sold off several when the market boomed, but she'd stolidly clung onto two, which she rented out. The twosome had asked her why she'd not sold up completely. Doris had tapped her nose, and said, "When antiques are slow, I still have income coming in, so I don't have to dip into my nest egg."

Inspecting herself in the car mirror, Kristie saw that her scarf was missing. She must have dropped it in the pub. Seeing Carole approaching, she hastily got out of the car. "Must have dropped my scarf. Be back in a minute."

Carole slipped into the driver's seat, took a cigarette out of the package lying on the dashboard and lit it.

She almost missed him. Her jaw dropped. Ponytail was calmly walking by with two dogs. He looked gorgeous! As deliciously tempting as he had at the garden centre. Just a damn pity about the dogs! She just did not like dogs. No animals, for that matter. Not one little bit! So, if Ponytail had dogs, that meant that Hazel Eyes might have dogs, too?

Kids and animals. She wouldn't have them around her.

Resolutely, she decided that they would have to go. She was not having any animals in her house. She was not sharing her space, let stand her affections, with some furry creature. Not even a goldfish! A man had to give her his full attention and devotion! End of!

But he was gorgeous. As one of the dogs squatted, the other one stood up against him, and Ponytail bent down to cuddle the dog. To Carole's horror he kissed the top of the dog's head! She saw red with such profound jealousy. Those bloody dogs had to go! No question about it. He was hers. All hers. Those damnable dogs had to go.

If looks could have killed, Carole's furious jealousy-driven and aimed daggers would have instantaneously killed the the lovable furry duo. Even more so when Ponytail caressed the other dog who was done squatting. With horror, she watched him remove something from the grass and continue his walk.

The car door opened, and Kristie got in. "What are you looking so pissed off about? I wasn't that long."

"He's got dogs!" Carole hissed. "Ponytail has dogs!"

Cautiously, Kristie asked, "How do you know?"

"How do I know?" Carole hissed. "I just saw him walk past. With two bloody effing dogs! He kissed them! Just like that, in the street, and in front of me. He kissed the damn mutts." Her voice had risen several octaves.

"Perhaps Hazel Eyes has pets, too."

"Exactly!"

"Can we follow him, or..."

"How can you lose anyone in this god-forsaken effing little village? He was walking slow enough with the mutts. He went thataway." She pointed left and started the car. "We're going thataway, too."

After a moment, Ponytail came into sight. He had walked through a white wooden fenced entrance, up a short path, and was opening the door to a large Cotswold stone cottage. The nameplate next to the door stated the cottage's name: The Old Forge. It looked like several cottages made into one. They drove by slowly, past another cottage, and they'd made it to the edge of the village, and found a spot to turn the car.

"Those mutts will have to go." Carole couldn't get over the shock of Ponytail being a dog owner. She felt horribly betrayed. "I'm not sharing my man with anything or anyone. All mine, and no one else's."

"He's leaving again," Kristie said.

The two pretended to check out a road map, while keeping their eyes on the large car exiting from a garage next to the cottage. Ponytail got out of the car to open a double gate, and closed it again once he had driven through. He drove in the direction of Hazel Eyes.

The two women kept a good distance behind him. Nothing suspicious about driving through the village, was there now? The Jaguar they'd seen in the pub's car park passed them on the other side. A small car was behind them.

"We'll park where we did before," Carole said. "We've got a good view from there."

"Yeah, OK."

Parked amidst the dense evergreen foliage, they kept an eye on Hazel Eyes' house. Ponytail had parked the car, taken out the two despicable mutts, and gone into Hazel Eyes' house.

As they waited, Carole remembered the scruff in the pub, and told Kristie what she'd seen and heard.

"I don't believe it!"

"I couldn't, either, but the barmaid huffily told me that Lord George Mayhew was well enough known. As if I would know every or any effing Lord in this arse hole of the back of beyond."

"If he is so well known, we might find him on Google."

"That's what I figured. We'll have a look tonight."

Neither said it, but both were infinitely curious about his Lordship's marital, or lack thereof, status.

Carole lit herself a cigarette, and handed Kristie the package. After a few minutes, their patience was rewarded by the appearance of the two men, minus dogs. They got in the car, and drove off in the direction of town.

"At least we know where they're off to," Carole said.

"They're a bit early, aren't they? They aren't expected at Peter's till about three."

"Maybe they're doing something else in the meantime?"

The car continued on to the supermarket on the fringes of town, where Ponytail drove into the forecourt and tanked up. A moment later, the car slid into an empty parking spot, and once again Ponytail got out. He hurried to the supermarket and, some time later, came out again carrying a large bag. They were plenty early still.

At the roundabout they took the last exit. There were several cars between the men and their pursuers. With added determination, the women set chase.

Spurred on by Carole's deepening mad obsession, Kristie followed suit.

While Donald took on the Saturday afternoon mayhem at Sainsbury's, Aidan scrolled through the photos Peter had sent him. If they looked equally good or more so in reality, Aidan decided to go for them. There was no turning back, for some force drove him to making these changes to his life, and he was listening.

The Snow Crystals

While Donald had gone to fetch his car, Aidan had taken pictures of every corner of his house. He shoved the cottage's floor plan, complete with room measurements, in his coat pocket, and he compiled a list of things he wished to replace, if not acquire new. He'd come prepared.

"This'll cost you an arm and a leg, Aidan," he mumbled to himself. "But it'll be worth it." With a satisfied sigh, he settled back to wait for Donald.

Unlike Donald, he wasn't particularly drawn to blondes, but this lady was a beauty. With interest, he watched her approaching, and for a wild moment he thought that perhaps his luck might be changing.

He could get out of the car, with an excuse to search for something in the boot... not find it and utter his frustration, and hopefully start a conversation. The plan had barely come to fruition when the sylph-like blonde stopped next to a balding man emptying the contents of his trolley into a large estate car. A pretty girl skipped up to her, and put her arms around the woman.

Aidan watched with a sense of envy as the blonde kissed the girl, then leant over into the car, where Aidan could only just see a toddler strapped into a car seat.

His heart plummeted when the woman cast the man a look of such profound love, that Aidan felt a stab of pain in his gut. *"Why not me?"* He felt worse as the couple exchanged a quick kiss, then laughed and clearly shared a joke. The man ruffled the girl's curly locks lovingly, and she and her mother got into the car. The man opened the driver side door, and for the first time Aidan caught a glimpse of his face. Yes, balding, and not the most handsome of men, but such a friendly, contented, happy, lovely, and especially open face.

CHAPTER ELEVEN

Aidan let out a shuddering sigh. If he had been a child, he would have taken his Teddy, and headed for a far-off dark corner, and let flow a few secretive tears. Never to admit that he had wept. Always that stiff upper lip!

Emotions swept through him, and despite his successful burgeoning business, he felt like an absolute and utter failure. He loved Donald unconditionally, but he was hardly going to snuggle up with him on the couch, was he now?

When his father died, Aidan had kept a stiff upper lip for his mother's sake. The last thing she'd needed was for him to fall apart. But after the funeral, with his mother carted off by Mrs. Becket to her Cornish home, Aidan had accorded himself the luxury of falling apart and grieving. It had been Donald's arms around him, as he had descended into uncontrollable, racking sobs. Donald had just held him tightly, let him cry till there were no more tears left.

The Snow Crystals

Donald was more than his best friend. More than a cousin. More so, Donald and he had discovered as children that they were like soul mates. Always there for each other through all that life threw at them. In truth, despite enjoying his independence and the London job for a while, Aidan had missed the proximity of his best friend.

Looking back, he knew that those London colleagues he'd called friends back then, had been anything but. They'd been colleagues, work associates, less than acquaintances. People he went to the pub with, or out to dinner with. They'd been pretentious and full of themselves. Love was a game to them, and their casualties mere notches on their bedposts. Good looking Aidan had been a babe magnet for them, and he had too late realised they had used him. During his last year in London, he had steered more and more away from any social involvement with these so-called "friends".

When he left London, they removed him from their Facebook pages, calling him a loser, as they mocked and ridiculed him. They'd had to find a new babe magnet. Aidan saw them for what they were. Deep down, they were jealous of him. What a pathetic emotion.

Yes, a pathetic emotion, but a moment earlier he himself had felt a hint of jealousy, as he had watched the loving interaction between that happy couple. "*The lucky sod!*" It made Aidan feel even more down than before.

What was the matter with him? He'd been all over the place since he'd discovered those crystals. Less than two days... and look at the strange magic they had worked on him.

Intuitively, he knew they were good. Positive.

There was nothing evil about them. They felt so right when they lay in his hand. He was drawn to them, and they clung onto the fringes of his mind, constantly there, never far away. Working their magic.

Did he believe in magic? Aidan pondered deeply and came to the conclusion that everyone had the power to create magic if one so wished.

He had dreamt and hoped long enough for a dream home near Donald... His visualisations had materialised. His dreams and hopes for Galbraith's, too, had been realised, and the company was thriving. Galbraith's had been a respected and much-loved local business under his father, but it was his vision, his dream, that had made Galbraith's known across the nation, and as far afield as the Continent, the USA and Canada, and Down Under. So, if he was capable of that kind of magic, then why the blazes couldn't he bring true love into his life?

Donald had the Midas Touch, too... but was equally sorely lacking in the relationship department.

He knew for a fact that Donald craved something more than just the two ladies padding around the place, just like he craved something more than the feline twosome thundering up and down the stairs on their daily mad half hour.

He had reached a low ebb. He felt something stinging in the corner of his eyes, and checked himself in the car mirror. The last thing he wanted was to look like a sad git.

"*But you are a sad git!*" He was relieved that his reflection confirmed that he looked passable. He was not worried about showing his emotions in front of Donald. He just did not want to look like a sad idiot in front of anyone else.

Just as he wanted to push the mirror back up,

something caught his eye.

"Oh God. NO!"

A head with hair like hay, and black and red...

He turned abruptly in his seat. He scanned the many cars parked behind him. Shoppers scurried or ambled along to and fro. Cars leaving, cars hastily parking, while the less fortunate continued searching for that elusive empty parking bay. But he did not spot the apparition that turned his blood to ice.

"*Am I seeing things?*" He turned back to the mirror, and the first thing he saw was a face pale with shock and two huge hazel eyes. His ankle throbbed in sympathy... or was it fear? Then he scanned the mirrored image of the cars parked behind him again. Nothing. A similar scene to a moment ago was reflected in the mirror. Aidan shivered, and noted that the hand moving the mirror up was trembling.

There was something about those hags that absolutely terrified him.

He thought about the blonde vision of loveliness, and his immediately crushed hopes by a scene of obvious marital bliss. But a hag hits on him. And her pal hits on Donald.

"There is something incredibly unfair about this! Why are we treated so unfairly? Is it Karma? Have we done something so damn wrong or bad sometime, somehow, in this or a previous lifetime?"

No matter how Aidan pondered it, as he had done often enough before, he just could not remember anything either he or Donald had done, to warrant this continuing bad luck. They had unwittingly and unknowingly pulled two hags today. Besides, they were so obviously much older than he and Donald. And the worst part was catching these glimpses of the cause of his agony. This was the second time today. Was he paranoid? A figment of a terrified imagination? Or was it for real?

Aidan pulled the mirror down again. Just to make sure. *"Am I going mad?"* Except for his still too-pale face and worried eyes, nothing unusual was reflected. Just the normal business of a December Saturday afternoon.

The memory of her clutching his arm was tangible. The agony as her heel had ripped into his ankle. The foul stench emanating from her being, her mouth. A foul form of hell-fire and brimstone.

He wished Donald would hurry up. He desperately wanted to get away from this parking lot... he needed to escape.

"But escape from what?" Common Sense asked him. *"The apparition of a hag?"* Common Sense sighed and chuckled. *"Gather yourself together, darling boy. You are in the process of changing your world. Concentrate on that. Forget about those hags. Of course they terrified you. They would terrify anyone! I am Common Sense, and they quite terrified me! But look on the bright side, something came into your life that incited you to make positive changes. Concentrate on that."*

Aidan shrugged and almost imperceptibly shook his head, as white straight jacket and padded cell came to mind. He was holding a conversation with his common sense... whatever next? Yet there was truth in Common Sense's musings; he had to concentrate on the good things happening. Forcefully, he banished the hags from his mind.

Aidan thought again about the crystals. He was sure that they lay behind this change in his life. But how? The strangest of all was that he had found the enigmatic beauties in the spot where his father had died.

Donald approached, toting a large shopping bag. He was grinning. He placed the bag in the back of the car, and got in.

"That's me done. Let's go and get you sorted." Smiling, he turned towards Aidan, and his face fell. "What's with you, mate? You alright?"

Lowering his eyes, and turning his face partially away from his friend, Aidan mumbled. "It's nothing."

"Yeah, sure. Nothing my foot!" Donald thought, but didn't pursue it. He knew Aidan as well as himself, and within mere minutes his friend would be spilling his guts.

The exit from the parking lot was a tour de force in itself. "And to think this mêlée will only get worse as Christmas approaches," Donald stated conversationally. "You should've seen the laden trolleys! Sheer madness. Oh, by the way, we're having some pasta concoction of mine tonight."

"Thought we were going to the pub for a meal."

"Not tonight, we're not. I saw that cookbook you bought. Gotta start sometime."

"Won't it be a lot of work?"

"What I have in mind, even you can't ruin."

"You know I have a Michelin Star in cremating food."

The further they got away from the busy supermarket area, the quieter the road got. There were a few cars ahead of them as well as a few following them. Just normal Saturday afternoon traffic.

Not even three yet, and daylight was already waning. The sky was heavily leaden. The greyness had sunk into the gently undulating landscape, and settled over bare trees, shrubs and hedgerows.

"If I didn't know better, I'd say it looks like snow," Donald said.

"Perhaps. I paid no attention to the forecast." Aidan shivered. The car was pleasantly warm, so why did he shiver? "I think I may be going mad..." He gave Donald a sidelong glance. Donald took his eyes off the road for a moment, to cast his friend a questioning glance. "I think I spotted one of those horrid hags in a car, back in the car park, as I waited for you. I saw black and red, topped off by that horrid hay bale hair. A moment later it was gone."

Donald frowned. "Maybe they've gone shopping, too?"

"A possibility," Aidan conceded. "But I spotted the same hag when we were at Trivia! So, I am either going mad, or..."

Donald didn't answer immediately. He appeared to be pondering Aidan's words. "Are you suggesting that they are following us?" he asked incredulously.

"There was something so desperate about them. And with that chap saying they'd timed it on purpose to bump into us..."

Donald nodded slowly several times over. "True. If we spot them again, God forbid, then we'll... But what can we do? Except for them crippling you, what have they done? It's our word against theirs. Certainly where it concerns your ankle. I agree they are freaky, Aidan. Seriously freaky! But let's not let them get to us. For now let's just get on with our lives, and if they cross our paths, whether we are together or not, we'll have to take it from there. For all we know they live in Combe-Norton and one is bound to run regularly into the same people in a market town, and even its surrounding areas."

"Sensibly spoken. And you're right. Maybe it was no more than a fluke." Aidan spoke bravely, but did not really believe his own words. It was this lack of conviction that made him blurt out, "But you can't deny their behaviour was utterly creepy. The way the hag desperately clutched and clung to my arm, with her foul gob in my face..."

"Yeah, ditto, ditto!"

"Donald, if it hadn't been for that, and the timing of their attack - for what else can you call it? - I might be inclined to call it a coincidence. Proclaim me mad, but I got some really bad vibes off those two."

"Like I said, we're just going to get on with our lives, and if they cross our path again, or we spot them, then we need to consider what may need doing next. If they end up on our doorstep, or in our village, then we may have stalkers on our hands."

"You uttered the words I did not dare bring out into the open."

As Aidan said this, Donald cast a glance in his rear view mirror. His hands tightened on the steering wheel. Was his imagination playing tricks on him, too? Did he really see what he thought he saw two cars down?

Such an incongruous small, old, dark blue car, like many other old, small incongruous cars on the road. He could have sworn he too now witnessed Aidan's nightmarish apparition... or had paranoia set in?

Seeing a chance to overtake the remaining car in front of him, Donald put his foot down, and a sigh of relief escaped him as he saw the dark blue car grow smaller, all but trapped behind several cars.

He sped up, and made it just past a farm exit before a cumbersome tractor could turn into the road.

The tractor was heading in his direction. With traffic heading into town, drivers would be stuck behind the tractor.

Knowing he had blessedly lost the car, he reduced speed some. Before long they were enveloped by the picture-postcard perfection of Thatch Hall.

CHAPTER TWELVE

Carole let out a husky cackle. "They think they can get away from us! Hah!"

"If we'd not know where they're going to, you'd not be so chirpy."

"That bloody tractor is a damned nuisance, but we know where Peter's shop is, so we know where our men are. So, in all, not a biggie at all." She demanded yet another cigarette off Kristie, and sat back, as they crawled at a snail's pace behind the tractor.

Neither of them reacted to the genteel beauty of the sizable village. Neither noticed that Christmas was starting to settle over this quiet community. In the encroaching gloom of the afternoon, the first outdoor lights had already been lit, and twinkled festively in several gardens. More festive cheer sprang forth from numerous windows.

Except for some cars, the road into the centre of the village was comparatively quiet. As they approached the square, it appeared busier. At a quick glance, the two women spotted a small convenience store, a bakery, a small butcher's and a greengrocer's, all of which struck the two women as surprisingly busy for such a backwater of a hole. A large Christmas tree with multi-coloured lights stood near the war memorial. Lights were strung along some of the shop facades, too.

"There they are!" Kristie pointed.

The men's car was parked by the Christmas tree, across from an elegant double shop front. Peter's antiques shop. It was exactly as Doris had said. The shop lay on the corner of a small lane, framed by lush evergreen vegetation.

"Where to park?" Carole looked around the square. "We have to be able to keep an eye on them."

"Someone's leaving. There, behind that tree."

Carole put her foot down and drove around the square, where she slid into the open parking bay. She rudely ignored the elderly driver who was just meticulously aligning his car to back up into the open space.

"That was lucky." She sneered. "Got there before that old fart with his poncy Rover."

"They're not happy at all." Kristie glanced at the angrily frowning elderly couple.

With amused satisfaction, Carole turned to have a look at the couple. "Stuck up corpses!" She pulled a face. She regretted that the two did not catch her giving them the finger. Would have served them right. "Shouldn't be allowed on the road. Should be locked up in a home. Key thrown away. Bloody nuisance, those old bags." Her face turned ugly with her deep ingrained bitterness and jealousy of all who were better off than she.

"We're here on a mission. They're not in the car, which means that they're already in Peter's shop," Kristie reminded her. "What shall we do? Wait here, and see what happens? Or do you want us to get out and snoop around some?"

"Have a quick snoop. See what we can find out."

The women got out, oblivious to the glances of passers-by. They did not fit in with the gentility of the village scene.

"Nice!" Donald glanced around him appreciatively. Aidan agreed.

A young woman, serving a couple, smiled at the men, and said someone would be with them shortly. A moment later, an elegant lady approached them smiling.

"Peter is expecting me... us. I am Aidan Galbraith. This is my friend, Donald MacIntosh."

The lady smiled. "Yes, we are expecting you. I am Peter's wife. He should be here shortly. Perhaps you wish to have a look around already."

"Yes, please. Peter sent me some photos. There are several things I'm interested in."

"Yes, I know. Come with me. The furniture in question is in the back."

She led them through a large room with fine antique furniture beautifully and artistically displayed, and into a large and well-lit warehouse-like area. Here, too, everything was perfectly displayed. From the many windows, there were pleasant views onto the picturesque lane which ran alongside the building. At the back of the room, the big windows showed that the lane gave way to a small green bordered by several ancient fairy tale-like cottages.

"Shall I leave you to it? If you have any questions..."

"We'll know where to find you." Aidan smiled.

Unlike Donald, who was casually biding his time, looking around and clearly enjoying himself, Aidan took out his phone, quickly scrolled through the photos, and went in search of his longed-for treasures.

Within mere steps, he discovered the desk he'd taken a fancy to. Seeing it now as it were in the flesh, Aidan knew this was what he wanted. There was a price ticket on it, so it wasn't sold yet. Next, he spotted the much-liked round table and chairs. Then the suite which would complement the two chairs he had already bought. Within the shortest period of time, he rushed around, best possible with his ever-worsening aching ankle, and ticked off the things he liked, tried out the sofa and chairs, sat at tables, and the desk, and he was ready for Peter.

A familiar voice called out their names. "Sorry, I was held up. I got your rug in the van, Aidan. See anything you fancy?"

"Thanks for collecting the rug. Much appreciated. And this is the list of things I took a fancy to. Please let me know how much that is going to set me back."

Peter saw a good-humoured sparkle in Aidan's eyes. "You've been busy!" He took the list and retreated to his office. A short while later he emerged and handed the list back to Aidan. He had written a figure at the bottom of the page.

For a moment, Aidan contemplated it, and then nodded with satisfaction. "Yes, you're on!" He held his hand out, and they shook hands on it.

"You're done already?" Donald approached. He

was carrying a large wicker basket and a chair. "Found these. Quite like them."

"I love customers like you two." Peter grinned.

"Give us some more time, and who knows what else we'll find." Aidan had forgotten his earlier problems, and was concentrating solely on his home.

"There's more upstairs," Peter offered.

Aidan had caught the bug, and succumbed willingly. Why hadn't he accompanied Donald before on his forages? Donald regularly went off to search for treasures at markets and fairs, and came home with at least one, if not multiple gems. Donald's home was cosy, inviting and felt warm and homey the second one crossed the threshold. Aidan looked at the chair and basket his friend had found. Who knows what he'd use them for, and where he'd put them. Aidan felt, where it concerned this area of life, that thinking a bit more like Donald would ultimately benefit him.

"I'm definitely coming back next week," Aidan assured Peter. "Better write out a cheque for you. When can you deliver it?"

"My son's fetching the lorry as we speak."

Aidan felt Peter's eyes searching his. As if Peter could read his soul. Tap into his mind, his thoughts.

"We'll load up, and can be with you later this afternoon. That is if you don't mind us arriving that late."

Once again, Peter's eyes scoured through the protective layers he had built up across the years. Layers he had only ever entrusted Donald to peel away. For as open and easy going as he was, Aidan had only ever truly opened himself up to his father and to Donald. And now here stood this near-on stranger, who for some peculiar and unfathomable reason felt so right, and who was reading him like a book.

"But I know you won't mind. Because you're desperate to replace the grey with these newly acquired treasures. I'm right, aren't I?" Their eyes were on a level. Peter's eyes were filled with a knowing twinkle. "So, hie thee home, and start emptying shelves and drawers, and whatever else needs doing, so we can easily offload and load again."

"You... you... won't mind?"

"I wouldn't be offering if I'd minded. Besides, I can't wait to hear from Mary. She'll be over the moon."

Aidan wrote out the cheque, and Donald paid for his chair and basket.

As they made their way towards the door, Aidan cast a last glance around him. He saw several more things he'd have liked. But they appeared to be the kind of things that he might equally be able to find at markets, now that he had finally decided to accept Donald's offer to accompany him on some of his forages. As he approached the door, he spotted something he rather liked, and made a beeline for it. It stood smack in front of a window overlooking the lane. "Peter," he called out, "I want this, too."

"Duly noted, mate." Peter called back from the other side of the room, where he was moving some furniture towards a door. "Now go home," he added, laughing. "Before we run out of lorry space."

Aidan laughed in reply, and cast a last satisfied glance at the cabinet. That is when he spotted the flash of black and red... Unmistakable! Topped off by that ungainly and vile bleached hair. He blinked in shock. A wave of icy cold sickness hit his stomach like a brick. Less than a second, and the horrid apparition had dissipated.

The Snow Crystals

"Aidan, come on," Donald called from the doorway. As Aidan turned to follow his friend, Donald eyed him worriedly. "You look like you've seen a ghost."

Numbly, Aidan nodded. "Yes, that or I must be going mad."

"Not again?"

"Since that catastrophic encounter, this is the third time, Donald. Either I am going totally mad, or that hag is following me... us... around."

Saying goodbye, Donald steered Aidan out of the shop. "Where did you see her?"

"In the lane."

"Stay there," Donald ordered, and went to have a look in the innocuously pretty lane. A moment later he was back. "I went to the cottages at the end, and didn't see a thing."

"See? Mad! Paranoid! If this keeps up, I'll be needing a padded cell next."

Both men looked around the square. The last of the daylight was fading fast. There were less shoppers around than before. Less cars in the square, too.

"Let's get ready for that delivery, mate."

They made their way to the car, and for a moment stood looking at the colourfully decorated tree.

"Looks cheerful," Aidan said.

"Your tree will be cheerful, too, once we set it up. Tomorrow I'll help you with the outside decorations."

"Thanks. I just had a thought. Now that I am being kitted out with a new interior, I'll want some more decorations. For the study, and certainly for the kitchen, to go with that new dining set. And let's not forget those gorgeous dishes. Daft or what, but I am seeing that kitchen in a new light, and I'll be using it lots more from now on."

"Whatever the season, the view across that garden of yours is a joy to behold. Anyway, the garden centre is open tomorrow, so if you feel like it, we can hop into town at ten. I'll drive. Chances are that you'll be hobbling worse tomorrow."

"Argh! Don't remind me!" Aidan growled.

"Let's wave cheerio to this pretty village. Get ready for Peter." Giving the square one last look, Donald got in the car. Aidan followed suit. Seconds later, the car drove off in the direction of West Woodside.

CHAPTER THIRTEEN

Oblivious to the cold, two women emerged from behind the Christmas tree, their eyes dancing madly.

"We'll be there, too!" Carole looked at her friend. "Shall we follow them now, or go home?"

"I am bursting for a pee. It's the cold."

They got in the car, with Carole once again behind the wheel. "What do you think of this? We go home. Change into warmer clothes. Have a hot drink, a fag or two, and we'll both need a pee..."

"Perhaps scoff a pork pie while we're at it."

"... and return to South Woodside, and have a look at what is happening. Maybe we'll find out a bit more. And tomorrow morning we'll be at that garden centre. Early!"

"Yeah, OK." Kristie smiled.

"Get me a fag," Carole demanded. She inhaled deeply and sighed with satisfaction. "I can feel him. Oh, he felt so good when I clutched his arm. I can just imagine what the rest of him will feel like. Kristie, they can't get away. They're ours!" As she drove the car back to town, Carole said, "We'll put on dark, warm clothes. That'll be best for this mission."

"And look gorgeous and sexy for tomorrow." Kristie wriggled in her seat. "Hurry the fuck up, will you, or I'll have to hang me arse out of the window."

"Your two flatten us with doggy love, and look at my two."

"That's cats for you."

"I'll move their highnesses to the utility room. They're warm and safe there. As much as I love them, and as sweet as they are, they're rather gormless. A bit thick, really."

Donald bent down to stroke the two. "Nah, they are just pulling your leg. They know that you adore them, and they're using it to their fullest potential. If I were a big feline tea-cosy, believe me, I would, too. You'd be my slave."

Aidan leant over and hugged his friend from behind. "Aw, you'd be my long-haired tea-cosy. And I'd love you to bits, and feed you Whiskas and Felix and Royal Canin, and lots more goodies. Buy you toy mice and rattly balls. And you could sleep on my bed, and go for walkies in the garden. Now, wouldn't you just love that?"

"Get orff, you idiot." Donald laughed. He was relieved to note that the earlier haunted look had left Aidan's eyes. Instead, he saw a twinkling mirth. "Would I get my own nice big private litter tray with one of those swing flaps?"

The Snow Crystals

"Yes, with your name above the flap, so that the other two would know that it is yours and yours alone."

Donald looked down at the two cats in mock surprise. "They can read?"

"Oh yeah. Surprised, eh? They might look, and even be, gormless, but the other day when I came home, I caught them both entranced by Wind in the Willows."

"That makes it easy then to buy them a Christmas present. A book!"

"Good idea. They've taken a fancy to Paul Gallico and James Herriott. Nietzsche and Kafka are a bit beyond them. As I said, a tad thick..."

The two looked at each other, and burst out laughing.

"If someone could hear us, they'd think we've flipped." He started singing in a high falsetto voice his own rendition of a once well-known song, "We're being taken away to the funny-farm, hee hee, ha ha, by little men in shrunken white coats, ho ho, hee hee..."

"Idiot!"

Chuckling, Donald picked the dogs' leads off the table. "You start doing whatever needs doing. I'll give the girls a quick stroll. Put them in the utility with your literates. Oh, and I'll pop your car in the garage."

Aidan wasn't quite sure where to start. Office, kitchen, sitting room? Might as well get the cats settled first. He gave them their dinner early, and placed it safely out of the dogs' reach.

He emptied the kitchen table, and a dresser which had served its purpose. Beyond serving its purpose and filling up an empty wall, he couldn't say anything positive about the dresser. It was also a rather sad and meagre display of the lack of kitchen paraphernalia and food stuffs he had in stock. He was just glad he could toast bread and fry an egg without cremating it.

"I need to take time out to start living," he mumbled to himself.

This reaffirmation appeased and satisfied him. His next port of call was the office. As he emptied his desk, he saw Donald talking to one of the movers. A moment later he came in.

"Your new neighbours are held up and won't be arriving till tomorrow. By now I am damn curious about them. Car keys in your jacket pocket?"

"Yes. And thanks, mate. The cats are already safely tucked away. I'm curious about the new neighbours, too. Perhaps two little old ladies... sisters or life-long friends who, à la Miss Marple, poke their pointy noses in everyone's lives and businesses. Hmm, I just hope they're nice."

Even his desk did not take long to empty. But when he reached the drawer containing the box with snow crystals, a sense of reverence overcame him. He could hear Donald chatting away to his two ladies. Aidan had to smile; they were both right softies and totally daft about their pets. He focussed his attention on the box again, and had a quick peek. Folding away the tissue paper, he was relieved to find the crystals still safely cradled and intact within. Their sparkle had intensified. Aidan could have called Donald at that moment, and shown them to him, but his friend was now obviously in the utility room. Better let him get on with it. He'd show him later. Or tomorrow...

Aidan hid the box behind some books, in the ceiling to floor bookcases which covered two walls of his office. They'd be safe there.

In a few more hours the state of the art desk and

accessories would be history. As would a large part of the remainder of the cottage's contents. He had never felt any attachment to any of it.

A starkly modern bed to sleep in, and whose linens were changed weekly by Mary. A kitchen table to have breakfast at, or even a quick dinner straight from the microwave. Two not particularly comfortable designer sofas, which hardly enticed one to sit and read for hours, or watch that film from start to finish without moving.

Why had he done this to himself? Except for Donald, who was a regular fixture, he rarely invited anyone to the house. Socialising was mostly done at pubs or restaurants, and not in his home. Filling some bowls with crisps, olives, and nuts, had painfully accentuated his inability to cook or even prepare the most basic dishes. He'd found it safer to banish the social grace of entertaining from his home life. But not for long, he promised himself for the n-th time that day.

Donald had dinner guests if not once a week, then certainly once per fortnight. And it was Donald who happily slaved away for hours at the kitchen counter and AGA, measuring, slicing and dicing, stirring and tasting, as he created culinary magic. It wasn't some hired help. Without the slightest hint of envy, Aidan wondered why he couldn't be just a bit more like his cousin.

"Come and get some tea while it is still hot." The holler reached him from the sitting room. Donald was sitting on one of the sofas, which he had pushed up against the other. The large grey rug was already rolled up. The boxed Christmas tree and decorations were piled up in the bay.

"Thanks." Aidan smiled. "You've been busy."

"It's easy, really. Let's face it, a blind elephant couldn't come to any harm here."

Aidan shrugged helplessly. "Pathetic, isn't it? Not much to show for myself, have I now? Minimalism in extremis." He sipped his tea in silence for a while. "If I were to move right now, except for the books, I could fit everything in my car. That, of course, includes the cats. But that should go without saying."

"And I'd need a stonking huge lorry of the HGV variety!"

Aidan laughed. "If not two. By the way, what are you going to do with that chair and basket?"

"Line the basket, and plant spring bulbs in it. It'll go in the conservatory. The chair will go in one of the guest rooms."

"How do you do it? What is that magic touch that transformed your house into a home?"

"As an artist, I have acknowledged that just because I am a man, life is not all about testosterone. I've accepted and recognised my feminine side. You've one too, Aidan. It's there, beneath all that..."

"Macho bullshit?"

"Nah! You're not a macho bullshitter! Far from. No, my friend, you need to be a bit kinder on yourself. Pause to smell the roses. Stop for a while to enjoy all the good things in life. I've said it before and I'll say it again: look around you. You've got a gorgeous home. I am so glad... no, more than that... delighted... over the moon... that you are finally doing something about this place. It's been howling for love."

"So, what does that have to do with my feminine side?"

"Everything. It finally threw a sizable paddy, and you paid heed to it. Look around you. This is the result of this recognition. Tonight we will be sitting in front of that fire, in cosy and comfortable wingback chairs, toasting your success with a bedtime toddy of whiskey. Oh, I am spending the night. After that whiskey, and the wine we'll have at dinner, I'm not driving home, even if it is to the other side of the village. Can't be bothered to walk either."

"I think Mary made the bed..."

Donald's phone rang. "My mother. What does she want? Hello, Mum, how are you? ... Glad to hear it. Yes, yes, I am fine, too. I am at Aidan's. We have the weekend all planned. ... Oh. OK. Well, that's a shame. I got you and Dad a Christmas present. Will have to wait... What? .... No, Mum! No way! ... Mum, please stop pushing. ... I'm adamant. One Christmas with my sister and that husband of hers was enough to put me off forever. So, no way! ... Mum, she used to be a lovely kid, till she met that fellow. He brainwashed her. ... NO! ... Mum, Aidan and I have already made plans for Christmas, and that is final. ... What? .... WHAT? ... I don't believe this! ... MUM! ... How dare you! That is totally uncalled for, Mother! ... Mother? ... Oh, hi, Dad. ... Yes, I am fine. But now quite angry, too. ... Dad, I am not going to be coerced into this. I am staying right here in England. Cosily at home in the Cotswolds. ... Dad, I've told you before how I feel about my sister and her family. And I am not going to wreck my life, peace of mind and Christmas by spending it with her and that sanctimonious, bigoted sod she unfortunately married. ... She's WHAT? ... Not another one! Bloody hell! Is birth control totally beyond their understanding? ... Oh, yes! Of course! God forbids that! ... My answer is final, Dad. Look, I love you and Mum. But my sister chose to live this life, and I want no part of it. Christmas and birthday cards are my limit. ... Oh, come on, Dad. You know there is no love lost between me and that sanctimonious git of a husband of hers. He can't stand me. Well, the feeling is mutual. ... OK. ... Yes! Alright! ... Well, take care, and have a good trip. And be seeing you sometime next year. ... Bye."

His face flushed with anger, Donald looked in frustration at his friend. "I am sure you could guess what that was all about." Aidan nodded and waited for Donald to continue. "The weather forecast for the US isn't too good for the coming week. Snow, apparently. So, they decided to get out before there were problems. My mother gets herself in a tizzwazz and Dad just kowtows to her every whim. Damn! She used to be a sensible woman. But it seems, since Dad retired several years ago, that she's gone somewhat loopy. Maybe he's too much under her feet. Add to that the power that sister of mine has over her. As does that clap-happy git. This past summer Mum and Dad were talking about spending Christmas at a country house hotel, or some hotel on the Continent. They were looking forward to it. Then Mum and my sister chatted on Skype, and suddenly they are going to the USA. Spend Christmas with that holier-than-thou lot. Oh, and the breeding machine also known as my sister appears to be up the duff again."

"I gathered as much from your reaction."

"Yep, and that bloody husband of hers will thump his bible on the table, preaching vehemently that it is God's will. Thou shalt procreate."

"How many does that make? I lost count."

"So have I! Eight or nine, I think."

"Jesus. Talk about breeding like rabbits."

"You said it." Donald got up, and went to the

dresser. He poured himself a measure of whiskey, and swallowed it in one. "I need one. You want one?"

"A teensy one."

He placed the glass in Aidan's hand, and sat down heavily. Should he tell Aidan what his mother had said? Not that it mattered. But it was the way she said it. It had been her voice, but the seed had been his sister's and her blasted husband's, and the vile seed had sprouted... and his mother had given voice to the bigoted nastiness of Deidre and Randy.

Randy! What an appropriate name for that idiot. Donald was not one to give over to the emotion of hate, but at that moment he acknowledged that he hated Randy Chalmers.

As for Deidre, the worst part, if truth be told, was that Donald never wanted to see his sister again. Both she and Randy had planted the seeds of vile allegations in his mother's mind. And even if it had been true... what would it have mattered? But it wasn't true! Those two merely had taken a beautiful friendship and vilified it in their caustic, blinkered brains. And for what reason? Donald hadn't a clue.

And if this wasn't bad enough, he still had to tell Aidan about also seeing that bloody apparition as they were driving to Peter's. But with Aidan finally relaxing some, and clearly looking forward to his new interior, Donald didn't have the heart to tell him. He would, later... or tomorrow... but not now. They'd always been open with each other. But also sensitive of each other. And he was not going to inflict this pain knowingly... He would have to, but not now.

Donald looked at Aidan. His dearest friend and cousin. The one person in this world whom he trusted most and above all. He had never hidden the fact that he dearly loved him. They were like twin brothers.

"Mum's upset with me for preferring to spend Christmas with you, over spending it in Boston."

He didn't give voice to the rest. His mother's allegations, incited by his sister and that man, had really thrown him. He was still reeling from the affront.

"That's a relief, for I'd rather not have to visit you in some American jail."

"Eh?"

"Come on, mate. That SOB, that Randy, is a GBH victim waiting to happen. Just meeting him that once was more than enough!

"He hated you!"

"The feeling was and remains mutual." Aidan went to the dresser for the whiskey bottle and poured them each some more. "He's the type of bastard one would happily take on a cliffside walk, and... Oh dear! Oops!"

"The eulogy would make me puke, but it would be so worth it."

"So, when is this next little horror of a Godly gift expected?"

"Sometime this summer, I suppose. They only just noticed that she's late, so they naturally assume that she's pregnant again."

"Hmph. Anyway, back to the matter in hand..."

Donald took the two glasses and went to the kitchen. "Yeah, back to the here and now. I'll finish off down here. Why don't you go upstairs?"

CHAPTER FOURTEEN

"What do you think? Will this do?" Kristie twirled this way and that, as she modelled her black outfit. "It makes me look so fat."

Carole looked up from tying her boots. "You and me both. But we'll be snug as bugs and cosily warm. And that's what counts."

"I've warmed up some soup, and put out two pork pies."

"Aren't you precious." Carole smirked. "I want to have a look at Google Maps. Find out about that village."

"While I get us the food, have a look, see if you can find out anything about that scruffy lordship fellow."

"Oh, yes. Of course."

Walking into the lounge, Kristie saw Carole determinedly stabbing the keyboard, and manhandling the mouse. "Have you found something?"

Carole looked up, a satisfied smirk on her face.

"Well, the good news is that he is a lord - and appears to be a rich one, too - who lives near the village. Breeds horses, and is well known in horsy circles. That might explain his scruffy appearance."

"I'm scared of horses." Kristie put the tray on the table, handed Carole the soup and pie, and sat down next to her. "They're so big."

"Yeah. The bad news is that he is married with three kids. There's a picture of his wife, some snooty stuck up cow."

"At least we know our boys are single."

"True." She took a bite of the pie, and pointed at the screen. "Look, there..." Tiny crumbs of pie scattered over the mouse and keyboard. "...that's where yours lives. There's a small lane there, off the main road, that appears to overlook his house. We've got the binoculars, so we can see inside."

"What if he closes the curtains?"

"Oh! Shi... let's just hope he doesn't!"

They ate their pies and soup, and having thoroughly acquainted themselves with the village, both through Google Maps and satellite, they got ready for their mission.

Kristie was entirely dressed in black, save for matching dark brown thermal wool hat, scarf and gloves. Carole didn't possess black accessories, and had donned a navy blue hat, a dark green scarf and dark brown gloves. Both their coats had hoods. They'd be warm.

Excitement coursed through them, and elevated their temperatures, as they stepped into the car. Carole demonstratively held up a digital camera. "Bless zoom! We should be able to see right into the house."

"Alright," Kristie said.

Donald tore open the packages with ready cut onion, mushrooms, and bell peppers and tossed it into the minced beef mixture frying in the pan. Spaghetti had already been placed in boiling water. "And now we add herbs, salt and pepper, and this pot of ready-made sauce to the mixture. You stir."

"As easy as that?" Aidan obediently did as told. "Smells good."

"Yes, as easy as that! Even you can do this. Crispy French bread and garlic butter, and some ready-to-use salad. It's hardly rocket science."

Aidan set the table and poured wine. "This furniture really suits the kitchen. I feel like a kid with a new toy." He looked around at the new dresser, already filled with his few bits and pieces of kitchen accoutrements, and the new country table and chairs. The rug he had set his heart on lay under the table. "We really should be having this dinner by candlelight, with two beautiful ladies."

"We can light some candles. Do you have any?" Donald asked.

"No. Nothing."

"Then you'd better get some tomorrow. They're also very useful in a power failure. As for the beautiful ladies, sorry, mate, no can do." He shrugged helplessly. "I keep hoping for a miracle..."

"Hoping against hope," Aidan mumbled.

Donald placed two laden plates on the table, sat down, and raised his glass. "Cheers, mate. Here's to your new home, and may it bring a new life."

"Thanks. I hope Peter will be able to sell my old stuff easily. It's rather out of the ordinary... I mean it's not his usual stock."

"He said he had some people in mind, so don't worry about it. Enjoy what you've got now, and start making this house a home."

Aidan nodded contemplatively. "Yes, I will." He continued eating. "This is really delicious, and so simple to make."

"I'll turn you into a cook of sorts yet. More wine?" He poured them both another glass, and was pleased to see Aidan relaxing. There was something his friend was not telling him. He could sense it. You're one to talk, Donald thought, as his mother's allegations came to mind, alongside the sighting of one of those hags following them to Peter's. In truth, he desperately needed to share this with his friend, but as he saw a contented smile lighten up Aidan's face, he decided that tomorrow would be early enough... or even Monday.

"After-dinner coffee?" Aidan asked. Seeing Donald's nod, he put on the kettle. "There's quite a bit left over. Enough for another meal."

"Well, there you go." Donald stretched himself like a lazy cat. "Monday's dinner." He emptied the last wine into their glasses. "I could happily sit here for a few more hours nattering about all sorts and our pathetic love lives, but that tree needs erecting..."

"Lucky tree!"

"Eh? Oh, I get it." Donald laughed. "Why don't you concentrate on Christmas trees and baubles, like a good boy?"

"I'm trying." Aidan downed his glass in one.

They took their coffees with them into the sitting room. Donald poured two brandies and placed them on the new side tables next to the two new wingback chairs on opposite sides of the wood burner. The two ladies padded on their heels and settled contentedly in front of the warm fire.

"I could get used to this."

A profound sense of peace, warmth and satisfaction filled Aidan, as his glance swept over a considerably fuller room. Gone was the previous chill. Gone, too, was the previously accompanying emptiness. Although it had niggled him all day, only now, as he purveyed his newly created life and home, did the true essence of his mistakes strike him. Best to learn from them, and move on.

Donald had started to unpack the tree, and was laying out all the bits and pieces.

"It's going to be a beauty." Aidan joined Donald on the floor. Between them and the instructions, the tree stood proudly in the bay within no time. "I was right, wasn't I?" Donald exclaimed. "Now the lights."

"Does it really need so many?"

Aidan's mother had always decorated the tree, and he had managed for years with the same, same old, which Donald would demand binning by tomorrow. He readily acknowledged that he really hadn't a clue.

"Yes, it does. Let me do it, and watch and learn." Donald peered good naturedly over his specs. "Next year you'll know what to do."

As Donald expertly distributed the lights around the tree, Aidan, with one eye on the proceedings, was readying the decorations for hanging.

"Done. What do you think so far?" Donald stood back to admire the effect.

With a frisson of delight, Aidan looked up at the tree. He felt like a child who had wandered into a fairy tale. "It's magical," he whispered.

Donald grinned. "It is, rather. Now the rest. Come

on, help me with this." He held out his hand, to help Aidan up off the floor.

Aidan continued to feel like he had wandered into an alternative reality. Was this really his home? This cosy home... this beautiful tree. Had he mistakenly strayed through a wardrobe door into his own version of Narnia?

He eagerly accepted Donald's occasional suggestions, as snow crystals and other baubles found their way around the tree. When he stepped back, the end result struck him speechless. It was everything and more than he ever could have hoped for.

"It's beautiful! Donald, I never could have done it on my own. Thank you."

As he had done often across their life-long friendship, Aidan hugged his friend. A hug which was heartily reciprocated. For several minutes they stood with their arms around each other's shoulders, as they took in the masterpiece which graced the large bay.

"How time flies when you're having fun," Donald observed. "Do you realise eleven's fast approaching? If it's alright with you, I'll let the girls out back. Shall we have a bedtime toddy? Hey, you're quiet."

Aidan felt star struck, and said so. "I'm rather gobsmacked about today. And that beauty is the icing on the cake." He waved in the direction of the tree. "And I owe it all to you." There was a mistiness to his hazel eyes. "Thank you for unleashing much-needed magic in my life." More magic came to mind. The enigmatical snow crystals in their safe box in the office. And it had all started with those crystals. From there on his life had snowballed. "I'll pour us the toddy, while you take the ladies out back."

Eleven o'clock came and went, as they drank their

whiskey and relaxed for a short while, amicably side by side on the cosy new sofa, talked about this and that, and stared at the twinkling tree.

Around 11:30 the lights were switched off on the tree, and the rest of the room fell into darkness, too.

CHAPTER FIFTEEN

Two women stirred in their car hidden amongst the dense foliage of a narrow lane leading out the village. They watched lights come on at opposite ends of the first floor. Almost simultaneously, some fifteen minutes later, these windows went dark, too.

Except for an olde worlde street light casting soft yellowish light over the three cottages in Old Orchard Lane, looming midnight ruled.

"Looks like Ponytail is staying the night," Carole said. "I hope Doris wasn't wrong."

Kristie fidgeted with her scarf and gloves, and secured the hat firmly over her head and ears. "Maybe there's a rear exit, and he slipped out without our knowing. Maybe one of those lit rooms was the bathroom."

"Could be. But..." She let out a shuddering breath of indignation. "But you didn't see them embrace. I had the goggles, and I saw them embrace."

"Are you really sure of that?"

"Of course I am sure! I have eyes in my head!" Carole snapped.

"Shhh. It's OK, honey. We're in this together. I understand. It's just that we're trying to get a peek from quite some distance, and through windows, and all we have to rely on are those binoculars..."

"I know what I saw!" Carole riled. "They embraced!"

"We embrace," Kristie tried to appease her friend as best possible.

"Just not the same. This was two mature men engaged in a full-blown embrace."

"We'll get to the bottom of this. Honest. Let's do as you planned. OK?"

Without another word, they got out of the car and, keeping to the shadows, they made their way across the quiet village street. They crept past a garden wall which would be a riot of foliage and blooms from spring onwards.

"We'd be in deep shit if these were rose bushes," Kristie whispered, following Carole as they pushed their way forward through the low barren shrubbery.

They stopped at the end of the wall, keeping themselves hidden amongst the evergreen branches of a rampant laurel bush, and observed the small lane.

"It's a dead end lane," Carole said. "See," she pointed to the left. "And that's the lane I saw on Google Maps. Looks more like a dirt track to me."

"Hey." Kristie dug her elbow into Carole's side. "Look, there's a For Sale sign on the cottage opposite Hazel Eyes."

"So there is! It's for sale through Coleridge's. We'll Google it when we get home." She nimbly moved forward with Kristie in her wake. They made it to the low wall encircling the cottage. "It looks empty from here." She pushed open the gate and hurried up the short path. "Phew! No security lights." She made it to the window and peered in. "There's some furniture, but it looks very unlived in."

"Maybe they're on holidays."

"Could be. We'll find out from Coleridge's. But if this cottage is unoccupied, it could well be very useful to us."

Kristie gasped. "You are not suggesting..."

"Why not? All's fair in love and war. If this place is really unoccupied, it could be just what we need." Barely able to see Kristie's worriedly shocked expression as they huddled in the shadows, she patted her friend's arm. "It is exactly what we need, hon. We can keep an eye on their comings and goings."

"Yes. But... but what about Ponytail? How are we going to keep an eye on him? He's got neighbours all around him."

"We'll just have to think of something, won't we?"

Kristie didn't dare voice her concerns. What was Carole thinking?

Suddenly, darkness fell around them. The village lights had gone off. Midnight.

Some light streamed from a nearby house, just beyond Hazel Eyes' cottage. Carole grabbed Kristie's sleeve and tugged her along, and led her across the road.

"This darkness is just what we need. We'll go and have a peek through those windows."

"There's people still awake there." Christie worriedly pointed in the direction of the lit-up house. "What if they see us... see something?"

"It's dark here, isn't it, you daft bat."

"What if he has security lights, or an alarm? Or CCTV?"

"Then we scuttle the hell out of here, back to the car, and drive back home. At least we'll have had a peek."

She easily made it over the low stone wall, and landed amongst shrubs. Quickly, she footed it to a thatch-covered bay on the side of the house. The light from the nearby house was just enough to see where she was going. She felt Kristie's hot breath on her cheek.

"What now?" Kristie almost squealed as she witnessed Carole taking several quick flash-lit photos of the interior.

Nothing happened.

Carole dragged her along the facade of the cottage to the other side of the porch. That's when the light came on. Both women jumped in shock.

"That was inevitable." Carole breathed raggedly. They were crouched under a window.

"What now?" Kristie repeated, her heart beating in her throat.

"Just wait. It's only a porch light." She sounded braver than she felt. "It could have been activated by a cat or a fox wandering about, too."

"Yeah."

Some minutes passed and the light dimmed, and once again darkness descended around them like a shroud. Carole raised herself to her full height and peered through the window. Unlike the rest of the house, the faintest of glints of light permeated the darkness of this room, giving it an eerie gleam. Its source - a mystery.

"Beautiful room!" Kristie sighed.

The darkness was speared by a flash as Carole took a photo. "Now we get the hell out."

Once again, the porch light sprung on, and by this light the two women dashed back into the shadows of the opposite garden wall, and hurried to their car hidden in the lane. As they settled back in the car and made ready to leave, the light faded and darkness descended. The lights in the nearby house had been extinguished, too.

Minutes later they were on the road back to town.

"We did it!" Carole exclaimed triumphantly.

"Shall we have a midnight snack and a glass of wine before we hit the sack? We do have to be at the garden centre again at 10."

"We'll be there! Yeah, let's not go to bed too late, for we've got to look gorgeous and sexy in the morning."

"We are gorgeous and sexy, because we're blondes. All men adore blondes." Kristie knew that this would meet with Carole's approval.

And it did.

"As the saying goes, blondes have more fun," Carole reacted, cock-sure.

"By the way, when are we going to do the tree?"

"Some time tomorrow." Carole gave her friend a satisfied grin. "Light me a fag, will you."

Sleep came easily for Aidan. It had been quite a day. As he slipped into the first stages of a relaxed sleep, the last he knew was hearing contented purring, and two warm furry bodies pressing into him. He was asleep.

The Snow Crystals

He dreamt he was in his former, starkly ultra contemporary office, digging the box out of his minimalist desk, and opening it. The crystal glory lit up the entire room. Secure in the knowledge that his treasures were still intact, he closed the box on their blinding brightness, and returned it to the safety of the drawer.

The box was closed and had been returned to the drawer - then why was the room still so bright? The crystals were locked away safely. The brightness persisted. And sound resonated off the crystals. He reached for the drawer with the boxed crystals...

An unusual sound permeated his sleep, and his eyes snapped open. The digital clock on the bedside table stated 12:05. The village lights went off at midnight. Light was filtering through the curtains at the front of the house. Nothing but darkness on the other side of the dual aspect room. A cat or a fox must have activated the porch light, was his next thought. But then, this rarely happened. His neighbours were all thoughtful about their pets, and Mrs. Manning's cats, who were elderly, like her, preferred the warmth of the kitchen AGA, whatever the time of day or night, let stand the season.

The light faded, as Aidan knew the porch light would, and the room was dark again. Perhaps a hungry fox after all, he thought.

He was just giving in to the land of Morpheus again, when a stark, sharp white flash stabbed his closed lids. His eyes flew open. What the hell was that? Had it been any other season but winter, he would have counted the seconds before the rumble. But it was winter and no rumble followed the flash. Mere seconds later, the porch light came on again. And once again he heard something. As thoroughly well-glazed as the windows were, his acute hearing picked up something that should not be part of this peaceful night-time village.

He gently pushed aside the cats, and flung back the covers. Within several steps he was at the window, and peered through a crack in the curtains. Yes, the porch light was on. He saw neither cat nor fox. The small lane was peacefully empty. He was at the point of turning away and returning to bed, when he caught a movement among the shrubs by Mrs. Manning's wall. Too big to be an animal. Aidan blinked, and strained his eyes to best see in the dark. The porch light did not reach that far, and besides, it was already fading, with darkness moving back in. Before the last shard of light disappeared, he saw it again. A hint of movement.

Uneasy, he stayed at the window. Had Donald not been in the guest room, he would have rushed there and hopefully caught a glimpse of whatever or whoever was wandering around the village. If it had been an animal, he could account for the porch light, but not that flash.

Was he imagining it, or did he hear a car motor being switched on? For a moment he considered that it could have been visitors of his neighbours... perhaps they had a dog and let it out before leaving... that could account for the light. The dog had wandered into the garden... It sounded plausible enough. But the flash...?

The sound of the car motor became louder, and Aidan expected to see car lights, but the darkness persisted. It was blatantly obvious that the car was near or in the main road right by his lane, and the sound did not move further into the village... it moved towards town. He could hear it go over the speed bumps, as it drove off into the night with its lights off.

Bare footed, he silently made his way downstairs, switched on lights and checked everything. All was as it should be.

Despite that, he felt uneasy. But he was tired. In the morning he would have a look around outside. Maybe there was a clue out there about what had awakened him so rudely. The porch light could always be explained, but that sharp white flash, the unlit car and the movement by his neighbour's garden wall, could not be explained. Burglars... Aidan could not eradicate the gut feeling that it weren't burglars. So if it weren't burglars, then what, or more importantly who?

But it was that same gut feeling that kept tugging at him, and cast another option into the outer fringes of his mind. No, no, that was not possible!

He returned upstairs and entered his bedroom shaking his head. No, it couldn't be possible.

Or could it?

Twenty Three Days to Christmas

The two women arrived home shortly after midnight on Sunday morning. Carole opened a bottle of red wine, while Kristie warmed up two pork pies in the microwave.

"Cheers!" Carole and Kristie toasted each other with a glass of cheap wine.

Carole was loading the photos she had taken onto the computer. "To be honest, I was a bit scared..."

"I sure was!"

Grinning broadly at Kristie, Carole said with smug satisfaction, "But we did it." She jabbed at the computer screen with a pink talon. "So, what do you think? The photos aren't great, but they worked."

The two women looked at photos of part of a spacious, beamed sitting room, with stylishly classic furniture. Carole had managed to get part of the Christmas tree into the photo, too.

"The tree is rather boring," Carole said scathingly. She did not appreciate the genteel beauty of the decorations.

"The rest of the room looks nice, though." Kristie knew better than to share that she found the tree quite pretty.

"Not to my taste at all..." Carole studied the pictures, flipping backwards and forwards. "But not to worry, once we've snagged them, we'll take care of the décor. They'll be putty in our hands!"

Carole cast Kristie a knowing glance. Yes, she'd ensure that they'd get what they wanted. Down to every last detail.

Kristie poured them another glass of wine. "What about that other picture? The one of that study?"

"Oh yeah, the study..." Carole brought it up on the screen. "What does he want with all them books?" She prodded her finger at the screen. "What a waste of good space. Think about all the dust those things collect."

"They don't look like my kind of books. Talking books, we haven't had a look yet at what Doris gave us." Kristie got up and fetched the loaded bag from the hallway, and unpacked it, stacking the books on the table. "Now these are more like it!" Besides the usual chick-lit romances, there was a hefty pile of erotic romances, too.

"Oh, nice!" Carole said appreciatively.

The Snow Crystals

They finished their wine, shut down the computer, and went to their respective rooms.

Standing in the doorway of her bedroom, Carole turned. "I know what I'll be dreaming of tonight."

"Yes."

"Sunday's our day!"

"It's already Sunday," Kristie reminded her.

The women exchanged goodnights and closed their bedroom doors, as erotic fantasies about two men they had taken a fancy to danced in their minds.

Pondering the day that had passed and the day that lay ahead, it was especially Carole's obsession that was gathering a frightening pace with every passing second.

CHAPTER SIXTEEN

Twenty four days to Christmas

Aidan woke minutes before his alarm was set to go off. Who needed an alarm when you had two big furry, purring alarm clocks ensuring you woke every morning in good time for their welcome and much-needed hearty breakfast?

"You two are scallywags." He caressed them, and got up. The strange occurrences of the night before came back to him, and gave him an uneasy feeling in his gut. The first hint of daylight was still a good hour and a half away, so he'd have to wait till then to check outside.

He quickly got dressed and followed his eager cats down the stairs. He saw to the needs of the spoiled twosome first. Then put on the kettle for a first mug of tea for himself, and switched on the coffee maker for

Donald.

Mug of tea in hand, he went into the sitting room and lit the Christmas tree and several table lamps. A warm glow of immense pleasure filled him. More needed adding to the room, but this already was a joy he had never envisioned for himself.

He heard footsteps on the stairs and called out a cheery good morning.

Donald's equally cheery, "G'morning, mate," paired with a yawn, wafted from the kitchen into the sitting room. A moment later, carrying a steaming mug of coffee, he walked into the sitting room.

"I let the ladies out back. Trust you're OK with that." Aidan nodded, smiling, as Donald sprawled out on the sofa next to him and took several careful sips of the hot liquid. "Oh, I needed that." He looked around the room appreciatively. "Starting to look good, bro." Then his face darkened. "What was going on last night?"

"You noticed?" Alert, Aidan sat up.

"Maybe the Wrights had visitors or just being their usual late selves. I noticed that their lights were on till just gone midnight. It could have been them, but I saw three subsequent flashes. Had it been anything but winter, I would have thought of an approaching electric storm. But it equally could have been someone taking photos. Elsie Wright is big into photography, but at midnight?"

Aidan's jaw dropped visibly. "The porch light came on twice. A fox. A feral cat... poor thing, especially in the winter. I was just nodding off again when there was a similar kind of flash. Only one. Immediately followed by the porch light coming on again. I went to have a look."

"I had a look, too, following those three flashes. But seeing the Wrights still up... well, you know... I went back to bed. I did hear something as I was dropping off. Sounded like a car. I figured that the Wrights' visitors were leaving."

"So it wasn't some weird dream after all." Aidan grabbed Donald's arm. "I had a peek from my bedroom window. The porch light was on, and as the light was fading, I thought I saw something amidst the shrubbery by Mrs. Manning's wall. A movement. And a moment later, I heard a car start. In the stillness of the night, sound travels, so I knew the car was near the lane. But saw nothing. By the sound, I could make out that it was heading out of the village, towards town. It picked up speed. But I never saw any car lights. I heard it drive over the speed bumps."

"Indeed, sound travels at night," Donald mused. "You saw no cars coming into the village?"

"No, nothing. I went downstairs to check and everything was OK. In daylight I am going to have a good look around outside."

"Absolutely. And with the Wrights on the Neighbourhood Watch Scheme, I will ask them if they noticed anything."

"Good thinking."

Some sharp barks from outside sent Donald rushing to the utility room to let his ladies back in.

"Slave!" Aidan laughingly called after him.

"Pots and kettles, " Donald called back.

While Donald dried the ladies' paws and bellies, Aidan set the table. "What shall we have for breakfast?"

"No offence meant, mate, but I'll cook us breakfast. Look and learn."

"You really don't trust my meagre cooking skills, do you?" Aidan chuckled.

"Eh... no!" Donald raided the fridge and placed all

he needed on the kitchen counter. "You can do the toast. I think I can trust you with that."

Had his mother or anyone else made this comment, Aidan would have felt hurt, even inadequate. But not so when Donald said it, with a good-natured smile twinkling in his eyes, and his lips curved in a crooked grin. "That looks like you are intent on the full works."

"Yeah. Several mushrooms each. One tomato each. Two sausages each. And some baked beans. You cut the mushrooms and toms."

A moment later Aidan watched it all cook with pleasure. "Smells good. And quite easy to do, too. Why haven't I ever learned to do this before?"

"You're learning now. That's what counts." Donald smiled. He chose not to add that he had often enough tried to get Aidan interested without success, concluding that it was better late than never. "Plates, please, maestro."

They took their time savouring every bite. Aidan had often enough enjoyed a fried breakfast, and quite a few prepared by Donald, too, but somehow this time around it was different. The atmosphere in the house had shifted yesterday, and he was relishing it. Maybe that was why this tasted like one of the best breakfasts ever. Sated, both men leant back in their chairs. "Another coffee?" Aidan asked.

"Please. Then I'll take the girls for a stroll. Pass by the Wrights, and ask if they saw anything."

"OK, I'll clear this all up. See," he laughed, "I'm learning. You might yet de-slob me. It is light enough out there now to have a look. See if I can find something."

"OK. How's your foot... ankle?"

"Could be lots better." He stuck out his leg, tried to move his ankle, couldn't and winced. "Bugger. Worse than I thought. I put more Arnica on it this morning... I damn well am not going to let this knacker our plans. But you'll have to drive..." He looked miserably at his ankle, and put it back down.

"Sorry, mate." Donald got up and squeezed Aidan's shoulder. "If it gets any worse, I'm taking you to A&E."

"The bloody woman!" Aidan spat out. The dogs and the cats looked up in shock at his raised voice.

Donald just squeezed his friend's shoulder again. "Just take it easy. OK? I'm out with the ladies."

With the strange goings-on around midnight, Donald looked around Old Orchard Lane with unease. It looked so incongruous, so innocent, so pleasant, even on this cold, leaden-skied morning.

Frost lay scattered like powdered sugar. No amount of inclement weather could ever make this village lose its innate charm. Even on this still early gloomy morning, with the cheerfully twinkling lights from Christmas trees behind several windows, the village exuded a welcoming warmth.

Donald ran into Maude Finchley and her Jack Russell and they chatted for a few minutes. Like old Mrs. Manning, Maude was one of the stalwarts of the village. He promised her that he wouldn't dream of missing the carol service she organised lovingly every year. Nor would Aidan. Donald wasn't a church goer, but he supported the ancient parish church on the green. It represented to him a vital and integral part of the village and its surroundings.

Yes, he loved this village. And he was glad that Aidan had also embraced this delightful place.

But something strange had happened last night

around midnight. Something that, as it had Aidan, gave him an uneasy feeling in his guts. He still hadn't told Aidan about seeing something akin to those hags following them yesterday. He hadn't caught a glimpse like Aidan had, while at Peter's, but by then he knew that his friend's sightings could not be doubted.

"Donald, good morning," Arthur Wright called out.

"Good morning to you too, Arthur. You're just the person I needed to talk to." And out poured the strange occurrences of around midnight.

Arthur frowned. "Definitely wasn't us. For a change, we had no visitors on a Saturday night. Elsie wanted to finish off making gifts for the Christmas stall next Saturday. And I was upstairs reading. We went to sleep just after midnight. Have you had a look outside?"

"Aidan should be doing that as we speak."

"Right." He continued frowning. "A car... hmmm... yes, I did hear a car shortly after we had switched off the lights, but thought nothing of it."

"One wouldn't, would one now?"

"No. Let me know if you see or find anything. I will also ask everyone to be extra observant."

"Thanks. Give my love to Elsie, and enjoy your day."

"You too, Donald."

As he turned into Old Orchard Lane, Donald saw Aidan bending over a shrub, recoiling, and freezing several steps back from the shrub.

"Yo! Aidan, I just spoke to Arthur Wright. Hey, what's the matter? Found something?" He quickened his pace as Aidan urged him on with a frantic arm wave.

"Look!"

"Jesus!"

The two men looked at each other in shocked

disbelief. Then looked back at the shrub under the study window. Tangled amid the skeletal twigs rested a long bleached blonde hair.

"It can't be..." Aidan looked to Donald for reassurance, but didn't get any from his shell-shocked friend.

"Do you have your phone on you?" With Aidan shaking his head, Donald rummaged in his pockets. "Got it." He took several pictures, and looked at the results. "Dated, timed when we found it, and possible proof that someone was here. I am sending these photos to both our email addresses, and also to Arthur Wright."

"Should we leave that hair there? It sickens me to think that it is there." He swallowed hard. "It could be..."

"Yes, it could be, and that freaks me out no end."

The ladies barked a welcome as Arthur Wright hastened towards them. "Just got your message, Donald. Good morning, Aidan." He looked at the shrub. "It's not an animal's hair. It's obviously human, and it's obviously not yours. Definitely isn't yesterday's removers, either."

"And it clearly isn't Peter's or his son's." With Arthur looking at him questioningly, Aidan said, "An antiques dealer, who delivered some new things for my home late yesterday afternoon." Aidan looked in disgust at the wiry bleached hair. "And I don't fancy blondes. My last lady friend was ages ago, and she had a dark brown bob."

"Just to be on the safe side..." Arthur took some photos with his own phone. "And I will remove the evidence."

"Please!" Aidan shuddered as he watched Arthur remove the hair and wrap it in a paper tissue.

"Did you find anything else? Footprints? Broken twigs? Anything like that?"

"I didn't get that far yet. I've been concentrating on the area around the house."

"We'll have a look together," Arthur offered.

"And have a look there. That's where I saw something... some movement." Aidan pointed at Mrs. Manning's stone wall.

Donald deposited his ladies in the house, and the three men scoured Aidan's relatively narrow front garden, circled by a low stone wall.

"It's easy to nip over this wall," Arthur said. "We had some drizzly rain Friday night, but of no consequence, so the soil is essentially dry. It was still above freezing when we went to bed. During the night the temperatures plunged, hence the ground frost this morning. Do either of you see anything?"

"No, nothing at all," Donald said. In the background, Aidan merely shook his head. "Let's have a look there now." He made for the high stone wall which was part of Mrs. Manning's property.

Here, too, they scoured the soil for any evidence that someone had been there. Donald grabbed Arthur's arm and pointed. "There. See that? Some broken twigs."

Arthur leant forward. "Could be fresh breaks." Once again, he took some photos. He straightened up and looked at his neighbours. "Besides the hair and the broken twigs, we have nothing to go on. We'll have to be extra vigilant, and I'll have a chat with my friend, Jonathan. I happen to know that he is conveniently on duty today." He scrunched up his face in a frown. "We could look at it this way: the hair could have come from someone in the village, and the wind blew it onto your shrub. Those breakages are low enough to have been made by an animal. Then we have the car without lights, those flashes, and your porch light coming on twice. The last could have been an animal. But the flashes and the car definitely weren't animals." He smiled encouragingly. "I know that you have a superb security system, Aidan, so you're alright. As do you, Donald." Once again, he frowned. "We may not cause panic, but everyone needs to know that they have to be extra vigilant, and report anything unusual."

Wishing each other a pleasant Sunday, the men parted.

Aidan shivered as he and Donald walked back to the cottage. "Winter sure has set in."

"I propose we have ourselves another hot coffee before we set off."

"You're on."

Had the men crossed the main road and wandered into the narrow, densely verdant lane that led out of the village towards various farms and hamlets, they would have found clear evidence that someone had been there.

CHAPTER SEVENTEEN

They complimented each other on their hair and their makeup, both adhering to their standards of feminine perfection.

To match her pale blue eyes, Carole had indulged in a substantial smattering of blue eye shadow, and numerous coats of mascara weighed down her lids. She regretted that the perfectly polished bright pink nails, matching her sexily pouting pink lips, were only there for the day, for tonight she would have to remove all her hard work.

That was what she hated about her job. The income wasn't too bad at all, but her manager was a Tartar when it came to the looks of her staff. "You are here to serve the public politely, not proposition them," the woman had testily reminded Carole, but also Kristie, several times.

Eager to keep their jobs, they had both toned down their appearances to suit the demands of the bloody woman, who was co-owner and manager of the Emporium since the place opened last year. The last Carole and her mate had heard was that the other co-owners were two sisters, who were shortly moving to the area. Neither Carole nor Kristie had ever met them. Nor had Doris. And not being close friends with the rest of the staff, Carole and Kristie remained in the dark about their other two bosses. All they'd heard was that they were lovely ladies. Huh! Sounded like two sad, boring old bitches, who wouldn't know real style if it hit them.

"Bet they'd never look as glamorous and gorgeous as I do!" Carole exclaimed as she turned this way then that in front of her mirror.

"Who're you talking to?" Kristie appeared in the doorway.

"Myself." Carole spun round. "WOW! You look fantastic."

Kristie tittered excitedly, grateful for any rare praise Carole lavished on her. "Oh, thanks."

She'd piled up her long hair in a do Carol considered beguiling. Dark smoky eye shadow, paired with heavy black mascara, encircled her nondescript grey blue eyes. She had outlined her thin lips with a dark brownish pink pencil to make them look fuller, and filled in with several shades lighter. Her nail polish matched the pale lipstick. She held up her hands. "These should pass the inspection tomorrow."

"I was just thinking of her." Carole sat down on the bed. She held up a shoe in one hand and a boot in the other. "Shoes or boots?"

Kristie studied them for a moment. "You're wearing those slacks?"

"You bet! It's effing cold out there, so I'm wearing

these slacks. They're also sexy."

"Oh yes, very sexy. Perhaps the boots? I'm wearing the same." She grinned encouragingly.

"We'll look the part," Carole chortled.

Both finished off the last of their preening, and simultaneously exited their rooms. They looked each other over, and smiled. Especially Carole thought they looked irresistible.

"You want some more coffee before we go?" Kristie asked. "The place doesn't open till 10."

Carole glanced at the clock on the mantle. December Sunday mornings were quiet in town, and they'd be at the garden centre in less than 10 minutes. "A small one."

As Kristie made the coffee, Carole fetched her coat, scarf and gloves. She double checked that the camera and binoculars were in her big shoulder bag. She returned to the kitchen, where she joined Kristie for a coffee and biccies.

Some fifteen minutes later they were ready to go. They had touched up their lippy and complimented each other anew.

Satisfied that they looked gorgeous and sexy, Carole started the motor of their car, and set out for the garden centre with vigorous determination.

Wincing, Aidan raised his leg onto a chair, whilst Donald made them coffee. He'd tried to forget the nagging ache was there as he had joined Donald and Arthur in search of clues. It had been getting worse. Before leaving, he'd put on the ankle bandage he'd thankfully kept following a sports injury at uni. And he'd pop some Paracetamol, too. The mere thought of complaining made him feel like a complete wally. More so because of the reason. Inwardly, he groaned. Donald was right. If this didn't get any better soon...

"Here you go." Donald placed the mugs and an unopened package of biscuits on the table. "Painful?"

"A little," Aidan lied. "Just resting it."

Donald's disbelieving glance spoke volumes, but he didn't say anything. If not A&E today, he'd be driving his mate to the GP tomorrow.

Donald took a deep breath. He had to tell Aidan. "In view of what happened..."

"You sound formally ominous."

"Yeah... I mean no. Oh, I don't know. Look, I didn't want to tell you sooner, because you were really freaked out about those sightings, and I didn't want to upset you more."

"I am not going to fall apart. Yet. I hope. Spit it out, man."

"Remember yesterday, en route to Peter's? When I suddenly revved up..."

"Of course I remember. How can I not? Speeding is more my thing. I must be a bad influence on you."

"Just shut up, will you, for a minute. I, as it were, took flight...God, I sound pompous. Because I spotted something a few cars back that looked exactly like one of those two hags. And it was following us!"

"And then I saw one peering through the window at Peter's..." Aidan's eyes were like saucers.

"Yes! And now we've found a bloody long straw-like hair in those shrubs." Donald gulped down part of the mug's contents. "They hit on us. In one of their attempts to catch our attention, one of them all but crippled you, and we keep spotting them. That hair and the other things... Aidan, I don't know about you, but my gut tells me there's something not quite right in the state of Denmark."

"My gut feeling tells me the same. But I'll be damned if I am going to let it affect my life!" He finished his coffee and banged the mug down on the table. "Wright is right, no pun intended, that we both have excellent security systems. Pity we don't have CCTV cameras. God, I'd hate having to spend money on that, too, because of some stupid tarts."

"Who could be nothing more than silly, desperate women..."

"Or dangerous bunny boilers!"

"Whoah, Aidan. Let's not get carried away."

"I am not. But I cannot deny that odd gut feeling that we have not seen the end of them. And, oh man, that is the part that really freaks me out. It also makes me want to scream at myself: 'are you a mouse or a man'?"

In sympathy, Donald put his hand over Aidan's. "You're not a mouse. Far from. Our guts are aligned, mate. We know what we have seen. We have to be careful. Vigilant, as Wright said. And like you, I'll be damned if I am going to let two obsessed hags impact our lives." He got up and rinsed out the mugs. "Let's get our butts over to that garden centre. I look forward to decorating the outside on our return." As Aidan made for the door, Donald added. "Do you still have that bandage from that injury you had during your wild years? If so, put it on."

"Yes, mother!" Aidan chuckled as he hobbled up the stairs.

"They're late." Carole had parked near a clutch of cars,

undoubtedly belonging to some of the centre's staff. From their position they had a good view of the entrance. They'd seen the first shoppers hurry in to escape the biting cold. The men were not among them. "Neither of their two cars is here yet."

"Maybe they're not coming." Kristie pouted. "I'd hate to think we went through all this trouble for nothing."

"Don't say that," Carole snapped. "We heard them loud and clear. They'd be getting some more things early this morning. Maybe they were held up. Light me a fag, will you?"

Silently, they sat smoking, watching and waiting.

Quarter past ten came and went. The women were getting restless. Impatient. The car's digital clock stated 10:22 when they saw the car approach. It was parked nearest possible to the entrance.

"They're here!" the two exclaimed simultaneously, with their hearts beating excitedly as they watched the two men enter the store.

"That's our cue. We're going in." Carole gave herself a last look in the car mirror, and got out. "And we're going to be coming out on the arms of our men! Because this time they're not getting away from us!"

Kristie's bright smile did not reach her troubled eyes.

Chapter eighteen

"A few more decorations for the tree in the sitting room. A tree and decorations for the kitchen. And anything else that takes my fancy. Or yours, for that matter. Herewith you've been promoted to be my very own personal interior designer... decorator... or whatever."

"Aw, such an honour." Donald laughed. "What's the whatever?"

"Whatever you want it to be."

They knew what they wanted and needed, and within the shortest period of time, they'd found and acquired the necessities. On Donald's advice, Aidan had chosen a table-top tree for the kitchen. They'd quickly chosen lights, as well as decorations for both trees. Some more items found their way into the trolley.

"As much as I am enjoying this, there is a sense of relief that I will not have to go through it again next year. Starting from scratch is quite a chore."

"Aidan, I bet you'll find an excuse next year to add to the collection. I always do."

"Who knows? You could well be right. Let's go there. I want to get some all-singing-and-dancing done-up little trees for my bedroom and the guest room."

"How about your office?"

"Oh, yeah. Forgot all about that."

"How about a jardinière with a seasonal arrangement in the window sill? I could help you make it. You've got all sorts of evergreens, ivy, and holly and more in the garden. Get some of those bags with decorative things. And oasis." Seeing Aidan's questioning look, Donald explained. "You stuff it into a jardinière, water it thoroughly, and stick the branches, flowers, whatever in, and it keeps it all fresh throughout the season. Oh, and mustn't forget candles! And I bet you've no candle holders, either." With Aidan shaking his head in denial, Donald added, "You'll need a few to get you started for now."

Concentrating on selecting the last bits and pieces before heading for the cashier, they did not notice the two women who stealthily crept towards them.

"Oh, hello, what a surprise! We bump into each other again."

Shock seared through Donald. A bag with decorations tumbled from his fingers. Quickly, he retrieved it and threw it into the trolley. Aidan, next to him, stiffened and groaned.

The shorter one of the two hags had moved right next to Donald and given the trolley an almighty shove. It hit an unlucky shopper who let out a pained cry. She ignored it. Instead, she focussed her attention on Donald, whose arm she clutched in a vice-like grip.

"We meet again. It was meant to be. It was fate."

Dreading the thought of chucking up his delicious breakfast, Aidan tried to move away, but his sore ankle - and more so, a persistent woman - kept him rooted where he was. Her pale pink-tipped claws had encircled his wrist. He could feel the vile nails digging into his flesh. "Yes, just like Carole said, it was meant to be."

"Now that we meet again, we'll go and have a coffee. And you can tell us all about yourselves," the shorter of the two said.

"Yes, tell us all about yourselves," the pink-taloned hag echoed.

"And we'll tell you all about us," the other hideous parody cooed, as she strengthened her hold on Donald. "Get to know each other better."

Not wishing to cause a scene, Aidan hissed. "Please, let go!"

A young man approached them, his face dark with anger. "Hey, you. That your trolley? It hit my grandad's leg..."

"Yes! It's OUR trolley. What of it?" the shorter of the two snarled. "Quit bothering us!"

Both Donald and Aidan desperately tried to escape the vile shackle-like clutches, but the women's determination merely exacerbated their strength. Neither man had ever hit, much less dreamt or thought of hitting a woman, but now it was a distinct and nigh-on-pleasurable temptation.

"My granddad..." The young man's voice had risen angrily, but was cut off by the shorter of the two women.

"You deaf, or something? You're bothering us!"

Several shoppers had stopped and stared with acute distaste at the unfolding scene, then hurried on quickly. The men did not look like the type who'd associate with such obviously vulgar and obnoxious women.

"My granddad's in the offices, being looked after..."

"Sod off, you whining windbag."

"Yeah, sod off," the other woman parroted.

Her pink tentacles felt like they were at the point of piercing Aidan's skin. He'd never hit a woman. He considered it evil and criminal. But as he felt the woman's body and nails invading his space and skin, he didn't care anymore. Scene or no scene. He had to get rid of those abhorrent claws.

"Let go. NOW!" he snarled at the bleached hag.

"But honey... we're shopping for Christmas..."

"Let go, I said. Or..."

"Or what?" she simpered.

Had he used his full strength, he would have broken her despicable fingers, if not her hand. Instead, as he forcibly removed her claw, one of the talons broke, and she let out a piercing wail.

All eyes were on them now.

Donald, without a word, had used reasonable force to slap his assailant's hand off his arm, and with a whimper she backed off slightly, nursing her painful hand.

"Alright, what is going on here?" A gruff, well-educated voice rose above the mêlée. "Ah, Aidan, Donald. What in the world is going on?"

"Mr. Forbes. Good to see you. Can we go to your office, please?" Donald exclaimed as relief flooded through him at the sight of the imperious proprietor of the centre.

"Yes, of course, Donald. What about these two women? Do you know them?"

Bristling, Aidan exclaimed, "Hell no, Sir! Haven't a clue who they are."

Donald's voice shook slightly as he added, "They've been hitting on us since yesterday."

Carole let out a wail. "They're our boyfriends!" She gave Kristie a piercing look, and she nodded emphatically in support.

Mr. Forbes looked from the two men to the two women, and said loudly enough for them to hear. "In your dreams, ladies." The word *ladies* was an emphatic sneer. "There's an elderly, diabetic gentleman getting first aid as the trolley injured his leg."

"What's that gotta do with us?" the shorter of the women cried out.

Donald glared furiously at the harridan. "She gave our, meaning Aidan's and my, trolley a shove so that she could grab my arm in a vice. The other did the same to Aidan."

Mr. Forbes and a store security guard escorted the small group to the offices. The two women were ordered to wait in a separate room. A sign from Forbes Sr. was enough for the security guard to understand that he had to keep an eye on them.

He took Aidan and Donald into his own office. An elderly couple sat in one corner. The man's injury was being tended by a first aider.

Donald and Aidan expressed their sincere regrets, which were graciously accepted by the couple.

"Understandably, our grandson is angry," the lady said. "I soon realised that those two women were making a right nuisance of themselves."

"You've no idea!" Aidan exclaimed. He lifted his right trouser leg, and pulled down his sock. The bruising was visible above the ankle bandage. "That is what the taller hag did to me yesterday. Supposedly accidentally bumped into me in the restaurant. All but speared me with her killer heels."

Even Donald gasped. It was far worse than Aidan had let on. The first aider advised Aidan to get it seen to.

"You had problems with them yesterday?" Forbes asked the men.

Aware of Aidan's pained face, Donald told him what had happened, but omitted the various sightings, especially the strange midnight goings-on.

"Oh, Donald, we might as well tell Mr. Forbes the whole thing." Aidan sighed miserably. "Yesterday, Susan suggested we go to Trivia in the marketplace. And lo and behold, I caught a glimpse of the tall one there. In the afternoon, as I waited in the car while Donald got some shopping from Sainsbury's, I once again spotted that hair."

"And I saw that same hair following us, several cars down, en route to Thatch Hall," Donald added. "Aidan saw one of them ogling him through a window while we were at Sullivan's Antiques."

"Some weird things happened around midnight." Aidan shuddered at the memory. "And this morning we found a long bleached blond hair in a shrub under my office window."

"Our Neighbourhood Watch man is onto it," Donald finished off.

A heavy silence filled the room.

"They sound like stalkers," Forbes said. "Do you want me to contact the police?"

Aidan shook his head. "No. We've got our Neighbourhood Watch man taking care of it with the police on our end. But perhaps you want to report them?" he asked of the couple.

"Leave it be." The man looked to his wife, who agreed. "It looks like we all are the victims of some very sad women."

"I'll have a little chat with them shortly," Forbes said. He looked toward the two men. "Go and collect your shopping, try to forget about them, and enjoy the rest of your day. I am so sorry that this had to happen to you. Get that ankle looked after, Aidan."

Having said their goodbyes, they retrieved their trolley and hastened to the cashier.

"That was freaky," Aidan whispered as Donald started the car. "How the hell did they know that we'd be at the centre this morning?"

"As they were in Thatch Hall yesterday afternoon, chances are they were hiding nearby, and heard us talking about it in the marketplace."

"Oh yeah, so we did. They're sick!" Aidan looked at his wrist. "I thought those talons were going to draw blood. Jesus, that bitch has strength!"

"So does the Cruella De Vil who clutched my arm."

"They're mad!"

"Maybe we should have gotten the police involved," Donald said.

"And then what? What proof do we have? Except for a mangled ankle, which could be construed as an unfortunate accident, we have nothing, Donald. Even that hair..."

"Oh, come off it, mate. We can ask Arthur for a DNA test on that hair. I bet it is one of theirs. Exact same colour!"

"OK, so, we ask Arthur to get that done. He has his

contacts. His friends. And then what? We have nothing to compare it with."

"Of course, true. It was a nice thought while it lasted."

"We don't know where they live. And unfortunately, they haven't conveniently moulted on us. The cards are entirely in their hands. They've got us over a barrel, mate."

"You could well be right. Best we can do is keep our eyes and ears open. It is all we can do."

"Yeah..." came Aidan's half-hearted reply.

They were silent until they reached South Woodside.

"We're going to enjoy a coffee with something warming in it, then we are going out in the cold and put up those decorations." Donald smiled encouragingly at his friend.

"You're on." Aidan sounded braver than he felt.

"He broke my nail. Look! My finger is bleeding!" Kristie cried out and sobbed theatrically the second Mr. Forbes entered the room with the security man on his heels. As evidence, she held up the middle digit of her right hand.

"I am sure you will survive," he observed coldly. "That was a very nasty and uncalled-for scene, ladies." Once again the word *ladies* came out as a mocking sneer. "You are very lucky that this matter will not be reported, although I personally would have. I understand that you have been making a nuisance of yourselves by annoying our customers... the second day running."

"Nuisance?" Carole bristled. "Nuisance? Those men

are our boyfriends. They promised..."

"Stop the fantasizing! They are not your boyfriends!"

"They are!" Dry-eyed, Carole sobbed. "We're engaged..."

Spotting Carole's penetrating side-long glance, Kristie patted Carole's arm comfortingly, and nodded vigorously. "As she said..."

Forbes Sr. let out a bellow of laughter, drowning out the women's hysterical utterances. The security man behind him couldn't contain his laughter either.

"What... what's so funny?" Carole asked indignantly.

Forbes Sr. silenced them with an imperious gesture. He was not accepting any more nonsense. "Ladies..." The sneer was blatantly evident. He half turned to the security guard. "This gentleman..." he turned back to face the women, his face angry, "will escort you to the cashier. He will also take your names and addresses, after which you will then be escorted off the premises. We have evidence of what happened on CCTV. We have YOU on CCTV. You are no longer welcome here, ladies."

CHAPTER NINETEEN

Well over an hour later, thoroughly chastised and feeling deeply humiliated, Carole and Kristie sat at their small kitchen table drinking coffee and eating a sandwich. Their Christmas purchases lay untouched and unpacked on the table in the sitting room.

"How dare they? How dare that old man?" Kristie was on the verge of tears again. She had wept over the snapped-off nail, and dramatically wrapped her finger in an oversized bandage.

Carole didn't say anything. She was thinking. They still had to put up the tree today. That was for sure. It would have to be tonight. But more importantly, they had to go to South Woodside, to see what the men were up to.

As Carole worked out a plan of action, Kristie rehashed their downfall over and over in her mind.

The security guard had asked for IDs, but Carole had vehemently claimed that they didn't have any on them. They'd only gone out to buy some decorations. They'd walked to the centre. No, they had no cards or driving licenses on them. Just cash. Kristie had clearly recognised the disbelief in the man's eyes, but all the same, he had taken their fake names and equally fake addresses. Thankfully, Carole had immediately been on the ball, and talked their way out of what could have been an even worse situation. Caroline Dobbs and Christina Evers... where did she get those names from so quickly without batting an eyelid? As for the address, it was in a street not too far from theirs...

Kristie was still trembling. She'd never have been able to do it on her own.

They'd been marched to the cashier, and Carole had paid in cash, artfully hiding the contents of her wallet from the watchful security man. Instead of heading for their car, Carole had grabbed Kristie's arm, and stated plaintively that they'd be walking back home now. For emphasis, she had added sniffly that their boyfriends had promised to drive them home. The man had cast Carole a harsh disbelieving glance, and rolled his eyes.

"Yes!" Carole exploded. "They'd promised to drive us home. And then we were going out for Sunday lunch... They were late, so we walked here, instead of waiting for them. We met them here as planned."

The man had pointed at the exit. "That's the way out." His eyes had burned into their backs as they left the centre's car park and headed back to town.

Out of the man's sight, Carole had shoved the bags into Kristie's hands. "You wait on the corner over there. I am going to fetch the car. He should have gone back in again."

And thus they had arrived home. Cold and

frustrated.

Having made them another coffee, Kristie found Carole at the computer in the sitting room, a satisfied smile on her red-smeared lips. "What're you doing, Carole?"

"Having another look at Coleridge's about that house, and getting to know the layout of the village. The gardens of the two largest houses on that lane touch, and are surrounded by stone walls."

"Stone-walled gardens are so romantic." Kristie envisioned herself in a summery garden, with Hazel Eyes bringing her a cool glass of wine... dotingly kissing her... and then they'd make love on the terrace. She softly moaned in ecstasy. But deep down she knew it was but a mere dream, and as fictional as the romantic novels she sought refuge in.

Carole ignored the moan, and pointed at the screen. "See? There appears to be a path, which runs behind the houses on the main road. Who would have thought there were some more cottages there? And there, too." She pointed to an area which lay behind the gardens of the cottage which was for sale. "There's a narrow path next to the house that's for sale, and that rambling big house at the top of the lane. It appears to lead to farmland which lies behind that big house. Could be an orchard."

"Which is probably why it's called Old Orchard Lane."

Carole nodded. "When I looked at the village plan yesterday, I was more concerned with the immediate area around Hazel Eyes' home. But now I am studying that part of the village in its entirety."

"So, except for hiding in that narrow lane where we parked yesterday, anywhere else nearby where we can park?"

"The lane's called Woodedge Lane, and leads to farms and hamlets." A long pink talon snaked out and pointed at the screen again. "Look, we can take that lane off the main road, just before we get to the village, and we take the first left... and then first left again... and end up where we parked yesterday... Woodedge Lane. Or we could perhaps park the car there." Carole pointed to another lane on the edge of the village.

"Or park at the pub!" Kristie exclaimed triumphantly. "We print off the details of that cottage. We go into the pub, have a tea or a coffee, and pretend interest in the cottage. When someone wants to buy somewhere, they want to know what the neighbourhood and neighbours are like..."

"What a brilliant idea! You're a star!"

Warmed by this unusual and high praise, Kristie added, "No one will think anything of it. It's normal."

"You're right." Carole eyed Kristie pensively for a moment. "We'll have to tone it down some. The inhabitants are rather dowdy codgers." Kristie gave her a quizzical stare. "It means we have to change our looks. We cannot be recognised." A woebegone look crossed her face as she raised her hands. "All that hard work. Oh, well. It would have to come off tonight anyway."

She got up, and took Kristie's arm. "We're going to wash our faces, and redo our makeup like for work. As little as possible." Kristie pulled a face. "It's for the best, believe me. And we'll dress like for work." She was silent for a moment. "And we'll put on those wigs we got off Doris..."

"They're perfect! You are so right, Carole. We'll be two middle-aged sisters who are house hunting."

"I don't appreciate the middle-aged, but you've got

a point. And we'll speak like we have to at work."

As they were preparing themselves for their venture, nearly ready, Kristie walked in on Carole. "I just thought of something. We'll be able to find out now, too, why those two embraced."

Half an hour later, Carole and Kristie, quite unrecognisable and presenting a demure spinster ladies image, walked to their car, and set off for South Woodside.

"The man's an absolute darling! He needn't have come back especially for us." Holly swept her long, wavy, mink-brown hair back, and deposited the broken hair clasp in the handbag at her feet.

Ivy, who was in the driver's seat, kept her eyes on the road, and chuckled. "You know what Mr. Locke is like. Generous to a fault."

She took the 3rd exit at the roundabout, and followed the sign for South Woodside.

A strangled meow curled up from the backseat. Holly turned in her seat. "We're almost there, Pye." The black, green-eyed long-haired cat let out another plaintive cry. Holly gently shushed him.

"Crystal's unusually quiet," Ivy said.

Holly smiled. "Eyes like saucers, the poor darling. She just doesn't like cars. Hope they will like their new home, though." Her fingers caressed the cage door, and a cold nose nudged them. The pretty long-haired white with aquamarine eyes gave her a doleful stare. "It won't be long now, sweetness."

"Have you given the Christmas party any more thought?" Ivy asked.

"It isn't like we have many employees..."

"No, hardly. But we may not forget the stand holders."

"No, I am not. We can rent a room at a restaurant or pub in town or, as we discussed, we can invite them to the house. Plenty of room. Get a caterer to supply some food. Unless you have some problem with it, I opt for a get-together at our home."

"Yes." Ivy nodded pensively. "We lock the doors to wherever the guests are not allowed. And Pye and Crystal can go in one of our bedrooms. The only problem I have is with those two Bridget told us about. Work-wise they can't be faulted, as they do a good job. Without saying so, it is obvious that Bridget doesn't like them. But then no one seems to like them, except for one of the stand holders."

Another wail rose from the back seat. "Shush, Pye. Almost. Almost." Having stroked Pye's nose, Holly turned around again, and stared out at the gloomy undulating landscape. "They might not be able to come."

"It's a possibility."

No one looking at them would have ever thought they were twins. Tall, willowy Holly, with her untamed dark hair and honey-coloured eyes, was a world apart from her shorter, more voluptuous, strawberry blonde, blue-green-eyed sister, Ivy. There were obvious similarities, such as an inborn elegance of body and movement. The slant of their thickly fringed eyes. The voluminous wavy hair. Their elegant hands. Gentle smiles capable of turning humorously wicked at a second's notice. Once people got to know them, their similarities became all too apparent. They were totally devoted to each other, as only twins could be.

"Mr. Locke said that our neighbour was really pleasant."

Ivy slowed down for a horse rider. "The couple who lived there when Gran did must have moved away. They were really nice. A bit nosey, but nice."

"Yes, they were." Holy chuckled. "Although their nosiness that one afternoon rather got to me."

"That's village life for you, Holly."

A few minutes later their car turned off into a short lane. To the right, a 4x4 was parked in front of a stone thatch-covered extension that appeared to be the garage of the sizable thatched cottage next to it.

Opposite, a For Sale sign stood in the garden of another pretty stone cottage.

Right in front of them lay the sprawling thatched house that had been in the Moreton family for generations. The only family house left in South Woodside. In front of their new home they saw parked a familiar, gleaming grey car.

"Mr. Locke's waiting for us." Ivy drove the estate up the driveway, to the garage which lay off to the side of the house. The garage door opened and Mr. Locke stood there, smiling a welcome. He moved aside as Ivy drove the car forward, and he closed the door.

CHAPTER TWENTY

"That was a perfect Sunday lunch." Aidan stifled a yawn. A heavy midday meal always had that effect on him. "Glad you suggested it."

"And now the hard graft starts." Donald, who thrived on coffee, poured himself another cup. "You?"

Aidan declined. "I've been thinking about doing something special for my employees."

"You're doing the usual yearly Christmas party, complete with Santa. You have something else in mind?"

"Yeah," Aidan said pensively. "We've had a good year. And the next is already well on its way to being an even better one. I couldn't have done it without all those wonderful people! They stuck with Galbraith's through thick and thin, and that's why I want to do something special, something extra for them as thanks."

Sipping his coffee, Donald pondered the matter for a moment. "There's the party..."

"Yes, although the Christmas party is *the* event of our company year, I do organise other social events for them."

"I know that! What I meant to say was that they get this super party, a well thought out gift, a Christmas bonus..."

"I just want to do something extra. They all mean the world to me, Donald. And heaven forbid the day my secretary retires!"

Donald laughed. "Stop fretting! Knowing her, she'll still be organising and bossing you and everyone else around, with a Zimmer frame parked next to her desk."

"I wouldn't put it past her."

"She's buying all the gifts, as usual, and organising the whole do?"

"She won't have it any other way."

"Gotta love her."

"So, any suggestions? I want to do something special for them."

"Hmmm... thinking. Oh... eh... sure you want no more coffee? Another drink?"

"I know you are dying for the dregs. They are all yours, mate." Aidan grinned. "I don't want another thing. Especially not a drink." He hid another yawn behind his hand. "Don't render me useless. Those lights are not going to put themselves up."

Donald poured himself the last of the coffee. "Ugh, you're right about dregs. Hmm... Special... Something special... How about a share in the company, or a percentage of the profit..."

"Discussed that with the company accountant and solicitor already. Didn't I tell you?"

"When? I can't remember..."

"While I was waiting for the purchase of the

cottage to go through. Both agreed it would be wise to see if the growth continued as forecast, and come back to it in the new year."

"Oh, yes... then... I'm so sorry, it must have passed me by."

Donald thought back bitterly to the past February and March. Work had taken him to the USA, and he had stayed with his sister and her obnoxious husband for several days on his mother's insistence. A memorable nightmare that had left lasting scars, and widened and deepened the hiatus between him and his sister even further.

Seeing the pained look cross his friend's face, Aidan remembered Donald's ordeal and lightly touched his hand in comforting sympathy. "How insensitive of me. How could I forget? Anyway, a share or such, is a possibility that could well be in the cards for them sometime next year. It's a wait and see situation depending on the latest figures. I know they're good. Pretty good, in fact. But, I agree, we want to be sure."

"Understandable. How about some extra time off for everyone?"

They both got up and put their coats on.

"That's a thought. Yes, I like that idea."

They each paid for their dinner, exchanged greetings with some villagers, and left the cosy warmth of the pub.

"Shall we take Marsh Lane? It's shorter and kinder on your ankle. How is it?"

"The rest helped. Thanks. I like that idea of extra time off between Christmas and New Year."

As they walked from the pub to Marsh Lane, they did not see the small dark blue car drive into the pub's parking. The inhabitants of the car did not see the men either, as a garden wall had already obscured them from view.

Two middle-aged ladies primly entered the pub. They appeared to be of similar height. The taller of the two was wearing simple, sensibly low-heeled boots, a dark grey skirt and matching warm sweater, under a moss green coat. Her slate-grey bob framed a demure, minimally made-up, bespectacled face. The shorter one wore higher, chunky-heeled boots, a dark blue wool dress, and a dark grey coat. Salt-and-pepper curls framed a narrow, similarly made-up, bespectacled face. They epitomised proverbial nondescript, prude spinster sisters.

As they walked up to the bar, they were pleased by the polite treatment they received, befitting their middle-aged status. They ordered coffee, and once seated at a small table, the salt-and-pepper haired lady demonstratively removed the estate agent's details of the cottage for sale in Old Orchard Lane from her bag, and placed it on the table.

The previous day's bar staff was not on duty that afternoon. The young woman who brought them coffee and biscuits saw the details of the cottage and asked in a friendly tone of voice, "You are interested in The Hollyhocks? It's only just come on the market. Lovely spot."

"Yes, we are interested." The salt-and-pepper head bobbed sagely up and down. Her diction was meticulously slow. "We are just having a look. So important to get it right."

"We've seen another house we like," the slate-grey

bob stated. Her diction was slow and impeccable. "But this one looks far nicer."

"After we've had our coffee, we plan to have a look." Pepper-and-salt stalled, and looked questioningly at the waitress. "How do we get there from here? Will we need the car?"

"Do you know the village at all?" the girl asked.

"No, we do not. We will shortly be retiring and are looking for a suitable home in a quiet location," Salt-and-pepper said. Slate-grey nodded emphatically.

"Why don't you leave the car parked here? It is a few minutes' walk to the right of here. You will find Old Orchard Lane just off the main road. It is pleasantly quiet. Across from The Hollyhocks lives a business man."

"Oh, a family man, then? We have nothing against children, but we do favour our tranquillity," Salt-and-pepper stated with urgency.

The waitress smiled. There was something utterly comical about the two. "No need to worry about noisy children. He's a single gentleman. There are only three houses in that short lane. The end house has been in the same family for generations. With the elderly owner finding it too much with stairs and a big garden, it has been unoccupied for a while. But it is no longer. A relative moved in." Seeing the horror in the women's eyes at the potential of nearby children, she hid her smile and quickly added. "No children from what I heard."

Satisfied at this revelation, both women smiled. "It is so important to get the area right, isn't it, sister dear?" Pepper-and-salt appeared to be the one in charge, and did not wait for an answer. "It is all about location, location, location!"

Keeping a straight face, the waitress made to move away, when the slate-grey haired lady spoke up. "You said a single gentleman... a retired gentleman, perhaps? We'd hate it if our peace and quiet was interrupted by wild parties and lots of noise..."

More graciously than she felt, the waitress put the woman at ease. "Hardly. He's a well-respected businessman. In his thirties. Lovely man. Really well liked here in the village. In fact, he and his best friend were here just now, having Sunday lunch. Always a pleasure to serve them. They're really nice."

The salt-and-pepper head quivered. "They... they... they are not g... well, you know... oh dear, oh dear, they are not... well, you know?"

"Oh no!" As if on cue, with her slate-grey bob trembling, the woman's hand fluttered to her breast. Her eyes were huge with shock, and her mouth slightly ajar. "The mere thought!" she gasped.

"You mean gay? No." This time the girl couldn't help laughing at the women's prude horror. Aidan and Donald, gay? Not that they were! And even *if* they were? So what? She detested homophobics. Naughtily, she added. "Besides, that would be incestuous." For a moment she revelled in the shocked looks. "They're related, as in cousins," she added for good measure, and picked up the tray. "Ladies, if you want some more information on the village, the person to ask is our manager. In an hour or so he should be happy to answer any village-related queries. I have to get on. Have a good afternoon."

Imperceptibly shaking her head, the waitress returned to the bar. Seeing her smirk, the barmaid asked what had transpired.

"Those two ladies were asking about The

Hollyhocks, the neighbours and the village. And oh, shock horror, that they might have children as neighbours, or worse yet... gays!"

The barmaid joined her in laughing as they moved towards the kitchen. "Gays? How...?"

The waitress told her, and they both burst out laughing. Then added, "They look like something out of Miss Marple goes panto. I am sure that Col. and Mrs. Howard would love them."

They returned to the bar, and a few minutes later watched the two ladies prepare to leave. The property details were meticulously folded and returned to a sensible black handbag. With genteel nods to the waitress, they made their way out of the pub with slow measured steps, befitting their prim and demure middle-aged status. Casting a glance through the pub's windows, the barmaid and waitress saw the two ladies turn right onto the main road.

"They're caricatures. Friendly, polite, very ladylike, yet there's something strange about them. Something fishy!" the waitress mused as she saw them disappear from view. "Like they're trying to ape the ladies in Little Britain."

"God help poor Aidan," the barmaid stated, and went to help some clients.

CHAPTER TWENTY-ONE

Having waved goodbye to Mr. Locke, Holly and Ivy sighed in unison, and went to the kitchen to see about lunch.

Holly switched on the kettle. "Locke really needn't have come out on a Sunday."

"You know what he is like. Perfect service all the way." Ivy emptied the shopping bags they'd brought with them, while Holly put the shopping away. Ivy selected some things for their lunch. She shook the contents of a bag of mixed salads into a bowl. She chopped tomatoes and cucumber, and added them. "Will a simple salad, cold meats and bread do you for now? I'm not particularly hungry."

"That's fine, love. As for you not hungry..." Holly giggled, "... that'll be the day."

"Honest! I really am not that hungry. Must be nerves. Moving here. A new life. Oh, look, our darlings." She swept up the two cats who had walked into the kitchen, and gave them each a kiss on the head. "How do you like our new home, precious darlings?" The black boy head butted her, as the white girl let out an impatient meow. "Alright, carry on. Have fun." Another kiss and she put them back down. Languorously, with tails entwining, the cats wandered off on their exploration. "Do you want to badger Bridget tomorrow, or shall we devote the day to settling in?"

"Let's continue the settling in bit tomorrow. I'm so grateful to Locke and his boys for unpacking almost everything. But we still have our personal stuff to unpack. Besides, Gran was right, it's such a lovely house that I look forward to spending lots of time here. Funny, really, now that I am older... Stop laughing! I am serious! I mean now that I am no longer a child, a teenager, I see the house through different eyes. I loved it then, but now... There's also something about this village. I can see why Gran always loved it so."

Ivy put her arms around her twin and hugged her tight. "I feel the same. Bridget has been doing a great hands-on job running the place all this time. I am glad that she's the one with the in-depth business sense, so that we can enjoy ourselves supplying the merchandise and such."

"Talking merchandise, which still entails lots of hard work, as well you should know, Miss Ivy, don't forget the auction on Wednesday. We'll have to go to the viewing on Tuesday."

Ivy grinned at her sister. "Oh, yes, the viewing. Of course. We also have to think about the party."

"At least our employees and stand holders know that we're having a party this Saturday. Thus far the only thing missing is the address."

"And we need to put up decorations."

"Talking decorations, is there no end to Locke's thoughtfulness? He truly is a treasure. I noticed that he has put all boxes with Christmas decorations in the storage room. I rather look forward to dressing up the house... hey, shall we start on it this afternoon? I really feel like it."

Having forgotten her lack of hunger, Ivy eyed the salad she'd prepared, and the meats, cheese and breads plate Holly had rustled up, with pleasure. "Looks good." She poured them each a mug of tea, and sat down. "Yes, let's think Christmas and decorations. Do we have enough outside lights? I'm a bit doubtful."

"We don't want it to look like Blackpool, do we? But you could be right. All we ever had was one fir tree."

"It was pretty, though."

A wave of nostalgia hit Ivy as she thought about their charming Georgian end-terrace back in London, and the many happy past Christmases. A young solicitor and his doctor wife were living there now. And they would undoubtedly be putting up lights in the pretty and perfectly-formed outside tree. And the bay window would be home to another tree full of twinkling lights spilling out across the small front garden, and into the lamp-lit avenue. Their previous home and life was a far cry from the world they had chosen to move to now.

Holly spotted the far-off look in her sister's eyes. "I know what you are thinking. I, too, have been thinking the exact same thing. I am so glad that our home was bought by a lovely couple who fell in love with it the moment they saw it. Our former tree will be bedecked lovingly for many Christmases to come."

An sudden rush of emotion she could not place surged through Holly. It went paired with a sensation...

like an electrical tingling... She reached for the pendant she always wore on a white gold chain around her neck, now safely hidden. She could feel it through her sweater. "We are now going to make this our home. And as soon as we've eaten lunch, we are going to start on it."

The sisters exchanged loving glances and continued with their lunch. Each eager for the planned afternoon and their new life. Yet each filled with a hint of nostalgia and all they'd left behind.

Following the banal occurrence of the morning, both men had pointedly avoided the subject and talked about everything but the two hags. By unspoken pact, each in their own way hoped that, as ridiculous as it might seem, by playing ostrich and ignoring the situation, it might just go away. Yet it was never far from their minds. Especially not Aidan's, as the aching ankle, no matter how determinedly he tried to ignore it, was a constant reminder. Although hours gone and forcibly removed, Donald continued to feel the pressure of the claw encircling his lower arm. For no matter how much they tried to ignore it, the hags had left their imprints.

Having reached the back gate to his garden, Aidan unlocked it, and he and Donald entered the large wall-enclosed space. Mature trees and shrubs in their shivery winter garb stood artfully dotted about, creating private and secluded pockets which came into their intimate element from spring through autumn.

Aidan studied the gate as well as the height of the stone wall for a moment. The wooden gate was such that no one could look into the garden. The ancient wall dwarfed him.

"Something the matter?" Donald asked.

"No. Nothing. Just... no. Nothing."

Donald did not push, as he had an idea what might be going through Aidan's mind.

They had unpacked that morning's shopping earlier on. Aidan gathered the outdoor lights and extension cords. "Might as well get on with it."

"We'll need a ladder."

"Use the one in the garage. It's sturdier."

"I'll get it. You're in charge of the lights."

A moment later Donald had placed the ladder next to a tree which rose up out of a bed surrounded by evergreen and other low shrubs. It lay next to the drive and by the office window. With his arms full, Aidan joined him.

"I feel rather useless," Aidan grumbled as he handed Donald the first string of lights.

"With that damned ankle, you'd be lots more useless if you came off this ladder. Besides, your help on the ground is quite invaluable."

He encircled the top of the tree several times, then guided the string downwards towards the back. "Can you grab it and hand it back to me? If that ankle can't take it, holler. I mean it!"

"I'm alright. Honest," Aidan lied.

They were unaware that they were briefly being watched from the house next door.

Donald got off the ladder and arranged the remainder of the lights around the tree. "Done. Now I have to start all over with a blue strand. You're OK still?"

"Yes," Aidan lied again.

As Donald repositioned the ladder and climbed

back up, Aidan held the blue lights at the ready.

This time, somehow, they worked faster, and within minutes they lit the tree, and stepped back to admire their handiwork as the lights sparkled in the gloomy afternoon.

"That really looks like a fairy tale." Aidan hugged himself as he shivered.

Donald noticed. "Let's get the rest done, so that we can get in and warm our frozen fingers on a mug of hot tea. We've got scones."

"Oh yes! A mug of hot tea and scones."

Decorating the low shrubs along the cottage wall with lights was easy. Donald had a knack for it. Aidan stood back, ensured the strings did not get tangled, and watched and learned.

"The temperature sure is dropping," Aidan complained.

Donald glanced up in surprise. "I've not noticed. We'll be ready soon, then you can warm up... Uh-oh, we've got visitors."

"Huh?"

"Inevitable, with that cottage up for sale. Look, two older ladies poking about."

Aidan looked in the direction of the cottage. A wave of nausea hit him.

There appeared nothing untoward about the two primly prudish women, but he could not take away that out-of-the-blue sick feeling which gnawed at his gut. Maybe it was that they were two women. He'd had his fill of women who appeared in twosomes. Especially like the twosomes that kept barging into their lives so persistently since yesterday morning. But these appeared to be two older ladies. Your typical spinster ladies who blush at the word knickers. No matter how much he tried to convince himself that everything was alright, Aidan could not eradicate that unsettling feeling.

A second later, Donald appeared to harbour the same sentiments as he voiced, "Be that as it may, I cannot help feeling..."

"Ditto," Aidan mumbled.

"Hmmm..." Donald went back to arranging the lights, while Aidan helped as best possible, as both kept an eye on the women.

The women wandered off into the lane which lay behind Mrs. Manning's garden, and which also led towards the back of The Hollyhocks. Inwardly, both men sighed in relief.

Donald stood back and appraised his handiwork. "I am not really sure." He lit the lights. "I was right. Too much to the right, and not enough to the left."

"Is it really necessary?" Aidan grumbled.

"Believe me, mate, this village really appreciates perfection." He undid the string, and told Aidan to step back some. "Hang on, and don't let it get tangled."

Neither saw the women prim-footedly inching towards the garden wall.

"What a lovely spot!"

Like being stabbed, the men swung around simultaneously.

They stood side by side, clutching their handbags and papers, their salt-and-pepper curls and slate-grey bob trembling in the icy breeze.

"What a lovely spot!" With meticulous and slow precision, the salt-and-grey curls repeated herself. "Location, location, location! It is so important, don't you think? Before we make an appointment with the estate agent, we want to make sure the house is in the right neighbourhood. So far, this village has made a very favourable impression on us. But the right neighbours are also very important. I take it you gentlemen live here?"

"He does," Donald stated inelegantly. "I live on the other side of the village."

"Oh, I thought... I am so sorry. It's something someone said..." The salt-and-pepper curls' flustered behaviour, as if on cue, was mimicked by the bob. The curls continued, "It is just that the right neighbours are so important. The wrong neighbours can devalue a property in an instant. As can rowdiness, late night parties, noise. Unsavoury occurrences..." She blinked, seemingly nervous, behind her specs. "A friend, a lady, even older than us... a couple moved in next to her." She swallowed hard. Looked at her frowning companion and shuddered theatrically. "She thought it was a single gentleman. But there were *two men*! Oh, the noise, the parties... the things she saw. Disgusting!"

A sharp glance from the salt-and-pepper curls made the slate-grey bob agree hastily, "Oh! Oh, yes, disgusting!" Her speech, too, was meticulously prim and slow. "Which is why we want to make sure the neighbourhood is perfect for two older ladies."

Trying to keep straight faces, Donald and Aidan exchanged glances. Were these women for real?

"We enjoyed a coffee at the pub, and the girl who served us," she pronounced it "gal", "was so kind as to tell us a bit about the village. She said something about a gentleman who lived in one of the cottages. We were led to believe it was an older gentleman..."

"Excuse us, but we do have to finish this before it either gets too dark or we freeze," Donald said, and continued with the lights. Aidan gave the women a brief nod, and joined him. They heard the women traipse off. A quick glance over their shoulders made their hearts sink, as the women had entered the gate to The Hollyhocks, and were peering in through the windows. "Genteel, my arse!" Donald said.

"Something not kosher with those two." On Donald's request, Aidan lit the lights. "You were right, this does look better."

"I knew it would."

Two high-pitched squeals of delight reverberated around the lane. "How lovely!" Primly tripping back across to Aidan's garden wall, the salt-and-pepper curls excitedly exclaimed, "From what we can see of the inside, it is delightful. And your charming lights have convinced us, too. Tomorrow morning first thing we will call the estate agent."

The slate-grey bob nodded gleefully. "Yes, delightful!"

"Yes, the lights are delightful," Donald lisped, and looked at Aidan. "Aren't they... eh... darling?"

Donald didn't know what made him do it, as he clasped Aidan around the waist, and drew him into a firm embrace. His mother's words, which had been planted by his bigoted sister, boiled angrily in his mind, as his mouth sought out Aidan's, and he kissed him long and hard. When he looked up, he saw the flustered shock of the two women, which quickly turned to red-faced anger. "Bingo!" he whispered.

"Best kiss I've had in ages," Aidan stated bemused and sotto voce. Then, following Donald's glance, Aidan saw the reaction of the two women. "Oh, bugger! And I thought it was a declaration of your undying love for me."

"I do love you. You're not a bad kisser yourself."

Donald grinned, continuing to hold Aidan in an embrace. "I think I just lost you the perfect neighbour status."

Seething, the women stood rooted in the middle of the lane for a moment, their mouths ajar.

"Disgusting!" Salt-and-pepper curls cried out. She hastily spun round and started for the main road. "Are you coming, sister?"

"Perverts!" The slate-grey bob wagged her finger like a school ma'am. The top of the middle finger of her right hand was exaggeratedly and excessively bandaged.

Aidan drew in a sharp breath. "Oh, fuck!"

"What?" With his arm still around Aidan, Donald felt him shudder.

"I knew it! It's them! Donald, it's them!"

The bob spun on her heels, and sped after the other woman. Their speed, following their previous prissily measured steps was rather unexpected as they hoofed it, and turned left onto the main road.

Donald let go of Aidan. "Please explain."

"The one with the bob wagged her blasted finger at us. Didn't you see? She forgot to hide her bandaged finger. The finger whose nail I broke this morning, as I pried her claw off my wrist."

Donald's eyes widened. "You sure?"

"Yes. Also, the bob was wearing lower heeled shoes than the curls. That's why they were the same height. The bob is taller than the curls. The same as those two hags."

"Jesus."

"I need a stiff drink!"

"Me, too," Donald agreed.

"Are we done out here? Oh, that still needs doing.

Tomorrow..." Aidan looked at the shrubbery under his office window.

"I can easily manage this on my own. You go in and pour us a glass. Also, make tea, and set out scones. And then put that foot up."

CHAPTER TWENTY-TWO

Aidan was on his second whiskey when Donald came back in. "Thank you once again for helping me." He held out a glass to Donald.

His friend sank down next to him on the sofa and emptied the glass without preamble. "I needed that." He poured himself another glass from the decanter. "So you're sure?"

"About those two? Yes, as sure as I can be. When I saw them, I got this strange feeling."

"Hmm, so did I. But still... if that was them, us kissing like that hopefully put them off."

Despite himself, Aidan had to laugh. "And supposing it wasn't them, we put off two very prim and prude *lay*-dies. Whichever way, it was worth it."

"You're a good kisser."

"Aw, you say the sweetest things. You're a good kisser, too. So then, why are we still single, with not a girlfriend in sight?"

"Aidan, me mate, I haven't a clue." He leant forward and poured them each a mug of tea. "I am starting to feel my toes and fingers again. You were right, the temperature's dropping. It feels and looks like snow out there."

They sipped their tea in silence. Donald suddenly got up. "Where are your secateurs? The shed? Garage?"

"Utility room. Top drawer near the door. Why?"

"Let the girls out, and collect some greenery before it gets dark."

As the two canine ladies hobbled about the garden, Donald cut off a varied selection of branches and deposited them in Aidan's waiting arms.

Neither were aware that someone cast them a fleeting glance from an upstairs window of the neighbouring house.

"You're an artist! That is beautiful."

Aidan touched the window arrangement in awe and appreciation. It was a masterpiece. He wished he had Donald's, always readily available at a second's notice, talent. Donald made it all look so easy, whether it were the indoor decorations or the outdoor lights. He'd enjoyed watching Donald create several table and window pieces in no time flat. He especially liked the one gracing his office window. A myriad of twinkling white lights lay hidden amid the profusion of varied evergreens, trailing ivy, red-berried holly, and some of the shop-bought decorations.

This reminded Aidan that he wanted to see the outside lights now that darkness had fallen, and he grabbed Donald's arm. "Let's go out and have a look at our handiwork."

They walked to the main road and turned around.

"Brilliant." Aidan threw his arm around Donald's shoulders and gave him a quick hug. "You're the best! Shame the cottage opposite is empty. It looks rather forlorn and barren."

"Not so the other house. Look. There's a tree in the window."

"Oh! I was so intent on my own home... So, they've arrived. I... we... well, certainly me... oh my God!"

"What now?"

"Ladies! The removers said that they are two ladies. They can't be...? Ye gods, I tell you, as much as I'd love me a girlfriend, I've developed a lady phobia." Shaking his head, he laughed. "I'm an idiot, aren't I?"

"No, definitely not. I admit, since yesterday, I have started to share your phobia, mate."

They walked back, and stopped in the middle of the lane to look at their decorative achievements.

To Aidan, the house had never looked more inviting. He had always loved the Christmas season. Then why had he never heeded its alluring call and draw, and let its seasonal warmth and cheer into his own home and life? Whenever he had shared in the holiday season with Donald, he'd felt in awe, and been full of admiration of his friend's exuberance.

Then there were the few meagrely soulless Christmases when his mother had not gone to Mrs. Becket. What had happened to his mother? She had overcome her obvious postnatal depression within a few years of his birth. Aidan remembered happy family Christmases... and then his father had died. And nothing had been the same since then. If it weren't for Mrs. Becket, Aidan knew that his mother would not do a thing.

As for himself, as he stood hugging himself with this new-found delight, he swore that this was a new beginning. Despite this positive affirmation, he could not help regretting that, for too many years, he had done little to nothing about it.

"I love it." Aidan started for the gate, then stopped in his tracks and turned to Donald. "The new neighbours... shall I... we... go say hello? Grab a bottle of wine. That is, if they drink. They might not drink..."

"Stop faffing, man. This will solve your dilemma. They're coming out of the house."

"Hello! We're your new neighbours." The voice was light, sweetly pleasant, and cultured. "We're the Moreton sisters. I'm Holly."

"And I'm Ivy." A similar timbre of voice, only slightly lower. Sexy, yet totally cultured.

Neither Aidan nor Donald could move. The two voices swept over them like a warm, enthralling embrace.

Donald found his voice first. Embarrassment surged through him, when he heard himself haltingly stutter. "H... H... Hi, I'm D... Donald." Mentally, he gave himself a smack around the head, and sternly castigated himself. *"Stop acting like a stupid prick! You're making a right arse of yourself!"* He stepped forward, hand extended. "Donald MacIntosh. And this is my best friend and cousin, Aidan Galbraith." He poked Aidan, who was stupidly staring at the two young women, in the back. "He usually isn't this quiet. He lives here. I live on the other side of the village."

They shook hands.

As Holly placed her hand in his, Aidan felt a warm tingling sensation, akin to an electric current, travel up his arm and spread around his body. A gentle hand, yet a firm, positive handshake. Firm yet soft. Cool yet warm. It was the same sensation he felt when he touched the enigmatic crystals. "Pl... pleased to m... meet y... you."

As he shook hands with Ivy, Donald felt a sensation cascading through him, reminiscent of all his Christmases and birthdays, and every other happiness that could be celebrated befalling him in one go. All he could think in that moment was that it was like magic.

Aidan felt a sense of loss as Holly's hand left his. She shook hands with Donald. Next, Ivy's hand lay in his, and as pleasant as the handshake was, Aidan felt no reaction. Nor did Donald when Holly shook hands with him.

"Holly and Ivy... such lovely seasonal names. Bet you were Christmas babies," Donald said.

"Winter Solstice babies, actually," Ivy laughed and looked at her sister. They'd been asked this question so often. "We dread to think what we'd have been called had we been boys."

"It's cold out here." Aidan felt stupid stating the obvious. "We might be getting snow... sorry, I'm blabbing... I usually am quite coherent and intelligent..."

"He really usually is. The cold must be affecting his brain..." Donald laughed. "I think what he is trying to say is that it would be nice to welcome you to the village with a glass of something. He doesn't bite. I don't, either."

"Yeah, can I... we... offer you a glass of wine? You want to come in? It's nice and warm inside. Oh, you are not allergic to or afraid of dogs or cats?"

The two women were enchanted by the two men's quite endearing reaction. Like two dumbstruck, enamoured schoolboys. They were quite lovely, Holly and Ivy conceded.

"Heavens, no." Holly's laugh had a silvery tinkle. Aidan was smitten by it. "We have cats of our own. And now that we live here, we may get a dog, too."

They walked up the short path and Aidan welcomed Holly and Ivy into his festively decorated home.

Across the road, in a small dark blue car, two women dressed as aging ladies watched the goings-on in Old Orchard Lane. Binoculars changed hands over and over again. The atmosphere, already fuggy with cigarette smoke, had been further exacerbated by their seething affront.

As Carole's fury reached new heights, Kristie's anger took on a new direction. It was an anger she could not fully comprehend, and it was directed at herself.

They drove home in total silence, each absorbed in their own tumultuous thoughts.

The moment they made it home, they tore off their wigs, kicked off their boots, and dumped their coats on a chair in the sitting room.

"Aaaarg!" Carole banged the wine bottle on the coffee table and, with a shaking hand, poured herself a large glass of red wine. She downed half in one go.

Kristie fetched a glass from the kitchen and also poured herself some wine.

After several minutes filled with a laden silence, Carole, having finished off the remainder of her wine, whispered with a trembling voice. "If this morning wasn't bad enough... I've never been so humiliated in my life."

They'd made it around the corner and back onto the main road in mere seconds. Kristie had wanted to run back to the car, but Carole had put a restraining hand on her arm. "You stupid? Or what? Remember we're middle-aged ladies. We don't run."

As they had traipsed genteelly back to the pub's parking lot, Carole suggested they have a coffee or tea at the pub, and see if the manager the waitress had mentioned might be available to supply them with more information. Although she desperately wanted to get back home, Kristie had dutifully agreed.

While sipping tea and nibbling biscuits, the manager had given them a few minutes of his time and assured them of the amenability of the village and its inhabitants. Old Orchard Lane was a charming and quiet spot.

The cottage's elderly owner had hoped to return home until recently, but had to concede that, following her illness, she would be better off in sheltered accommodation.

He had assured them that The Hollyhocks, although small, was chocolate-box pretty both inside and outside. In the summer, with all the roses and other cottage garden flowers, it truly came into its own. Whoever bought that cottage was coming home to a treasure.

And the new owner or owners would be delighted with their across-the-lane neighbour. A really nice man.

With all this praise of the really nice neighbour, Kristie had hoped to cautiously ask for some more information. But Carole, unable to hold it any longer, had blurted out that there appeared to be something going on between that nice neighbour and another man. A man with a ponytail.

The manager had burst out laughing. "That's his cousin. They should have been twins. I've known them and their families for ages. The village is richer because of them." With that, he had wished them good luck with their house hunting, and a good day. And he had resumed his duties.

The two women had quickly drank the remaining tea, and returned to their car.

Instead of heading back into town, Carole had driven past Ponytail's home, where the outside lights twinkled merrily amongst the shrubs in front of his house. White sparkling lights from a Christmas tree in a wide window spilled out into the encroaching wintry afternoon darkness. With pinched lips, Carole had glared at it. At the end of the road, she'd turned to the right, and turned right again into a narrow lane further along. Moments later she'd turned right once more.

"What are you doing?" Kristie had asked.

"Spying!" Carole had snapped. "What else do you think we are here for?"

"Oh, yes, I see. That is our stake-out spot."

With the gloomy afternoon darkening, and sufficiently hidden by the trees and shrubs around them, they had a good view of Hazel Eyes' festively lit and decorated house. Carole had taken out the binoculars, but seen nothing of any interest. Some lights had suddenly appeared in the window located between the door and the driveway. And minutes later, the men had come out of the house. Both women had gasped in horror as they'd watched the quick exchange of a hug between the men as they stood at the crossroads of the main road and the lane.

"Do you believe me now?" Carole had snarled at Kristie.

Then the men had walked back and paused to look at the house.

"Bet they're admiring the lights," Carole had stated, unable to keep the boiling bitterness from her voice.

What had really stung was that, a moment later, two women had come out of the large sprawling cottage at the top of the lane, and approached the men. They'd shaken hands, and then, to add insult to injury, the women had gone inside with the men. The binoculars were powerful enough to show movement inside the house.

"That should have been us!" Carole had wailed. Fury had taken hold of her. With no answer forthcoming from Kristie, she had started the car with trembling hands, and carefully inched it forward. Once they were on the main road, she had switched on the headlights. In dead silence, they'd driven home.

Kristie poured them each another glass. "They were obviously women. Could you see what they looked like?"

Carole stopped the furious biting of her lower lip to down some wine. "No. You know damn well that it was too dark to see anything. They were women. You know damn well that they were women. It should have been us."

"So, what are you planning to do next?

"I don't know!" Carole looked at the sinking contents of the bottle. "I hope we've got another bottle of wine..."

"We have to work tomorrow. The manager will give us hell if we are late, or she catches booze on our breaths."

"She can eff off, for all I care!" Carole couldn't contain her fury. "This is so damned unfair!" She sniffed. "Blast!" She felt a tear prick the corner of her eye, and wiped it away. Out of the blue, the wind went out of her sails. "You're right. We have to work tomorrow. The thing is that we're in limbo. Are they or aren't they straight? Maybe they were fooling around. The pub's manager said they are like twins."

"And don't forget what Doris heard."

"Yeah. Let's have something to eat. Put up the tree. And over the next 24 hours decide what we are going to do about our men."

Kristie got up, took the nearly empty wine bottle with her and headed for the kitchen. "Oh!" She stopped on the threshold to face Carole. "You have a decent job. You also do some extra part time..."

"What are you getting at?" Carole had sank back into a foul mood.

"Well, I was thinking. You have a steady income. You had that lottery win. You've saved money across the years. If you're so set on that cottage, why don't you give Coleridge's a call to view it? Who knows, you just might be able to afford that cottage."

"You're out of your mind!" Carole yelled. Her eyes widened behind her glasses, and her jaw dropped ever so slightly. "Oh! Maybe you're not..."

Smiling to herself, Kristie walked into the kitchen. For once, this was her triumph. Carole always was the one in control, the dominant one, the one who claimed to have any and all brains. For once, she, too-submissive-Kristie, had won. And it felt so good.

As she prepared their simple dinner, she sighed over and over. There was something niggling at the back of her mind. It had been there before, and she'd paid little or no heed to it, but back in their stake-out spot she'd become aware of it. Something she could not quite lay a finger on. Something that had been eating away at her for a while already, and just wouldn't fully form.

A brash holler from the sitting room brought her back to the present.

"Hey, you, been calling you for several minutes already. You deaf or something? Bring me another glass of wine."

Kristie closed her eyes for a moment and sighed once again. Thoughts and ideas were frantically racing through her mind, but she hardly dared formulate any of them. Yet Carole's callous command had made Kristie acknowledge one thing... she wanted to be her own woman.

"Own up, Marianne Christina Etherton, you want to be your own possession!" As an afterthought, she added, *"I'm not your possession, Carole Leach!"*

Carole obviously thought differently, as she bellowed once again for a glass of wine. Kristie shut out the string of expletives that followed, and made her way to the sitting room with the demanded bottle of wine.

CHAPTER TWENTY-THREE

Twenty Two Days to Christmas

Sunday slipped into Monday and, for Donald, sleep wouldn't come. He'd set the alarm, switched off the light, and for the next half hour he'd lain on his back staring into the darkness. All he could think of was Ivy.

Midnight came and went, and he was still wide awake. And he was in love. That was the part that baffled him most of all. From the first second he'd seen her, as she and her sister approached, he'd felt his heart leap with joy. If he were to paint his perfect woman - dare he think it? His perfect wife - it would be Ivy.

He loved everything about her. That luscious femininity that started with her long, untamed curly hair, those beautiful, lively, sparkling eyes, that smile...

oh, that smile which made him melt... He could listen to that voice for the rest of his life. As for that body... he could feel his own body reaching out to her in desire, but also with love.

Love. He had loved before. Or had he? He had married the woman he thought he loved. Looking back across his adult life, he had all too often mistaken lust for love. It was only over the last few years, as he had tried to find love and dated this and then that woman, that he'd concluded, despite all the positive elements in his life, his love life was a barren wasteland.

Bemoaning their shared fate, he and Aidan conceded that they might be denied their dreams of love, but at least they had each other. Always constant. Always there. Yet, as dear as Aidan was to him, and as much as he loved him and recognised that they were soul mates, he knew all too well that neither could give the other what they hoped for deep within. Nothing and no one would ever take away his pure love for Aidan, but he so sorely wanted and needed a female companion. The yin to his yang. Find the balance he sought for his life. He wanted someone to wake up next to. Someone to go to sleep with. Someone who sat next to him as he painted, and inspired his art. Someone who made his heart sing. The possibilities were endless.

And way, way back in the farthest reaches of his mind, hardly daring to voice it... terrified of jinxing himself and dashing his hopes... perhaps someone who would bear their child... or two... or more. He longed to hear a sweet young voice pipe up and call him Dad.

Yes, he loved Aidan. That special bond between them was undeniable, but it was a love totally separate from his deepest desires and hopes.

Mere hours ago, this vision of loveliness had walked into his life. Remembering all the feelings and emotions that had presented themselves throughout his life, he knew what he was feeling now was totally different. This was an emotion which was totally new to him. Love.

As soon as their hands had touched, their chemistry had been confirmed. He had read the signs in her eyes as they sought out his. She knew, like he knew.

The hours had gone so fast. Too fast! They'd only just met. Total strangers. Two hours later, they had sat around the kitchen table, chatting, laughing, toasting each other as they started a meal. It had been like a dream.

In shock, Donald sat up and switched on the light. The digital display stated that it was 12:25. Twenty five minutes into Monday.

Had it all been a dream? He was at the point of phoning Aidan to ask for confirmation that the evening had really happened, when he saw the business card lying next to his specs... the business card of Ivy Moreton. She'd written her private mobile number on the card. "Only family and special friends get this number."

He had walked her back to her house. Yes, he remembered that. As they had said their goodnights, they had kissed. How desperately and dearly he would have loved to have kissed those beautiful lips, but they had kissed each other quite primly on the cheek. One last look, a wave and a "See you tomorrow", and the door had closed, and he had barely been aware of Aidan clutching his arm and speaking to him. All he could think of was Ivy's promise, to see him tomorrow. Tomorrow... oh my God... tomorrow! Tomorrow? That was today! Already.

She'd said she'd be with him at 10am. She wanted to see his paintings. "... and have the coffee ready." But her eyes had said more. Her mouth may have spoken those words, but the look in her eyes had said otherwise. And that was just one reason why he was now wide awake and head over heels in love.

As they'd walked up the path to Aidan's house, he had finally become aware of his friend talking to him. "She's gorgeous!..." and on and on he'd gone about Holly. Just like he was totally smitten by Ivy, so was Aidan totally engrossed and enamoured with Holly.

There was no denying it. He and Aidan had fallen in love with two gorgeous sisters.

Wide awake, and too excited to sleep, Donald put on his dressing gown and went downstairs. He made himself a mug of coffee and went into his studio. And started painting Ivy.

At 12:25 Aidan had had enough of tossing and turning. His cats had repeatedly cast him annoyed glances, as he kept waking them from their peaceful sleep.

He slipped on thick house socks and his dressing gown and went downstairs. Maybe a mug of hot chocolate would do the trick. He really could have done with talking to Donald, but his friend was more than likely fast asleep by now.

Cradling the mug, and enjoying its warmth, he went into his office. He switched on the desk lamp, and sat down. The house at the top of the lane was merely a shadowy outline in the darkness.

Had the evening really happened? Or had it all been a dream? He saw his own and the room's reflection in the window, and beyond that lay night.

There wasn't a hint confirming that it had been real. The extra dishes in the dishwasher did not mean a thing. The two empty wine bottles did not mean anything, either. His head most certainly did not feel like he had drank too much. Donald had cooked. Maybe he had used extra wine... in the sauce... Or maybe it had all been for real?

From the moment he had laid eyes on her, the world around him had all but disappeared. He'd had eyes only for her. Such lovely perfection. The moment she laid her hand in his, he had known. And all he could do was hope that she felt the same.

His thoughts turned to the crystals which lay boxed and slumbering safely in a corner of a desk drawer. Since finding those crystals on Thursday evening, his life had been a roller coaster of changes and happenings which had taken him by surprise. Willingly, he'd let himself be swept along on its unusual tide which had taken him on a journey of discovery.

And in the midst of this sweeping and energetic symphony of occurrences, a series of discordant and brashly harsh notes kept ruining the beauty he was experiencing. How could he forget those two hags, when his ankle continued to be a ruthless and constantly throbbing reminder.

She had touched his ankle. Her fingers probing, pressing. She'd shaken her head, with that gloriously divine mane of gleaming dark hair, her honeyed eyes worried. "This is something I cannot and do not wish to handle. I am taking you to A&E in the morning."

Donald had piped up, "I did suggest that, or the GP, but he assured me that it was better."

Crouching at his feet, she had looked up at him, and smiled that knowing, wise smile, and chided, "Liar." She'd put the bandage back on, and sat down beside him again. "Ivy has a date with you tomorrow morning, Donald, so I will take Aidan to A&E. How did it happen?"

How could he tell her? It was too bizarre! Too

utterly mad. How could he tell her that he and Donald were being stalked by two bat shit crazy hags who had developed some obsessive crush on them? That this was a little gift from one of the hags, so he wouldn't forget her. Just thinking about it, he realised it sounded totally ludicrous.

He finished off the last of the drink and switched off the desk lamp. Total darkness out there. It probably had all been a dream. He wandered into the sitting room and looked around for a sign that it just might have been real, but saw nothing.

With the empty mug, he returned to the kitchen, and as he was placing it in the dishwasher, he suddenly spotted it.

A ring... a gold ring with rubies. He remembered, as she had placed her right hand in his, that she was wearing that ring. Her left hand ring finger bare. She had forgotten to put the ring back on after helping out with preparing their dinner. Or had she? Had she left it as a sign perhaps? He picked it up and held it in his hand. A warm glow of intense relief and pleasure filled him. She was real!

Clutching the ring, he returned upstairs, took off the socks and the dressing gown, and had to push Tom and Tessa aside. He laughed, as they'd typically taken over his bed. Before switching off the light, he tried the ring on his pinky finger. His hands and fingers were firm but slim, yet nothing had quite prepared him for the delicacy of her fingers. For the ring barely made it over the top of his pinky. Yet it was safely lodged there as he switched off the light.

He raised the ringed finger to his lips and kissed the ring. "I love you, Holly Moreton." And as strange, even new, as the words sounded to his ears, in his heart they felt totally right.

Within minutes he was sound asleep.

CHAPTER TWENTY-FOUR

It was a mundane Monday morning in Carole and Kristie's small Victorian terrace. Still dark outside. They'd showered, gotten dressed in their work clothes, and Carole had smoked her obligatory pre-breakfast cigarettes. It would be a long day without. Breakfast was eaten in silence. Toast, cereal, coffee, followed by more cigarettes for Carole.

It was almost time to leave. They gave their minimal makeup a final touch up, and assured their hair was coiffed as the manager demanded.

The fact that the simple makeup and hairstyles, as well as the required smartly-tailored dresses, made them look far more appealing and even added an element of attractiveness, totally escaped Carole.

Kristie had given her mirrored self a second appraising look and wondered... Once again, those half-formed thoughts inched forward, trying to make themselves heard and, more so, understood. Puzzled,

The Snow Crystals

Kristie moved away from the mirror.

It was Carole who most hated their work-life looks.

"You are good at your jobs," the dreaded battle axe of a manager had told them. "So, please endeavour to look the part."

Yes, they were good at their jobs. But time and again the battle axe had rapped their fingers for being too "friendly" with some male customers.

The salary could always be better, but compared to some of their previous dead-end jobs, this was the best they'd ever had. Work was a short walk from home, and by lunching at home they saved further money. That was not counting the many other benefits this job brought them. Their lack of education had always rather limited their possibilities; thus, they'd begrudgingly continued to obey the battle axe.

That morning, instead of seeing two nice-looking middle-aged women in their mirror, Carole saw stupidly boring ugliness.

"Time to go." Carole sounded thoroughly miserable and angry.

"Do you still plan to contact Coleridge's today?" Kristie waved the estate agent's details about.

Carole sighed and shrugged. "Why not? I'll give 'em a call during my coffee break." She snatched the papers off Kristie and stuffed them in her bag.

They both donned their coats, scarves to protect their hair, and put on gloves. They set off at quarter to nine. They'd be there in barely ten minutes.

Daylight was reluctant to appear on that cold, grey day.

In surprise, Kristie looked up as a few sparse snowflakes fluttered and floated lazily about her, caressing her face and lashes. She'd always loved snow.

Those amazing heavenly crystals always turned ugliness into beauty. She'd seen it time and again - that, like a carpet of colourful summery flowers, a carpet of white transformed the most ugly view into something magical. Delighted, she held out her hand and caught some of the crystals and smiled. This was a promise of more to come. "It's snowing!" she crowed happily, and pushed her scarf back to fully delight in the fluttering flakes tickling her face.

Without turning around, Carole snapped, "You're barking mad! It's damned sleeting! If this keeps up, it'll be effing treacherous underfoot."

She hurried on, grumbling and muttering to herself, while Kristie followed some steps behind, enchanted by the snow gently floating down around her.

As their workplace came into view, Carole finally spoke. "Before sleeping, I did a quick calculation. It is touch and go... a squeeze." She sighed miserably. "Of course, it'll be up to the bloody bank."

Kristie smiled. "Call first, and take it from there."

"Yes! I know that, too, you stupid moo," came the irritated reply.

Carole wanted her man. She could feel the ache of desire, of need. The men each had their own home. But to get her man, she had to live near him. Wear him down, till he could see that she was the perfect woman for him. Yes, she'd call. Her optimism returned. *"Well, who knows..."* she thought and opened the door to the Emporium. Instead of holding the door for Kristie, who was several steps behind, she let it fall in her face.

Shaking her head as more half-thoughts and ideas fought for recognition in her mind, Kristie pushed the door open and followed Carole.

The Snow Crystals

Inwardly, Carole groaned as she caught sight of the battle axe talking to one of the stand holders.

As Carole and Krisie placed their personal belongings in their lockers, she saw them, finished her conversation with the stall holder, and turned towards the two women, bidding them good morning.

"I'm afraid that it is just the two of you today, so separate lunches. Miss Grayson will help out, best possible, when and if necessary."

She'd have said something about their looks today, but knew that it would not be received with good grace. Why did they make such parodies of themselves, when they could look so pleasantly attractive, like today?

Donald woke with a start. He was cold. More so, he was stiff. And what the hell was he doing in his studio? Unsteadily, he got up, stretched, and tried to dislodge the annoying crick in his neck. A half-filled mug with unappealing-looking cold coffee stood farther on the table.

Slowly, it all came back to him. Sleep wouldn't come last night, so he had gone down to his studio to paint. The not quite finished watercolour study of Ivy which he had done from memory was pinned to his easel. He must have fallen asleep looking at it.

He picked up the revolting cold coffee and, yawning, walked to the kitchen. The two ladies were whining and anxiously waiting by the door to go out. That is when he spotted the wall clock. "Oh, my God!" He quickly let the ladies out, and ran to his bathroom. It was 9:30 and Ivy would be with him at 10.

He showered and brushed his teeth in no time flat. No time for shaving. He hoped designer stubble appealed to Ivy. He rushed back down to let the ladies in and feed them. And a moment later he was back in his bedroom, donning clean clothes. Halfway down the stairs he remembered his hair needed brushing, and back he ran to the bathroom. He was tying a leather cord around his ponytail when he heard knocking on his front door.

"Sorry I am a bit early. But I had no clue how long the walk would take."

Donald stepped aside to let her in. "Great to see you. I've not got round to making coffee yet..."

"You look flustered."

Should he tell her? Should he tell her what he had done? It seemed so silly. Sillier yet might be assuming that she shared his feelings. But the chemistry between them had crackled. Was it still there?

He switched the coffee maker on, and turned to face her. "I overslept. I cannot remember oversleeping, ever. And of all mornings, I overslept today." A questioning lift of her eyebrows and an inviting smile encouraged him. "I fell asleep painting in my studio. I'm not really sure how many hours of sleep I've had or not. I rather like about seven of 'em. Sleep, that is. *"I'm waffling again,* jagged through his mind. He'd never had problems talking to anyone. Talking to women came easily, too. Then why now did he sound like an absolute fool?

"I'm dying to see your work. Can we take the coffee to your studio... that is, if it's OK with you?" She placed her hand on his arm, and said apologetically. "I have to leave around 11. Some things to do before lunchtime."

Her words, although spoken gently, washed like a cold shower over Donald. He had hoped to spend the morning with her. Perhaps have lunch together.

She saw the disappointment in his eyes. "Bridget advised someone in town who could perhaps cater Saturday's party. Spoke to her this morning, and she can see me at 11:30. And I promised Holly I'd get some shopping." She gave him an encouraging smile. There was something endearingly sensitive to his crestfallen look.

"The coffee's ready," Donald said stiffly. Why was he reacting so ridiculous? Of course she had a life, as did he. She and her sister ran a business in town. He'd gathered that Bridget was their manager, and largely the business brains, but that didn't take away from Ivy's necessity to do her share. Just like he needed to work. Staring soulfully into her gorgeous blue-green eyes wouldn't butter his bread. He poured them each a mug, and handed her one.

"The studio's that way." He followed her down the short hallway, and stopped in his tracks as he remembered the painting. But it was already too late. He felt himself go hot.

"Donald, that is beautiful!" A wide smile lit up her face. "So that is what you were doing instead of sleeping." She put down the coffee, and gave him a hug and a kiss on the cheek. "I love it." His beet-red-faced shyness enchanted her. What was there not to love about this man? "You're a marvellous artist, Donald."

The hour passed all too quickly and Ivy looked up in shock at the clock on the studio wall. She uttered an unladylike expletive, which had Donald bursting out in laughter.

"I'll drive you into town," Donald offered.

"You're a darling. Thank you."

With the ladies in the back seat, they set off for

Combe-Norton.

Halfway into town, Ivy let out another expletive. Donald loved her feistiness. "You'll be on time."

"Yes, I know. I just remembered that I had to get some things from Sainsbury's."

"You sort your caterer, and I'll amuse myself for however long it takes. When you're ready, phone or text me. Then we'll go to Sainsbury's."

Before she got out of the car, she looked him intently in the eyes. "Donald, where have you been all of my life?" She leant over and gently kissed him on the lips. "We'll continue this conversation later." And she was out of the car.

Donald watched as she hurried to her appointment. His lips tingled from her kiss. Did she harbour the same feelings?

A car honked impatiently behind him, and he drove on. He'd take the ladies for a walk, which was also a great opportunity for him to clear his head and organise the emotions and feelings scurrying around in his head. But nothing could take away the love which was growing.

He parked the car, put a leash on the ladies, and set off on a walk to the park.

She'd kissed him! No one would have guessed from looking at him that inwardly he was jumping and dancing for joy. He remembered last night's fears and doubts and smiled happily to himself. Best of all, she was real! And not some figment of his imagination.

The winter season always turned this otherwise attractive park into a bleak and uninviting place. No wonder the park was deserted. He let the dogs off the lead, and sat down on a park bench.

As he watched the dogs run and play, he kept his

phone at hand, eagerly awaiting her message.

Yes, he was in love. It had hit him like a lightning bolt out of the blue. He repeated her name to himself over and over like a revered mantra... Ivy Moreton... Ivy Moreton... Dared he think, much less utter what really lay within the depths of his mind and soul?

There was no denying it. He was in love. But he was also filled with trepidation. Just because he'd never given up hoping didn't mean that he was expecting any romantic miracles. Yet here was lovely Ivy who, he so dearly hoped, harboured the same emotions and feelings as he did. She'd kissed him! Yet a kiss could mean anything... friendship... amicability... but it could also mean love.

Ivy Moreton... Ivy Moreton... Out loud, he whispered, "Ivy MacIntosh."

They came slowly at first. Gently, lazily... snowflakes. In surprise, Donald looked up at the sky as more of the glacial beauties fluttered down over and around him. How exquisite they were. Mother Nature's wintry creations... all different... all sizes. He held out his ungloved hand and, mesmerised, he watched as they landed.

Much to Donald's surprise, the flakes did not melt. Not even when he touched them. He picked some up and stared in baffled wonder at their lace-like perfection and solidity.

Strange. Odd. Peculiar. Amazing. And creepy. The words came and went in his mind, as he placed the crystals in a tissue paper, fully expecting them to have melted before the next minutes passed.

From the corner of his eye, he spotted a man enter the park with his small dog. He'd encountered the pair before. Man and dog were annoyingly alike. Aidan called his ladies, who rushed to his side, and he put their leads back on. Hastily, he left the park and returned to the car. Before he reached the parking lot, his phone beeped. A message from Ivy. She was ready. Warmth and well-being enveloped him. "Or perhaps you'd rather be called Ivy Moreton MacIntosh?" he whispered. In his mind, he could hear her sweet, sexy laugh - for yes, she definitely had a sexy laugh.

Before starting the car, he took out the tissue paper and peered at the crystals. "The mind boggles!" They lay sparkling up at him, in pristine perfection.

CHAPTER TWENTY-FIVE

The woman of his dreams was standing in his kitchen preparing him a much-needed coffee, and rooting through his fridge for some lunch, but he still felt like howling.

She'd pulled out a chair and ordered him to prop his leg up. A pair of crutches were at hand. Just great! Just bloody great! He'd not be able to drive for a week or two... perhaps more.

Damaged muscles and tendons which needed time to heal. And all because of a damned woman who had taken a fancy to him. He realised that it could equally have happened to Donald. But it had happened to him. He had so looked forward to this holiday season. He'd so looked forward to returning to Peter's shop this week, and accompanying Donald on one of his foraging trips on Sunday. The whole damn thing had gone to pot. And he felt immensely, and quite unreasonably, sorry for himself.

Holly sensed Aidan's misery, but avoided reacting to it. Intuitively, she knew he would share when he was ready. "Do you want the leftover pasta and some salad?"

Attempting a smile, Aidan nodded. "Sounds good."

A bit later, as he watched her put away the lunch dishes, Aidan finally spoke. "I am sorry. I am not myself. I know I am grumpy as hell. It is just... How can I make it sound less ludicrous?" Inwardly shuddering at the memory, he told her what had happened to him and Donald since Saturday morning. "One of them did this to me to grab my attention."

"How in the world?"

"Killer heels. Vicious killer heels."

"Ah. That explains it." She put her hand over his. "Aidan, it may not be much comfort, but it could have been much worse."

"The doctor said the same."

"Any idea who they are?" She continued holding his hand.

Aidan shook his head. "We heard the names and address they gave the security guard at the garden centre were false. If they are capable of all this, then heaven knows what else they are capable of."

Giving Aidan's hand a comforting squeeze, she got up. "I have to go back home now. You'll be alright?"

Aidan motioned towards the crutches and chuckled. "It's not like it is the first time. But the cause is quite novel."

She leant down and kissed him on the cheek. "See you later for dinner." She straightened up and reached for her handbag. But something in his eyes made her lean forward again, and this time she kissed him on the lips. It was all the confirmation she needed. He was as lost in love as she was.

"I'm going to the estate agent," Carole announced. It was her lunch time, and she wanted to know the latest news on The Hollyhocks.

Kristie sighed. "It's under offer!"

"It is not!" Carole bristled. "When I called at 10:30 the price was being negotiated. He said that he'd probably know at lunch time. So, I am going to get in there..."

"Give it a rest, Carole," came the calm reaction.

"Give it a rest? Give it a rest? Are you mad? I will gazump the bitch who wants that cottage! Come hell or high water, I'll get that cottage!" Her voice was too loud. Her face was contorted with a strange maniacal, fanatic determination. Her eyes glittered unnaturally. She cast Kristie a withering glance and stormed out to the staff room to fetch her coat.

Kristie was immensely grateful that a client required her help. Grateful that Carole had left her proximity. Grateful that her thoughts and feelings could be her own for the next 45 minutes. But in the background of her mind dwelt a nagging worry that she hardly dared give voice to. What was wrong with Carole? What had gotten into her?

With it being Monday, it was not as busy as other days, but Kristie felt immensely pleased with two particularly good sales. Both clients had thanked her profusely for her kindness, patience and her excellent help. Kristie was basking in this warm glow of pleasure and satisfaction, when Carole stormed in as if borne on an ill wind.

"I tried everything. But no! They said that they had

other similar cottages for sale. I said I wanted The Hollyhocks and that I'd offer more. No! The old fart had the audacity to tell me that they didn't stoop to gazumping, and asked me to leave. Hah! Uppity bastard!" Fury had raised her voice several decibels.

"Carole, can I please see you for a moment? In my office." The manager smiled at Kristie. "Are you alright for another five to ten minutes? Sorry for the delay."

"Yes, of course." Kristie smiled back. She knew that her boss had seen how successful the last 45 minutes had been for her. It felt good. How she revelled in that feeling. She liked it so much that she craved more.

"The bloody battle axe!" Carole grumbled and stormed out again.

Barely ten minutes later, Carole was back, her face flushed deep red, her eyes flashing darts at her boss, who pleasantly told Kristie that she could go for lunch now. Relieved, Kristie escaped the charged atmosphere.

Normally, she would have rushed home and had herself a sandwich, some soup, and smoked a few quick cigarettes, but for once none of these enticed.

Instead, she chose to stay within the bustling commercial part of town. She strolled by festively decorated shops and her heart longed to be part of it all. When she passed the charity shop, she spotted a dress. It was beautiful!

She smiled as she envisioned herself wearing it. In her mind's eye, she saw herself: from the charmingly stylish hairstyle and colouring, and the makeup she'd favour, to that heavenly dress, and feeling attractive, even classy.

Then her heart sank as she thought about her life. It just wasn't right for the pub. Always the same pub. The same people. The same conversations. It wasn't suitable for the club Carole dragged her to every few weeks, either. More so, Carole would hate the dress! But Kristie did not, for it reached out to her.

The sad truth hit her... the dress represented everything she wanted to be, but could not with Carole around.

Well, sod Carole! The thought hit her like a mallet, and the shock sent her rushing into the shop. She made it to the dress, saw the price ticket and the size. She had to have it.

A woman hovering nearby turned away in disappointment. Kristie fingered the velvety material and smiled happily. It was perfect! She called over one of the shop assistants and next she knew she was the owner of the most beautiful dress she had ever dreamt of calling her own.

And chances were such that she'd never be able to wear it. Going by the life she'd been living for too many years now, she knew more of the same constituted her future. This thought made her exceptionally sad. It also shocked and frightened her. *"Oh, please, not more of the same..."*

She carefully folded the bag to easily fit her large handbag, and left the shop in a turbulent state of mind, as both elation and deep sadness collided with each other.

"What am I going to do about you, Carole?" flashed through her mind. For that was what it all boiled down to, wasn't it?

Next to the charity shop lay Coleridge's. Kristie cringed at the thought of Carole making a right fool of herself. But then she recognised and admitted to herself that she was equally guilty. It was something she had never given any thought to, and it surprised her that she now contemplated out of the blue her life, her behaviour, her attitude.

Looking at the properties for sale in Coleridge's double fronted windows, she spotted The Hollyhocks. A sign had been placed across it. Under Offer. Hardly surprising, Kristie thought, as it was such a pretty cottage, and located in such a delightful village.

A moment later, her surprise was complete, when she found herself inside the estate agent's.

A lady asked if she could be of assistance. Kristie smiled a thanks, "Just browsing..." The next words which tumbled out of her mouth totally took her aback. "Actually browsing for a one-bed flat or even a cottage. An extra box room would be nice, but not necessary."

In awe, she saw her hands were being filled with a pile of brochures. The agent clipped her card to the top one. "Have a look at these. Having the time to find the perfect home is a luxury not afforded to many. With the Christmas and New Year season, things do slow down. You might find your little piece of heaven amongst the homes appearing on the market in the new year. Do keep dropping by. Or check our website."

Christie shook her head. "No computer... yet. Perhaps in the new year. I'll drop in from time to time, instead." She looked at the pile of brochures in her hand. "Unless my dream home is here."

She folded the brochures, and safely stashed them in her bag next to her treasured dress. She'd ensure that Carole would see neither the dress nor the brochures. With barely fifteen minutes left, she hurried to the deli and bought a sandwich. She ate it as she hurried back to work.

As she put away her coat, she spotted something half hidden under the collar. It appeared to have gotten stuck, and embedded itself in the fabric. It looked like a small snow crystal. Such a pretty little thing. It had snowed some this morning. How strange, Kristie thought, that this small snow crystal had remained intact in this warmth! It should have melted to a pinpoint water droplet within seconds of entering the building. But here it was, quite intact, and more so, quite firm to the touch. Such an enchanting little thing! She left it where it was.

A glance at the clock sent her scurrying to the ladies. As she washed her hands, she looked in the mirror, and was surprised at the smiling face that stared back at her. Not pretty, but pleasant enough. What's more, the makeup quite suited her. Why had she never noticed this before? All that was missing was the hairstyle and colour she dreamt of.

And that is when she spotted it... as she appraised herself... the tiny solitary snow crystal which sparkled in her hair. She blinked a few times in surprise. How? Just like the snow crystal on her coat. As perfect as when it had fluttered down around her this morning.

Like the dress and the brochures, Carole could not be allowed to see the crystals, either. Thankfully, her coat collar hid the one crystal, and with a slight alteration to her hair, she hid the other.

Nothing in her life had ever truly been her own. Not even the man she'd married, whom she'd ended up sharing with another woman. Of course, Carole had always been there. Since their schooldays. "We are bestest friends. We don't keep secrets from each other." And this pact had lasted since they were both 7 years old. Carole had made sure of it. Kristie had upheld her end of the pact. Had Carole? Even without that ever-growing niggling feeling that had crept into her life since late yesterday afternoon, Kristie knew the answer. No!

"Well, no more! These are my secrets and I plan to cherish them," Kristie vowed, and quickly returned to the shop, where a glowering Carole was waiting.

CHAPTER TWENTY-SIX

Donald had picked up an elated and relieved Ivy.

"We love cooking and entertaining, but this is such a load off my mind, as it will be off Holly's. Bridget assured us this lady is a superb caterer." She'd sat back with a contented sigh as Donald set off for the supermarket. "What shall we have for dinner tonight?"

"We...?"

"Yes, we. Holly and I will do the cooking. You and Aidan will come over and help us eat it."

He chuckled as a warm glow of pleasure spread through him. She could serve him roasted twigs with a crushed bricks sauce for all he cared. If she had prepared them, he knew that he'd love 'em. "Anything I... we can do?"

"No. Just be there by 7 pm. So, what shall we have?"

Aidan was in his office when he saw Donald's car park in the lane. He watched him and Ivy unload their shopping, and go into the girls' cottage. Shortly after, his friend came up the path, spotted him in his office, and gave him a sign to open the door.

"Bloody hell!" was Donald's greeting, as he found Aidan leaning on a crutch.

"You could have used your key," he grumbled. "Holly's diagnosis was pretty close." Irritation over his situation darkened his face. "If you want tea..."

"I'll make us some."

Aidan followed Donald into the kitchen and sat down wearily. "I've been thinking. All because of this." He waved his hand in the direction of his foot. "Those women... been thinking about those two. There's something I noticed about them, and wonder if you did, too. In retrospect, it hit me."

Waiting for the kettle to boil, Donald leaned against the kitchen counter. "OK, tell me. To be honest, I've been trying to avoid thinking about 'em."

"Yes, me too. But now that I am stuck with this, I've been replaying everything in my mind. It is the shorter one who hit on you. She initiated it."

"Yes, I suppose she did," Donald replied pensively. "It was over the baubles."

"The shorter one appears to be in control. The taller one mimics and echoes everything, and aims to please at all costs."

"Yes, I think you've got a point there."

"Yesterday, those two in the lane... It was the curly-haired shorter one who was in control. The other one just aped her. Mind you, I could be totally wrong, but from what I saw of them, there's a likelihood that the shorter one put the taller one up to crippling me."

Donald poured the boiling water into the teapot, and sat down at the table, facing his friend. "Hmmm. That's a possibility. The dominant force, and the obedient submissive who relies on the other for guidance."

"Or gets cowed or bullied into it."

Donald nodded. "The abused seeks to please the abuser."

"In order to avoid at all costs the otherwise inevitable abuse. Whatever form that abuse may be... verbal... physical... mental... The possibilities are numerous."

"Darn. I forgot mugs." Donald rifled for mugs, sugar and milk. "So you think this is the case here?"

"Call it intuition. Yes. At first sight, they're like clones, but as much as they dress, behave and talk alike, there's no balance. The short one's the dominant figure. The tall one, for whatever reason, is her minion, who gets drained to supply extra power to the other."

"You could be dead right, Doctor Freud. Or they could be two obsessed sick bitches. Not sure I want to find out."

"Nor me."

They drank their tea, lost in their own thoughts. Downing his last sip, Donald got up and placed his mug neatly in the dishwasher. "Work to do. I'll walk with you over to the girls tonight. You know we're...?"

"Yes, I know. We're having dinner with them."

Putting on his coat and scarf, Donald asked casually. "What do you think of them?"

Leaning on the table with his arms crossed, Aidan grinned. "Knowing you as well as I know myself, you know exactly what I think of them. Need you really ask?"

"Ah. Yes, of course.. Eh... yes... so that means you know that I am..."

"Yes! Ditto!"

Donald finished tying his scarf. "Well, glad to know we agree on that." His dreamy smile was answered with a similar one from Aidan.

Aidan hoisted himself up, propped the crutch under his arm and walked Donald to the door. "See you later. And remember, I want to see flowers, village scenes and landscapes by the end of this month, not variations on a theme of Ivy. As lovely as she is."

Donald laughed, stuck out his tongue in answer and headed for the car.

Sitting side by side in their office, Holly and Ivy pored over the auction house's online catalogue. The printed-out version lay between them.

"I really don't care what Bridget says," Holly placed a tick by lot number 178, "I refuse to bid on something I've not seen in person."

"People are doing it all the time, darling," Ivy answered reasonably. "We'd be bouncing all over the country, if not the world, like demented maniacs, to buy in stock. As much as I agree with you, sometimes we have to give in. We can't be simultaneously in London, Glasgow and Cheltenham, can we now?"

"I know that! But I prefer to see what I am buying," Holly stated stubbornly. In a calmer tone, she added. "Remember that vase which took our breath away online?"

Ivy groaned. "Oh, please! Don't remind me!"

"Exactly! We'd never have paid that price..."

"Much less bought it. I know! I know! Holly, you are right. But we can trust the reputable auctioneers. They have much to lose."

"We've never been here, so we go to their viewing days and their auctions till we are sure."

"Maybe Donald knows."

The way her sister uttered Donald's name made Holly smile. "What do you think of our new neighbours?"

Ivy took a deep breath before she answered. "From the little I saw of his home, I really liked it. Donald has excellent taste. And he is a superb artist."

"Yes, but what do you think of *him*?"

"I... you are not going to let this rest, are you?"

"No! So, tell me." Holly minimised the screen, to avoid Ivy's eyes wandering there. "Oh, come on, darling."

"I think that he is a very nice man."

Holly rolled her eyes. "Nice? Is that all you can say? Nice. Such a pitiful little word! Ivy Moreton, I can read it in your eyes."

"Well, then you know."

"I want to hear you say it. Out loud." Holly grabbed her sister's hand. "Saying it out loud will make it real."

"Will you tell me what you think of Aidan?"

"You first."

Ivy closed her eyes, and a soft smile crept over her face. "He's lovely. A genuinely sensitive and kind soul. The way in which he treats and dotes on his dogs is so endearing. His home is welcoming, and radiates his personality. His character. He's very special, Holly." A hint of sadness crept into her eyes. "It's so easy to..." She swallowed, not daring yet to utter the words that lay in her heart. Instead, she softly added. "I wish he'd shown up lots sooner in my life."

"Oh, darling!" Holly squeezed Ivy's hand.

Both girls had grown up into independent, strong minded, feisty, successful business women. But since they'd embarked on the path of love and men in their teens, all of their experiences had turned so badly wrong. Ivy had been hurt the most. So much so, that she had built a wall around her heart. Holly had followed suit.

There had been boyfriends. Some had been nice enough. All as insipid and trite as the word nice.

And suddenly two men presented themselves in their well guarded lives, who solely by their presence chipped away at these walls. Two men who wore genuine kindness and ingrained integrity like a cloak of honour. Two refreshingly open books. A far cry from their previous experiences.

"I feel the same way about Aidan," Holly said. "I don't dare say it yet either, darling. But the feeling is here, in my heart."

"Do you think...?"

"I hardly dare hope. Yet my intuition tells me yes."

"Mine does, too." Ivy's eyes sparkled brightly. She blinked away the tear she felt pricking the corner of her eye.

something so divine. But with Carole manipulating her every move, her every thought, her every breathing and living moment, Kristie knew that it was out of the question. Besides, something stopped her from sharing it with Carole. "Maybe I needn't bother with shopping. Maybe I have just the right thing in the wardrobe."

"We'll see. If need be, I will have to buy you something. I know your size. You can pay me later."

Carole headed for her wardrobe and started pulling out a variety of outfits, and held them in front of her as she eyed herself in the full length mirror. One by one, the garments ended up either in a heap on the bed, or slipped onto the floor. Carole held up a dress, nodded to herself and started to undress.

"This might do... Hey, instead of standing there like a lonely prick in a nunnery, make yourself useful and put these clothes back in the wardrobe."

The next revelation hit Kristie like a kick in the gut. Since school, she had been nothing more than Carole's devoted servant. Actually, nothing more than a lackey. Any attempt at individuality, Carole had squashed in her usual harsh manner. She had ruled over Kristie's life under a guise of so-called love.

There had never been any love, save for Carole's self-love. And her all-absorbing egotism. Why had she never seen it before? All those years she had catered to the wiles of a selfish woman, who had sweet talked her into believing her wildest manipulations. She remembered a part of a TV program she'd seen a while back, about Hitler. Ranting and raving egomaniacal Hitler, who had brainwashed millions into following him. In a way, Carole was like Hitler. It made Kristie feel sick.

"Well? Are you gonna continue standing there like

the stupid pillock you are, or are you gonna help me, or what?"

"I've got to go to the loo," Kristie lied and hurried off. She sank onto the closed toilet lid, and felt tears pricking her eyes. How could she have been so stupid? She felt trapped. Trapped into sharing a life with a bullying, manipulative woman, whom she had mistakenly called her dearest friend. Did Carole care about her even getting a man friend in her life? She doubted it. As long as Carole got the man she had set her sights on.

Looking back over the last few days, Kristie felt utterly foolish. She had let herself be swept along on a tide of Carole's making. Of course, both men were good looking. Very good looking, in fact. But she and Carole were both in their fifties. These men were young and, beyond a shadow of a doubt, far more interested in younger women. Perhaps they wanted families... children even.

Kristie, now that she had realised how wasteful her life had been, also wished that she was still young. But it went no further than a wish. Unlike Carole, who had started to imagine herself in her thirties. So much so, that when asked her age, she'd lisp sweetly that she was thirty seven or thirty eight, or even thirty six.

Kristie wiped away some tears. The silly woman! Neither she nor Carole could ever, in a month of Sundays, pass for women in their thirties. She knew all too well that age had crept up cruelly. Smoking and drinking, all urged on by Carole, had done the rest.

She cringed at her complicity and involvement in Carole's nasty game. Those poor men. It had been Carole's vicious prod that had sent her stumbling into Hazel Eyes. She'd seen him limping. All her fault. And

Carole's. Kristie felt so ashamed of her involvement.

She could not turn back the clock, but she could stop now and step off Carole's ever-madder merry-go-round. But how?

The loud impatient banging on the door brought her back to the present. Carole's voice made her cringe. "Fallen down the pot, have you?"

In answer, Kristie flushed the toilet. "I'm busy." For emphasis, she flushed the toilet a moment later, again. When she came out of the bathroom, she heard sounds coming from downstairs. The TV or the radio. She found Carole dressed in her chosen outfit, dancing madly around the room.

"Carole." She had to raise her voice over the noise. "Stand still for a moment, will you? You're off tomorrow afternoon, and I am tomorrow morning. We need shopping. Are you doing it, or shall I do it?"

They should have done it on Saturday or Sunday, but they'd been off on what Kristie now recognised as a ludicrous, but more so, maniacal wild goose chase.

"No, I'll do the shopping." And she continued dancing.

Kristie left her to it.

The veil had lifted a fraction more. They had both paid half for their cheap, small, old but infinitely useful car. They both paid half the road tax, insurance and petrol. But it was one more thing on the growing list that Carole was in charge of. Kristie rarely got to drive the car. Carole made sure of that!

As the eye-opening revelations about her life, and the relationship with the woman she had considered her best friend, piled up, Kristie felt the noose tightening. She had to get out. She had to escape. But how?

She showered, made a large mug of sweet, milky tea, and looked in on Carole. The woman's face was highly flushed as she lay sprawled on the sofa, breathing heavily... and laughing madly.

In the quiet safety of her room, Kristie retrieved the property brochures from their hiding place in her bag and started studying them. A small glimmer of hope lightened her mood. She had always managed to save some money. Always tried to live as frugally as possible. There was the lottery win.

Maybe, just maybe, she would be able to afford one of these one-bed flats or cottages. She tried not to think about Carole's inevitable reaction - she'd go ballistic!

Kristie folded up the wad of brochures and hid them again. With the remainder of the - by now - tepid tea finished off, she switched off the light. For a while, she lay staring at the street light filtering through the curtains, and that morning sprang to mind.

They'd been the first snowflakes of the season. She'd held up her hands and turned up her face to catch the small, fluttering snow crystals that had descended around her. She'd been mesmerised by their magic.

Magic?

It must be, for they hadn't melted. On her arrival home tonight, beside the one she'd found earlier on, she'd discovered several more crystals under her collar. An inspection of her scarf had revealed even more.

And just now, as she prepared for bed and removed the pins from her hair, after giving it a good brushing, more snow crystals had fluttered down. None of them had melted, so she had put them in a tissue and placed them in the bottom of her jewellery box. So out of place... diamond-like treasures surrounded by the cheapest of trinkets.

She had never seen anything so pretty and so unique as those mesmerising snow crystals. Kristie was all too aware that, with the arrival of those snow crystals in her life, changes had started steadily creeping in. Changes in her attitude, and her thoughts.

Before those crystals, she'd been Carole's always put-down, subservient clone. Now she recognised her own self-worth, and sought independence. Yes, there definitely was something magical about those snow crystals.

How jarringly painful Carole's irritated answer had been, proclaiming her mad. Carole had not seen the snow, playfully fluttering down.They had not fallen on her. She had complained about sleet.

Whatever had happened that morning, Kristie's eyes had been good and truly opened. While Carole's worst traits had all been exacerbated - of which Kristie was acutely aware there were many - the true Carole had emerged. Whatever had happened that morning had unleashed the monster in her.

As Kristie was pondering her life and hopes for a new future, Carole, despite knowing she'd be working in the morning, indulged in an entire bottle of cheap red wine.

She danced and drank, relishing the thought of Saturday's party until, laughing hysterically, she fell breathless onto the sofa. A moment later, she slipped into a comatose sleep.

In South Woodside, two couples ate, drank and talked, as they got to know each other better. Later on, having parted for the night, all four went to sleep in their own beds and homes, hugging the same feelings closely to their chests... feelings they did not yet dare sharing... stirrings of feelings they had feared would be eluding them forever... All four were in love.

CHAPTER TWENTY-EIGHT

Twenty One Days to Christmas

Aidan, who had been picked up by Gary that morning, was fussed over all day by his devoted secretary, as well as his employees. Nothing was too much for them. The morning meeting with a new client went better than he had hoped for. Lunch with some associates led to another client. When Gary dropped him off back home, Aidan complimented himself on a successful day.

Except for the cheerfully lit Christmas tree, the house next door lay in darkness. The object of his affections was not at home.

Since he came to live here, he'd never paid attention or much cared about the property being unlived in. But now it was foremost in his mind. He knew that the sisters had gone to a viewing day at an auction house, and that they were planning to spend the rest of the day at work. Like him, they too had their work life laid out for them. It was something that he had to keep reminding himself. Perhaps, when he was not at home, Holly felt the same as he felt now?

He phoned Donald, but he was asked to leave a message.

He couldn't put a finger on it, but disappointment and loneliness stealthily crept forward. Was it because he was hobbling about on crutches that he felt so miserable? Was he just feeling sorry for himself? It wasn't as if his world and life had caved in or come to an abrupt halt. He merely couldn't drive his own car for a week or two or more. That was all.

His home had taken on a new life. Yes, of course he was delighted with the result. But he couldn't help that flat sensation of loneliness. He longed to see Holly. He longed to feel the gentle touch of her hand. Last evening they'd kissed hello and goodnight. The pecks on the cheek of friends. Yet he'd read more in Holly's eyes. What was keeping her back? And then he remembered that they'd only met late Sunday afternoon.

"Stop being ridiculous!" he chided himself.

It was just that he longed to see and talk to some people. Why not hobble to the pub? Spare himself the trouble of preparing a meal for himself. He phoned Donald again, and left a message asking him to join him.

The Snow Crystals

As he exited from the house and made his way to the main road, then turned left towards the pub, he did not know he was being watched.

The small dark blue car was well hidden by foliage, and had only just arrived. Its solitary occupant, a middle-aged woman dressed entirely in dark clothes, had earlier on discovered a safe place from where to watch the large house on the other side of the village.

She'd seen visitors arrive at The Old Forge, and darkness had set in when they left again after an hour. They'd each been carrying a well-wrapped package.

Shortly after, she'd watched the house's occupant get in his car, which headed in the direction of town. Like possessed, she'd driven along her earlier discovered detour consisting of narrow country lanes, and she was now parked at her other stake-out position, to discover to her dismay that her quarry's car was not parked where she had expected it to be. Ponytail was not at his friend's home.

That is when she saw The Cottage's owner, on crutches, head towards the centre of the village. She decided to risk following him. The village was quiet. The occasional car passed through, and no more. It was, after all, dinner time. The street lights showed that he was heading for the pub. She'd find a convenient spot to keep an eye on him. Not that she was particularly interested in him. Far from it, but chances were great that the object of her affections would join him in the pub.

She'd forgotten completely that she should have gone to the supermarket. Completely forgotten that she would get shopping in, and that she should be at home, preparing dinner.

Kristie switched off the bedside lamp and, with mounting despair, she lay reminiscing the past day.

Her morning off had started on waking at 8 am, instead of 7:30. That half hour extra in bed, on her day or half-day off, was a small luxury she enjoyed indulging in. She'd dressed quickly, and gone downstairs. She was planning on a relaxing breakfast shared with one of the books Doris had supplied. Afterwards, she'd do some hoovering, then prepare herself for work. That would give her a few hours of window shopping, and enough time to have a coffee somewhere. She'd also drop in on some of the other estate agents in town. Kristie was looking forward to her morning off.

On entering the sitting room, she found the remnants of Carole's excesses of the previous night strewn about. An ashtray full of lipstick-stained cigarette ends. An empty bottle, and a half-filled glass of sour-smelling wine. The dress Carole had selected for Saturday's party lay forgotten on the floor. Kristie stumbled over some shoes. Books had tumbled off the table onto the floor.

"What a mess," Kristie mumbled to herself, and went into the kitchen. Not a sign of Carole. Usually, by now, the kettle would have boiled and coffee would have been made, and the smell of toast would be meandering around the house.

"Carole," Kristie called. No answer. With a resigned sigh, Kristie went upstairs and knocked on Carole's door. No answer. She turned the handle... at least, she tried. The door was locked! Did Carole always lock her door at night? She called out Carole's name several times over, without a reaction. There was no choice but to bang on the door.

"What?" finally came the woozy reply.

"Carole, it is 8:30. You have to be at work by 9."

Several seconds of dead silence followed. Then a string of screeched expletives erupted from the closed room. There were crashing and banging noises. The lock was turned, and Carole tore open the door. "Why didn't you wake me on time, you stupid, useless, effing bitch?"

Kristie stepped aside, as Carole stumbled to the bathroom, cussing and swearing every obscenity known to her.

"You have an alarm clock, Carole," Kristie stated, calmer than she felt. "I'll make you a strong coffee, and some toast," she added. She doubted Carole heard anything of what she'd said.

The verbal abuse continued to drift down to Kristie, as Carole got ready for work. The obligatory coffee and toast stood ready on the counter when she finally appeared in the kitchen. She was dressed, wore makeup, and her hair had been done in some sort of fashion. The truth was that she looked a mess.

With excitement for the party having taken over, she had barely touched her dinner the previous evening, drank too much, and this morning she suffered the hangover from hell. And blamed it all on Kristie. At just gone nine she slammed the front door shut.

Kristie sank onto a chair and took several deep breaths. "I am not her keeper!" she exclaimed to the empty room, feeling like crying.

"I have been there for you my entire life, Carole. Always trying to please you. Do things for you. Doing them your way, because my way was never good enough for you. Because I was too simple. Too stupid. Degrading me. Always degrading and humiliating me. Setting me to your hand, to your wiles and whims. Only when I followed unquestioningly in your wake were you satisfied.

"Oh, I see it all so clearly now. All those lost years! How I despise myself for having been so blind. How can you call me stupid? We had the exact same education, and left school at 16, and started work. You're the same level as I am. No better, no worse. But for once, I suppose I am better than you, Carole. Because at least I woke up. I can see myself and my life clearly. I don't like in the least what lies behind me, so I am going to make damn sure that I will like my future.

"I may never be more than a shop assistant, but at least I can be a happy and contented shop assistant, and be good at my job. I will not let you destroy my life anymore!"

She banged her fist on the table for affirmation, and sat still for a moment. Voicing it all aloud had, strangely enough, helped. It had given her strength.

"Breakfast and coffee." As the water boiled, with bread toasting, instead of selecting one of Doris' books, she fetched the property brochures, and longingly re-read them as she had her breakfast. Afterwards, she compiled a shopping list for Carole and placed it in clear view on the kitchen counter.

She cleared the sitting room and took Carole's discarded things upstairs. Once again, the room was locked. She left everything in the box room instead.

As she quickly passed the hoover around, Kristie wondered about the locked door. She had no key to lock her own door. Had there been a key to Carole's room? Not that she knew of. As strange as she found it, Kristie acknowledged that it was just one more item to add to the list that strengthened her resolve to gain her independence. And independence meant moving away. Finding a place of her own. In the time frame of just over twenty four hours, it had become imperative.

She looked around the room she had once considered a vital part of home. Although she had helped pay for it, Kristie saw nothing in here that represented her. Everything was to Carole's taste. Despite its pretty decorations, the pink tree looked tawdry and shop-worn in the midmorning winter gloom.

Together with the tree, the decorations dotted around the room had taken on a showy vulgarity that took Kristie aback. She swore to herself that in her own home she'd have a real tree, no matter how small. And she'd do it up traditionally.

Puzzled at her years of blindness, Kristie went upstairs to ready herself to go out.

CHAPTER TWENTY-NINE

Several hours later, Kristie arrived at work, smiling to herself. She'd enjoyed window shopping, then enjoyed lunch at a nearby tea-room while studying several more property brochures. The more she saw, the more she was assured that she might just be able to afford her own bolthole. It was this smile that her boss noticed and commented on. But more was to follow, as Kristie was asked to follow her into her office.

"No prying ears here," her boss said, and the smile that had lit up Kristie's face disappeared, as she closed the door behind them. "Carole is your friend. She was unacceptably late this morning." She appeared to want to say more, but chose not to, and instead asked, "Do you know what is wrong with Carole? Is she ill? Is something bothering her?"

Had this question been posed two days ago, she'd have been affronted with loyalty to her friend, but since just before nine am yesterday morning, her eyes had been opened. Why should she protect, or lie for the woman who had used her for most of her life?

"I noticed, too." Kristie studied her nails as her mind chased around in loops. Suddenly, she made up her mind, and looked her boss straight in the eyes. "If I'd not called her, she'd have been even later, or perhaps not come in at all. She drank too much last night. I am sorry, but I will not be held responsible for her behaviour. She is a mature woman."

"I am not blaming you, Kristie. Far from. And I agree, Carole is responsible for herself. But, I thought, with you two being such good friends..."

"I don't think we ever were friends. I was useful to Carole..." Pleadingly, Kristie looked at her boss. "I'm telling you this in confidence. Please keep this between us."

Kristie found Carole scowling behind the counter. She looked awful. Pale, with dark circles around her eyes. No amount of makeup could improve her looks. The anger emanating from her was palpable.

"This shite dump's all yours. I'm off." Without another word, she hurried away.

The afternoon sped by pleasurably for Kristie. As the shop closed at 6, a heaviness of heart descended on her. She'd have to go home now and confront Carole. Home... the word had taken on such an ugly ring to it.

She took her time walking home, savouring the lights and the cheer spilling from the shops and homes she passed on her way. Absorbing as much positive energy as possible, to counteract the inevitable negativity which Carole would be radiating.

As she approached the terrace she'd called home for years, she was surprised to be greeted by darkness. Carole adored that pink tree. Then why wasn't it lit? She called out her housemate's name, and the only reply came from the hum of the refrigerator in the kitchen.

On entering the kitchen, Kristie saw that the shopping list lay where she had left it. The only sign that Carole had been at home was in the box room, where her work clothes lay discarded in a heap.

More worrying to Kristie was that her bedroom door stood slightly ajar. She knew she had closed it! At first glance nothing appeared to have been moved or touched. Then she saw that her wardrobe door, too, had been left ajar. Anxiety and anger flashed through her, as she went to try Carole's door. Once again, it was locked. Back in her room, she climbed on a chair and checked if the suitcase on top of the wardrobe was as she had left it. It was still safely locked. Her treasured dress and the brochures were safe. The suitcase's key was attached to her own key ring.

The betrayal was an ache she could not drive away. And it worsened as she searched the fridge and cupboards for dinner. They were down to the bare bones. There was nothing much to speak of for breakfast, either.

Kristie was tired and hungry. She made herself a mug of tea, and tried Carole's phone. It was switched off. She found it hard to concentrate on a magazine. Perhaps Carole had forgotten the shopping list. Perhaps Carole wasn't back from the supermarket yet.

Seven o'clock came and went, and soon 8 pm loomed. Still no Carole.

Frustrated, Christie donned her coat, grabbed her bag, and went out.

As she had suspected, the car was not in its usual spot in the lane behind the house.

Fuming by now, she hurried to the chip shop. A

warming cottage pie would have gone down a treat on this cold winter's evening, but she'd have to do with fish and chips instead. She'd get some mushy peas with it. She was hungry.

She tried Carole's phone again without result, as she waited for her food.

Kristie left the porch light on when she went to bed at 10:30. She made one last attempt to reach Carole and left a message.

With her mistrust now complete, and lacking a lock on her door, she shoved a chair underneath the doorknob. "What a day!" she muttered to herself, the day's occurrences flashing past before she fell into a fitful sleep.

"The stupid bitch!" Carole grumbled as she found the porch light on. Almost midnight, and she was wide awake. Seven thirty would be here all too soon, and she did not fancy a second bollocking from that stupid, uppity bitch.

She poured herself a glass of wine, and sat down for a moment on the sofa. She'd fallen asleep on it last night. Around four she'd awoken, feeling dreadfully ill with the hangover from hell, and had hoisted herself up the stairs to bed. Not fancying a repeat of the previous night, she finished the wine, and went to her bedroom.

But sleep refused to come. Between the excitement of next Saturday's party and the evening's happenings, her adrenaline was racing.

She'd followed Hazel Eyes to the pub, and was glad she'd hung around the car park, for her determination was rewarded about an hour later. Ponytail had arrived with his despicable dogs.

How she'd longed to enter the pub! Get a drink. Banish the chill from her bones. Instead, she lay low in the car, and took an occasional sip of hot coffee from the thermos flask. The binoculars were trained on the pub's windows, and she was sure she'd caught sight of the two men talking, as well as chatting and laughing with several locals. They'd appeared to be in high spirits.

As last orders time had approached, Carole was also ready to call it a day.

Excitement had shot through her as she saw the men exiting the pub. Most of the pub's patrons left on foot, a few by car. Ponytail had walked Hazel Eyes back home. The going was slow, as they were held up by the mutts and those damned silly crutches. Kristie deserved an ass-hat on crutches. What a wuss!

As the last cars left, not wanting to draw attention to herself, Carole had also driven away from the pub's car park, and turned onto the main road. Up ahead she'd seen the two men. Their going continued to be slow. That's when the idea had hit her! And what a brilliant idea it had been, too!

She had not switched on the car lights. The intermittently dotted streetlamps would suffice.

She wasn't interested in the waste of space on crutches! He was a liability and on a level with the mutts. All three of them obstacles hindering her in attaining her goal. Obstacles which needed removing.

She'd have liked to whoop out loud. But didn't. For in the silence of the ever more sleeping village, an element of stealth was of the essence. Instead, to celebrate her brilliant idea, she'd punched the air, and watched the movements of the two men.

241

Her beloved Ponytail had walked on the inside, his mutts sniffing at garden walls. The wuss was hobbling along on his crutches on the road side. They'd been slowly strolling past garden-fronted houses that had given way to stone houses bordering the narrow pavement. Followed by a sharp bend in the road to the right... ideal!

Quietly she'd partially mounted the low pavement. To any onlookers it would have appeared the car was parked.

In her rear-view mirror, she saw a car approaching.

She'd seen the men stop, and at first it looked like the wuss was taking a breather. Then she saw that they were waiting for the dogs.

The car had passed her at a sedate speed. Keeping her car half on the pavement, Carole had moved forward slowly, following the other car close on its tail. The car passed the men. They'd paid no attention to it. Good! That would mean that they'd not pay attention to her either.

A second or two, if that, and she'd approached them. Their attention was still focused on the mutts.

She'd revved up...

It was over before it fully hit home. She'd driven the car into Hazel Eyes. She'd heard his cry and, in her rear-view mirror, before she'd disappeared from view around the bend, she'd seen him fall.

Her heart racing, she was relieved to notice that the car she'd been following was nowhere to be seen. She made it in no time flat, to the - by now familiar - hidey hole.

For want of something far stronger, she'd opened the flask with trembling fingers, and had some more coffee. She'd lit a cigarette, and waited.

The Snow Crystals

A variety of scenarios had crossed her mind... Any minute she'd expected to hear the wail of sirens. The police. An ambulance. Even the coroner.

What a shame that circumstances denied her the chance to see the results of her handiwork. In her mind, she'd seen a sobbing Ponytail cradling the bloodied, broken and dying Hazel Eyes.

She'd bring solace to the grieving Ponytail. She'd make herself indispensable. He'd be lost without her!

The mutts! She'd then remembered the mutts. Those would have to be dealt with. She'd think of something. He'd be grieving for those despicable creatures, too... Oh, he'd be reliant on her. She'd make so sure of that!

And from thereon it would be happy ever afters...

A car had passed on the main road, heading for Combe-Norton. Shortly after, another one drove through the village from the direction of town. No sirens. No police. Just another late, quiet village, winter evening.

Forgetting the cigarette abandoned in the ashtray, she lit another one, and mentally replayed what had happened since she'd left the pub's car park. She'd hit Hazel Eyes. That was for sure. She'd heard the cry, and seen him fall... If not dead, then he should be wounded...

From the corner of her eye, Carole suddenly detected movement. She leaned forward, trying to peer through the foliage, when she spotted shifting shadows approaching on the road. Squinting, she leaned even more forward, trying to focus on the figures still shrouded in partial darkness. When they reached the yellowish gleam of the streetlamp, Carole's fingers went icy cold, and started trembling. She nearly dropped her cigarette.

It was them! The two men and the abhorrent mutts were approaching at a slow pace. Worse yet, Hazel Eyes was still very much alive, seemingly unhurt, and hobbling along on his crutches. They turned into Old Orchard Lane, and entered Hazel Eyes' house. Half an hour later, Ponytail still had not come out. Shortly after, the lights went out around the house.

But something was not right. Why had Ponytail not left?

She'd failed. The hobbling wuss was alive to see another day.

Consumed with jealousy and rage that Hazel Eyes was still very much alive and kicking, she'd driven home.

What had she gained?

Confirmation that they were well-liked in the village.

Confirmation that there was something going on between those two.

As she stomped up the stairs, she swore that she'd get her man. Whichever way, she'd get him. No matter what it took, she'd get him!

Replaying the evening over and over in her mind, sleep finally came for Carole. And she dreamt of entrapping Ponytail, and keeping him all to herself. Hazel Eyes and the mutts had been taken care of.

When the alarm clock buzzed angrily next to her, she woke and smiled with satisfaction as she clearly remembered her dream. She knew exactly what to do next!

CHAPTER THIRTY

Twenty Days to Christmas

"How are you this morning?" Donald eyed Aidan up and down. "Slept OK?"

"That nightcap knocked me out." He grinned. "Mum would not have approved."

"You needed it." He poured them another coffee. "Any muscle aches, or bruises?"

"No! None. Stop fussing. I really am OK." He reached for his mug. Why did coffee made by Donald always taste so much better?

"I wish someone had seen something. It doesn't sit well with me, Aidan."

"Donald, like I said last night, it could have been a drunk driver. The pubs had just closed. Neither of us saw anything." Aidan shrugged. "I was lucky. In all, I came off lightly." He held up his scraped and scabbed hand. "It could've been lots worse."

"Yes. You could've been in hospital... or worse." Restless and irritated, Donald commenced pacing around the kitchen. "For once, I can't read you. Are you really taking it so lightly, or is it a put-on?" He stopped to face Aidan, who pointedly avoided returning the gaze. "You think that there is more to this, don't you? Well?"

Aidan concentrated on the coffee before answering. "It could have been a drunk driver. It equally could have been... well, you know..." Aidan looked up at Donald, reluctant to voice his suspicions.

Donald sat down again, and resumed drinking his coffee. "Precisely!"

"But we have no proof. We didn't see anything. It came from behind us, and it clipped the crutch from my grasp. I lost my balance and fell, more from shock than anything else. The car was long gone by the time I looked up."

Donald's usually good-natured face was grimly set. "It's just one more on the list of strange occurrences."

The doorbell rang. "That'll be Gary." Aidan got up. "Please don't mention this to anyone. Least of all Holly and Ivy."

"If that's what you want. How about Arthur Wright?"

The Snow Crystals

"I'll phone Arthur from the office as soon as I can talk privately."

Donald nodded. "Good. Thanks for the coffee, and glad to see you're OK." He smiled. "Hope the girls are ready. See you later."

"Have fun at the auction."

Waiting patiently in the company car for Aidan to appear, Gary saw Donald leaving The Cottage. They waved at each other. Gary liked the affable Donald.

Gary watched Donald head for the house next to Aidan's, and knock on the door. Without waiting for an answer, Donald returned to his car.

Gary needed a quick word with Donald, so he got out and headed for Donald, who stood waiting, leaning against his car.

"Good morning, Gary. Aidan will be out in moment."

"Morning to you, too, Donald. Can you drop by the office? What we talked about the other day, I want to pass by you. Been working on it for days and, last night, I think I finally nailed it."

"That's great. Will have to be tomorrow morning. I'm off to auction now."

"That's perfect," Gary grinned.

Simultaneously, the front doors of both houses opened. Holly rushed to meet Aidan, and greeted him with a quick hug and kiss on the cheek.

"Missed you last night." Aidan could have kicked himself. Talk about mouth before brain! "I'm sorry, I don't mean..."

"As I missed you. We were at Bridget's. Didn't get home till well gone midnight." She touched his gloved hand lightly. "Laters. OK?"

Had she seen the scabbed wound on his hand, he was sure she'd have questioned it. He was glad that he'd had the foresight to put on gloves before leaving the house. If only he'd worn gloves last night...

Having wished his friends a good day at the auction, Aidan got into the passenger seat. Gary placed the crutches on the back seat. They drove out the lane first, followed by Donald, then went in opposite directions.

Giving Aidan a sidelong glance, Gary said, "Gorgeous new neighbours you've got." The reaction he'd expected from Aidan made him smile. About time his boss got lucky with love.

"Donald's quite taken with Ivy. She's the pretty strawberry blonde." Aidan could feel his face reddening. How ridiculous was that?

Even though Aidan was his boss, having known him his entire life, Gary felt no compunction in stating, "And you are very obviously taken with that lovely brunette."

"Eh... yes. Her name's Holly."

From the way Aidan said her name, Gary knew the

The Snow Crystals

man was in love. No doubt whatsoever. Totally and completely in love. Hook, line and sinker. His mother would be over the moon.

CHAPTER THIRTY-ONE

Seventeen Days to Christmas

Donald had presented his auction purchases to some contacts, who had no qualms about paying the requested price. Before the weekend set in, Donald had pocketed his profits with great satisfaction.

Thursday, over lunch with Aidan, he'd sung the praises of Gary. The young man was an absolute and invaluable computer whiz. A gem! Gary had achieved what Donald had envisioned. Thanks to this intrepid young man, this new line of his work would be mesmerising.

Ivy boosted his already limitless energy. Since she'd come into his life, his inspiration had soared to new heights, as he artistically sought out for him as yet uncharted territory.

Except for the way she looked at him, the way her eyes lit up and smile softened and widened, the way her hand found its way into his, no verbal intimacies were exchanged. For days, they'd kissed on the cheek when they got together and parted. For days, there had been no repeat of Monday's kiss. Donald concluded that she was as cautious as he was after a life of disastrous entanglements.

With their party taking place on Saturday, he'd asked if they'd like dinner at his place on Friday evening. He'd asked casually. Half expecting that they'd be too busy preparing... but no, they'd enthusiastically accepted. Ivy had added that she'd been looking forward to seeing the rest of the house. But it was the unspoken message Donald had read in her eyes that had made his heart leap.

He always found cooking a relaxing and enjoyable hobby. But that late Friday afternoon, ensconcing himself in his large cosy kitchen, he was all set to work his magic for the woman of his dreams. Even though Aidan and Holly would be present, he knew they'd be lost in their own rosy world. As much as he loved Aidan, and was growing fond of Holly, as he'd set the table for four, it was all about and for Ivy.

With dessert still to be had, and the coffee maker on, leaving Aidan and Holly giving each other meaningful looks, he had taken Ivy on a tour of the house.

Her reaction exceeded his expectations. She loved it! That he had done it all himself, delighted her even more. Yes, he had painted, wallpapered and decorated everything himself. Yes, he had spent years foraging for everything... at auctions, antiques markets, fairs and centres, carboot sales and charity shops.

They'd been on the upstairs landing, when they both knew for sure. That it was inevitable, and no escaping it. Their kiss held hungry love and passion. With regret, they both remembered then that they were not alone... But the seed had been planted for more to come.

As Donald got ready for the party, all he could think of was Ivy. Days earlier, he'd known that he was in love but, since that kiss, he was all but consumed by her. Had he finally found the woman he wanted to spend the rest of his life with? A voice deep within cried out full of joyful agreement, yes, she was the one!

As he walked to Old Orchard Lane, he brushed aside the last shreds of doubt.

The unexpected phone call that Saturday morning had lifted his mood no end. Except for the elated text message that she had arrived in Cornwall, Aidan had heard nothing from his mother. He knew that all was more than alright, as Mrs. Becket had kept him regularly informed by email, as she was want to do.

His mother hadn't sounded so cheerful in ages. Cornwall always agreed well with her. More so, the company of her best friend. She chatted happily about their shopping trips, decorating the indoors and outdoor trees, dinner at a mutual friend's home, a film they'd gone to see, how she was looking forward to the Carol Service the next weekend.

And then she had told him what was burning on her tongue all along. She had accepted Mrs. Becket's offer to share her home. The pretty cottage was more than plenty big enough for the two of them. With the sale of her flat, she'd buy half off Mrs. B.'s. She asked Aidan to put the flat on the market. She'd be back in a month, or two, or more, to collect all she wanted to keep.

Aidan had spoken to an equally excited Mrs. B. The two widows were ideally suited to share each other's company into their old age.

If Aidan hadn't been hampered by his disability, he would have indulged in a happy dance. Finally, what he and Mrs. Becket had known all along would be best for his mother had materialised. Deciding that there was no better time than the present, upon putting the phone down, he made an appointment with Coleridge's.

With immense satisfaction, he poured himself another coffee and sat down at the kitchen table to continue reading.

The sense of loss he'd felt Tuesday evening was long forgotten. Since then he'd fully embraced the new warmth of his home.

The strangely frightening occurrence of Tuesday evening had been noted by Arthur Wright, who had passed it on to the police. Aidan had shared his thoughts about it being a drunk driver, or even possibly those stalkers. At the end of it, Aidan had nothing more than a rapidly healing scabbed hand to show for it. As the days passed, he had started to wonder whether it was perhaps nothing more than an idiot who'd drank too much. He hoped that was the case.

Mary Jennings' praise for the new interior had bordered on ecstatic. Cleaning had suddenly become a joy to her. She'd begged him to please continue on in the same vein. Aidan had assured her that between Donald, and now, too, Peter, this was inevitable.

As much as he hated not being able to drive himself, he enjoyed the twice daily company of Gary. What the young man had managed to achieve for Donald was beyond commendation. Aidan decided that Gary was due for a promotion and a raise. It would be the perfect Christmas gift for this immensely likable young man.

A meeting with the accountant Friday morning had put Aidan in an even better mood. He was relishing the memo that would be making the rounds next week telling everyone that Christmas Eve through to the second of January was a paid holiday for everyone. If anything would turn up that needed immediate attention, then whoever was needed would receive overtime. With foresight and due planning, Aidan expected nothing untoward to happen during that time, but the accountant had agreed it was best to cover all grounds.

Best of all had been the friendship that had been growing with his delightful new neighbours.

He could see how smitten Donald was. They'd talked about it extensively. Aidan hardly dared think it, much less voice it aloud, but he was in love. And dinner at Donald's last night and the company of the two lovely women had brought it all home to him. Holly was the perfect woman for him. The stolen kisses in the kitchen had confirmed it all. Had he been with her in his own home, he knew they would have ended up upstairs... He'd seen the longing in Holly's eyes. The promise of more had come just before Donald and Ivy returned to the kitchen. Aidan knew his cousin as well as himself, and could see that magic had happened. Magic had finally entered both their lives.

With everything ready for the party, save for the arrival of the food later that afternoon, the twins sat at their kitchen table reminiscing their first week in South Woodside over sandwiches and tea. Who would have thought that within mere hours of their arrival they'd become acquainted with two wonderful, single, good looking, successful men.

Ivy loved how Donald's slim line specs regularly slipped down his nose, and how he'd mock professor-like address you as he peered over them. She'd asked if he really needed them. "Absolutely," had been his serious response. He had lenses, but rubbing your eyes with paint-daubed fingers was not wise, so back to specs it had been. As he'd once again pushed the specs back into position, he'd laughingly called it the misfortune of a straight nose, and mourned the fact that it was bumpless.

She loved his unruly mop which refused taming. That slightly crooked smile. His humour. That wisdom that surfaced at the right time and kept her entranced.

He was a big man who liked his food and freely admitted that if he didn't watch the calories, or exercised, he'd end up round.

But most of all she loved his eyes, which mirrored his soul. With no one closer to her than her twin, Ivy still didn't share her deepest feelings for Donald with her sister. Ivy feared she'd tempt fate if she said those three little words... I love him.

Holly had listened with growing delight to her sister's lyrical praise of Donald. She might not say it, but it was obvious that she was in love. And going by the loving teddy bear that Donald was, he, too, was in love. Even though he was anything but hefty, let stand fat, Holly couldn't help thinking of him as a lovable teddy bear. Someone to hug, whose reciprocating hug made everything all right. He and Ivy were so perfectly matched.

The chemistry between her and Aidan had been instant.They'd both felt it simultaneously. She'd seen his eyes widen, and how he forgot to breathe for several counts. Take away the charming good looks, and that obvious bastion his life had make him erect around himself, and you were left with a loving, vulnerable, sensitive soul.

Donald had ready access to the real Aidan, as did his employees to a degree. The love with which he spoke of the people who had remained faithful to him following his father's death gave great insight into the character of this man. She was flesh and blood, too, and of course she adored his good looks. His habit of running his fingers through his plentiful hair ensured that it permanently looked unkempt. But Aidan without the wavy chaos wouldn't be Aidan.

She couldn't imagine Aidan in a suit, either. He'd worked in the city and told her that he was glad to be out. Yes, it had laid a firm foundation to his own know-how, and been instrumental in making a success of the business he had inherited from his father, but he was glad to be away from the clamours of city life. Glad to be back home where he really belonged.

It suddenly flashed through her mind, that she and Aidan would have beautiful children. She shot to her feet, so that Ivy wouldn't see the blush that spread like wildfire, and hastened to make them some more tea. She loved Ivy more than anyone in this world, but she just could not bring herself yet to voice what lay in her heart: that she was in love with the lovable, wonderful Aidan.

CHAPTER THIRTY-TWO

With Trivia of Cabbages and Roses closing earlier that evening, because of the party at the Moretons' in South Woodside, Carole had shot out of the door like possessed, and arrived home long before Kristie.

Except for Carole's continuous putdowns of her housemate, the women had hardly spoken to each other since Wednesday morning. Carole's glowering discontent grew with each day, and clients sought out the pleasantly smiling and helpful Kristie instead. This merely exacerbated Carole's foul mood. Their boss had taken each aside separately. To praise Kristie and to admonish Carole.

Every evening, following a sparse dinner, Carole locked herself in her room for a few hours, preparing herself for the party that she had claimed would change her life forever, after which she stormed out of the house, to return, sometimes noisily, sometimes stealthily, gone midnight.

Kristie was just relieved that no more wild goose chases following the men were demanded or expected of her. Instead, she spent the evenings doing the usual chores and reading. Even though she paid half of the internet and half of the computer acquisition itself, it remained strictly off limits to her. On her lunch breaks she'd pick up any new property brochures and longingly studied them every evening before going to sleep.

Friday night, Carole had spent much of the evening in preparation, convinced that she'd be the belle of the ball, the belle of the party. It was late when she'd rushed out on one of her mysterious missions.

Kristie knew that it had to do with the men, and in particular Ponytail. She never heard her come home that night.

Carole had long lost any and all interest in Kristie. As long as the woman wouldn't show her up at the party, she didn't care anymore. It was all about her and her desires, and nothing else.

Kristie was a liability, just like Hazel Eyes. They deserved each other. As soon as this thought hit her, she promptly changed her mind. No, Kristie did not deserve Hazel Eyes. She deserved something else... The seedling of an idea which had been growing for weeks now suddenly had come to fruition. Everything was slotting into place, as the timing couldn't be more ideal and right. Carole smirked.

With a few hours to go before the party, when Kristie arrived home, Carole was already ensconced in her room. Her radio was turned up loudly.

It did not take Kristie long to prepare herself for the evening, and she was enjoying a mug of tea and a snack when Carole emerged from her room.

Carole screamed her dismay. "You look bloody awful! I knew it. If I am not there to tell you what to do, you look a right disaster area. But it is your funeral. Looking like that, you'll never get your man. And serve you right!" she sneered. Then sniffed disdainfully, as she preened herself in the mirror over the mantelpiece. "I am ashamed to be seen with you looking like that! If it weren't for the fact that I'll need you to drive me home - for I damn well am going to enjoy some drinks tonight - I'd leave you at home." She kept on grumbling for a few more minutes, then her face lit up. "With some luck, I will be going home with him. How can any man resist me? I'm sexy and gorgeous!" Then she glowered at Kristie. "Unlike you! And don't you dare get in the way! Or I'll..." Carole had meant to add "... kill you!" but decided against it. She shut her mouth, a satisfied sneer on her lips, and turned away.

Kristie chose to remain silent. Kristie liked what she was wearing. She'd found it at one of the charity shops in town the other day, and like her special and secret dress, it had drawn her in immediately. It was attractive and simple. More so, there was a quiet elegance to it that appealed to her. She was grateful she did not resemble Carole anymore. Her days of being Carole's clone were over. For tonight - of all nights - Carole's vulgar bad taste had reached new heights.

But aside from the looks, Carole's bizarre behaviour started to worry her, and in fact frighten her. Silence was by far preferable.

What had happened to Carole? She had always appeared quite level-headed. The one in command. But now the scales were tipping into the fanatical.

Of course Carole drove them to West Woodside. She would have it no other way. For the duration of the drive, she kept up a steady stream of verbal abuse aimed at Kristie.

As the lights of the village approached, her mood changed like the flick of a button. By the time she reached her destination and entered Old Orchard Lane, she was in super sexy party mood, smiling widely, and batting her excessively mascara'd lashes.

On entering Moreton's residence, she slammed the door shut, full well aware of Kristie following her at several paces.

With the two women who worked in the gift shop having finally arrived, Holly and Ivy introduced

The Snow Crystals

themselves officially. They wanted to get to know everyone, and with help brought in for the evening, they could devote themselves entirely to their guests. The caterer had excelled herself, and the twins knew they'd be using her again.

The party was in full swing when Aidan and Donald arrived.

"Sorry we're late." Aidan kissed Holly on the cheek. "Donald and I got talking... some good news from my mother."

"What you'd been hoping for?" Aidan nodded. "Oh, I am so glad for you!" she squeezed his hand and ushered him into the room.

Alone in the porch with Ivy, Donald drew her close and kissed her deeply. "Been longing to do that all day!" he admitted. "If it weren't for that party..."

"Me too." Ivy grinned.

The men soon spotted Peter and his wife.

"Had half expected you back on Monday or Tuesday, but then Mary told us what happened." Peter cast Aidan a sympathetic glance. "Mary loves the place now, by the way."

"So do I! Really want to get some more things, but I can't drive." Aidan sighed. "I hate having to rely on people to shuttle me to and fro. Sucks, really. Makes one appreciate nimbleness of limb and good health."

"I've got me a very interesting house clearance this Monday. Once we've sorted everything, if you're still dependent on others, I or my son can pick you up. You still want to replace the bedroom suites?"

Aidan nodded. "Absolutely! The beds themselves are excellent, it's just the furniture... too starkly modern."

"And grey!" Peter chuckled.

"Will I ever live this down? I just want it to be history."

As they were chatting, Aidan suddenly noticed the solitary woman with the pale straw-coloured hair. She was perched in the corner of a window seat. A glass of juice in her hand. A plate with some food by her side, on a small table. She looked lonely and lost. She also looked uncomfortably familiar. For she did, yet didn't, look like the woman who had crippled him.

She had spotted him, too. He could see a series of emotions flit across her face, before she resolutely got up and approached him. Intrigued, Aidan extracted himself from the group.

There was a gentle, shy huskiness to her voice. She smelled fresh and flowery. It couldn't be... or could it?

"I apologise for what I did to you. It's unforgivable. I was forced to do it, and when I expressed my trepidation, I was shoved. That's how I bumped into you."

"It was a bit more than a bump." Aidan reacted angrily. "You speared me with those accursed killer heels. These damn crutches were supplied by the hospital, and are testament to the damage you did! "

Tears glistened in her eyes. "I am so sorry! You have no idea how sorry I am! She's controlled me most of my life. That's no excuse, of course, but it's all I can offer. And I am truly sorry."

"She? Your friend?" Despite his anger, Aidan was more than intrigued by now. Even though this woman was one of the twosome who had stalked and terrified him and Donald, her sincerity seemed genuine. More so, she couldn't be further removed from the horrid harridan of last weekend.

"Yes. My *friend*." A sad smile crossed her face. "That's what she led me to believe for most of my life. That we were *best friends*. I know differently now. She used me for years. Sorry, that is really none of your concern.

All I wanted to do was apologise. I am not responsible for her behaviour, but I still apologise on her behalf. She isn't remotely sorry, but I still apologise. I would like to leave now, but I can't, because I have to drive her home." A bitter laugh escaped her. "I am allowed to drive her home, in the car which is half mine, because she wants to drink tonight."

Aidan was surprised that her grey blue eyes, which had appeared nondescript before, with tastefully subtle makeup were in fact friendly and pleasant. She wasn't pretty, but again the word pleasant came to mind. Overall, she now looked like a pleasant middle-aged woman.

"Not that it changes much for my situation, but the apology is appreciated." He wanted to move away, but he felt compelled to ask. "What made you do it? Why did you stalk us?"

"I can only speak for myself. The truth is that I haven't quite gotten to the bottom of it yet. Perhaps it was self protection? Perhaps a deep rooted fear of the inevitable "or else" if Carole doesn't get what she wants, that I went along with everything she demanded of me. Even now I am in the grip of that fear. I've stopped looking like she demanded of me, and refused to get further implicated in her ridiculous schemes, earlier this week, and I've borne her abusive rants ever since." She smiled sadly up at Aidan. "You have no idea how sorry I am."

As she turned away, to return to her window seat, Aidan saw tears in her eyes. His anger at her had dissipated. Her remorse was so genuine. This appeared to confirm his earlier thoughts, that she perhaps was nothing more than a pawn in a delusional woman's cruel, manipulative game.

The woman had spoken of being "in the grip of fear". Aidan could sympathise, for going by Carole's instigations, she could well be capable of anything. It enforced his own suspicions that it wasn't a drunk driver who had bowled him over the other evening. That Carole was behind it.

The Snow Crystals

Now that he knew who they were, he still could not take the matter to the police. Except for one hair, he didn't have an ounce of proof! The hair... but that could equally belong to the sad-eyed woman who had resumed her window seat. It could have been borne on the wind.

She and Carole could have viewed the cottage across from his earlier on. Nothing illegal about that. He glanced at her, and their eyes met for a moment. She smiled at him. A shy, gentle smile. She couldn't be further removed from the bleach-haired tart who had crippled him. Her smile lit up her eyes, and for a fleeting moment, Aidan saw more than a pleasant middle-aged woman... he saw a hint of attractiveness shine through.

"Put a bit of flesh on those bones, do something about that hair, and she'd be able to turn a gentleman's head," Aidan thought. Despite having to suffer the result of her involuntary actions, he realised that his pain probably was minimal compared to hers.

Despite knowing now that Carole was clearly behind it, they still didn't have a shred of evidence. For neither he nor Donald had seen who had tried to run him down. Nor had anyone else. All he and Donald could do was to be extra vigilant, and once again inform Arthur Wright. What else could he do?

And that is where the clinch lay. The woman appeared to be as much a victim of this obviously mad Carole as he and Donald were. Like an evil Jack-in-the-box, Carole had popped into their lives a week ago and caused mayhem. What must it be like for the kowtowed woman who had assumed Carole to be her "friend"?

Aidan smiled back at her.

CHAPTER THIRTY-THREE

Hazel Eyes didn't have a clue how precious that smile was to her. It gave her strength. Courage. She'd get through this. She didn't have a clue how. But she now knew that her life and circumstances were worth fighting for.

She had experienced kindness this week from numerous people. Since she had shed the persona Carole had for too many years demanded of her, she had felt reborn, with her true self finally emerging. The unsightly chrysalis from whence a beautiful butterfly escaped and, spreading its wings, soared upwards to get kissed by the warm sun, and dance amongst the multitude of colourful flowers. She smiled to herself. Yes, she was indeed like a butterfly. She'd shed the ugly uniform Carole had forced her into and, like the butterfly, she'd chosen to soar. But foul weather, in the form of Carole, loomed on the horizon, and thus she continued to be a frightened butterfly. A butterfly who could at any moment have its wings clipped, be crushed, its life destroyed forever.

Her heart sank.

Maybe she was a weak person?

Or maybe Carole had some supernatural hold over her? Kristie didn't know.

Although he was a handsome man, and a pleasure to look at, Kristie was acutely aware that, had she had children, she could've had a son his age. Hazel Eyes' friend was of a similar age. Either or both could have been her or Carole's sons. What was Carole thinking?

Even though hell might yet lie ahead of her, Kristie was relieved that she had come to her senses.

More than likely, she would never be able to tell him that his well-meant smile had given her additional strength, for which she was immensely grateful. She'd ride this storm somehow.

She might come out battered and bruised, for a sixth sense alerted her to that inevitability, yet she was going to give it her best shot.

For one, it meant moving away from Carole and starting her life anew. She'd need to consider this sooner rather than later.

If only she wouldn't like her work so much. It might not be the best job in the world, but she enjoyed it. And she felt at home in Combe-Norton.

If only Carole was somewhere else! Carole was the vile cloud on what could be a bright horizon.

Kristie had read once in some magazine, "be careful what you wish for", and talked about it with a former colleague. The woman had confirmed it, and admitted it had worked for her.

"Write your wish on a piece of paper, light a candle and send it off into the universe by burning it." Beyond

The Snow Crystals

that, she'd not given Kristie much to go on. This came back to Kristie now, as she sipped her fruit juice and watched everyone enjoying themselves.

She closed her eyes for a moment, and without any malice to her intentions and hopes, she silently made her wish, and sent it off into the universe. Back at home, she would find a candle, and repeat her wish.

As she'd silently uttered her wish, she'd stared at the twinkling Christmas lights, and the precious snow crystals came to mind. Those crystals meant something. They'd come into her life for a reason. As she thought of them, a sense of peace crept into her heart, but then ran straight bang into the dire worries and troubles which lay there. *"Have faith!"* Kristie thought.

Soon after her arrival, Carole had asked for the toilet - the perfect excuse to go off and investigate - and had been directed to either the downstairs, or the upstairs one. With everyone congregated in the sprawling sitting and dining rooms, she had taken advantage of the quiet atmosphere in the rest of the house to acquaint herself with as much of the layout of the place as was possible.

En route to the downstairs loo, she'd discovered a large store room beyond which she assumed lay the attached garage. Behind the store room she found the large utility room and, off it, the toilet. This area gave way to the enormous back garden. Peering through an opaque glass window, she could make out the spacious kitchen which lay next to the utility room, and also overlooked the back garden.

A room on the left side of the front door was locked. Walking up the path, she'd wondered about that room. The cavernous L-shaped room to the right of the hallway served as sitting and dining room. And was now filled with party goers.

She'd also wandered upstairs, under the pretext of going to the loo, and found all doors locked, save for the bathroom. Behind one door she heard some sounds, and put her ear to the door. She couldn't place the sounds, till she heard some meowing. She recoiled in disgust. Cats! She hated cats even more than dogs.

With footsteps sounding on the stairs, she'd quickly rushed to the bathroom, and closed the door. Several minutes later, she opened the door, to find one of the guests waiting.

The woman gave her a perfunctory smile, and closed the bathroom door behind her. Carole didn't recognise her from Trivia, and assumed she was the wife or girlfriend of one of the dealers or male employees. Carole allotted herself a couple of minutes more to nose around this floor. When she heard the loo flush, she hurried downstairs.

As she made her way to the sitting room, Carole saw the strawberry blonde entering the locked room. The woman left the door open as she picked up something off a desk. Not wanting to be caught gawping, Carole hurried into the sitting room. Her curiosity had been more than satisfied. The locked room was an office.

Picking up a glass of ready-poured wine, Carole moved over to the food display and stuffed one of the finger foods in her mouth. She had no idea what it was, but it tasted good, so she had another one. She'd fill up a plate in a moment, but first things first, as she had other matters on her mind.

She turned away from the food, and looked out across the people-filled room, some standing in groups, some sitting down, all chatting, laughing, eating and drinking, and clearly enjoying themselves. Seasonal orchestral music was playing in the background.

This wasn't the place for her type of bawdy, belly slapping humour. Nor was this the place where you downed several pints and, in between raunchy flirting, staggered reeling to the loo every half hour. This certainly wasn't the place where you drunkenly complimented your drinking buddy's obviously substantial assets in the hope of a one night stand. Even Carole could see that all this would never be acceptable here. If it weren't for her mission, she'd be bored to death!

Well, well, well! One of them was here! It was the wuss. Hanging on his crutches, still very much alive, and unfortunately none the worse for his little accident earlier that week, had moved towards that stupid bitch, Kristie. God! She looked a right sight. Failure written all over her.

Carole watched the discourse between Kristie and Hazel Eyes from across the room. So the stupid cow got to talk to her lover boy after all. But he walked away from her. Serve her right!

Stifling the urge to laugh out loud, she turned back to the food, inelegantly stuffed some more in her mouth, and washed it down with several gulps of wine. She cast a quick glance over her shoulder, and revelled in Kristie's downcast face.

Hiding her ever-widening grin, she turned back to the food. She selected something which looked particularly appetising and shoved it, in one, in her mouth, and picked up another glass of wine. The wine was good. Better than the plonk she drank at home or in the local, but the glasses were rather small.

Armed with a glass of wine, Carole, on her impossibly high heels, minced her way towards the window seat.

"Sent you packing, did he?" Her snorted laugh dripped with cruelty. "What do you expect, looking like that? Who wants a sad, boring old bag like you? When I think of all the hours I wasted on trying to teach you how to look gorgeous and sexy. Look at where it got me! Is that how you repay me for all my effort? You are nothing but an ugly, useless piece of baggage. I just want..." She was going to say more, but like before, she swallowed her words. Instead, she shut her mouth with grim satisfaction. Better not to give away too much. Keep the stupid cow in the dark.

She drank half of the wine, then, casting Kristie a hateful, condescending glance, she walked away as a secret little smile started playing around her lips. Silently, she complimented herself, for she'd just had another brilliant idea.

Even though she detested the three bitches who were her bosses, she noted with satisfaction that Hazel Eyes had his arm around the dark-haired uppity tart. Serve that stupid Kristie right! That could have been her, had she listened to and done as she'd been told. But no, the stupid mare chose to do it her way. *"You'll suffer the consequences, Kristie!"*

Carole wanted another drink. And some more to eat. The food was good. No doubt about that.

Lost deep in her own thoughts, she was unaware of Doris till her arm was gripped and she was pulled away from the other guests.

"Guess what I just saw?" Doris' smirk rose Carole's hackles even more. "If you want Ponytail, you'd better get moving."

The Snow Crystals

"What do you mean by that?"

"Don't snap at the messenger, honey pie." The smirk remained firmly embedded. "I saw him in the kitchen with one of your bosses. The voluptuous strawberry blonde one. They were rather wrapped up in each other."

Doris had played along with the game, of which Carole would have been the initiator, and which Kristie would've automatically followed as she always did. But seeing fury reddening Carole's face, she now doubted this was a game anymore. Carole couldn't really be serious about this!

Doris knew a good thing when she saw it, and the man Carole was so taken with was a good-looking one. But for crying out loud, Carole was a middle-aged woman and so obviously, too, lots older than him. He could be her son! As for the looks department, Carole could never measure up to the strawberry blonde in a million years of Sundays.

Talking looks, Doris thought about Kristie, who had started to look really nice, attractive even, over the last days. And tonight she looked quite charming. Doris eyed Carole critically, and wondered why she didn't follow suit. It would be a vast improvement. But now, with her face working furiously with pent up rage, she found Carole downright ugly. *"An ugly, aging tart!"* Doris thought.

"What do you mean by "they were wrapped up in each other"?"

Doris sighed. This definitely was no longer the game of a romance, love and sex-starved woman. This had become creepy. "Doing what people do, who are into each other."

"Doing what?" Carole's voice was loud enough for

some of the guests to look up.

"Kissing."

"Are you sure?" Carole's voice had risen an extra octave.

"I know kissing when I see it. Love, too."

"Love?" Carole didn't wait for a response from Doris. She was consumed by fury, hate and jealousy. How dared he? He was hers, and hers alone!

Plans. Plans. She needed to make plans. By Christmas, he would be hers. Hers alone. She left Doris staring after her, as she hurriedly grabbed another glass of wine, and headed for the kitchen.

The kitchen door was pushed to, but through the crack she could see Ponytail and the despised strawberry blonde. They were standing close. Carole thought that she was going to burst an artery when she saw his arms encircling the woman, and drawing her to him, while her arms snaked around his waist. Her smiling face turned up to his...

Carole knew what was coming next, and didn't wait for it. She downed the wine and slammed the empty glass on the first surface she came across.

She needed to make plans. She knew what needed doing. But she needed to plan and time everything meticulously.

Pushing people aside, she rushed to Kristie. "We're leaving now!" She grabbed Kristie's wrist in a vice, and dragged her to the hallway, where she found her own coat. She didn't bother putting it on as she ran for the car.

With reluctance, Kristie followed her. "What in the world is going on? What happened?"

"It is that I had several glasses of wine, and don't want to get the blasted cops on my case. I have no choice but to let you drive me home." She glowered nastily at Kristie. "Well, get in! You better not screw up, you stupid, dozy mare."

As she got into the car, she glanced with loathing at Hazel Eyes' cottage. Not because she hated the cottage. Far from! It was chocolate-box perfect, especially now, with the cheerfully twinkling lights both inside and out. But because it was his.

It was then that the green-eyed monster, never far from the surface, once again hit Carole with a punch. It hurt. She could feel the ache spreading, constricting her throat, squeezing her stomach, and sending her pulse racing.

It merely strengthened her resolve. Yes, Ponytail would be hers! She'd make sure of that! She cast a last look at Hazel Eyes' house, revelling in the fact that Ponytail's house was far larger, when she spotted the two cats sitting in the window sill of The Cottage. One on each side of a window decoration.

And another idea was born...

Best to get back home soonest possible, so that she could set her plans in motion.

"Get a move on, you stupid woman!"

All the way back into Combe-Norton, Kristie was subjected to Carole's unending abusive tirade of vitriol.

Back home, the abuse continued.

Even though her hands trembled with sadness and anger, Kristie calmly asked if Carole wanted a mug of tea or coffee and something to eat.

Carole flung her aside with a furious expletive, and stormed up the stairs armed with a bottle of wine and a glass. The bedroom door slammed shut. In the silence of the house, Kristie heard the lock being turned.

"This is the final straw..." Kristie felt the first tears as she made herself tea. Except for a streak of light at the bottom of the door to Carole's room, there was no sound coming from it. Kristie went into her room and once again wedged a chair under the doorknob.

CHAPTER THIRTY-FOUR

Sixteen Days to Christmas

While Donald and Ivy, and Aidan and Holly, delighted in each other's company all day Sunday and lunched at the pub, it was a grim Sunday in Carole and Kristie's home. The pink Christmas tree never got lit, and stood forgotten by the window.

Carole went out mid morning. She took the car, and only came back late afternoon, upon which she locked herself in her room again.

Kristie had spent the day doing sums, and going over and over the property brochures. The problem was that renting was dead money. She just might be able to afford to buy a small, cheap studio or a one-bedroom flat. It would be by far preferable to the current situation. But what would she do about furniture? Carole truly had her stitched up, as she had paid half of everything in the house. They each owned half of everything.

And what about her job? She liked her job. She liked working there. She felt she was in a cruel catch 22 situation. She wept herself to sleep that Sunday night.

Fifteen Days to Christmas

Monday morning came and Kristie had not seen hide nor hair of Carole. She got ready for work, and decided to check on her before she left the house. She knocked on Carole's door.

"Carole, it's time we set off for work. Are you ready?"

The door was torn open. "I'm not feeling well." Her usual looks belied her words. "I'm staying home."

"Oh. OK. Take care. Hope you'll feel better soon."

"Yeah, I bet." She slammed the door shut, and turned the lock.

Kristie wished she could lock her own door. Unable to do so, she had taken some precautionary measures. She had little to nothing of value that meant anything to her, except for the dress she had bought the week before. She also had some important papers. She'd gathered them together yesterday and bundled them in

The Snow Crystals

a carrier bag. Together with the dress, she had placed them in her big handbag. The batch of property brochures were safely secreted away at the bottom of her bag.

Since she had discovered Carole could lock her door, and found her own door and wardrobe door open, she had felt uneasy about leaving anything important to her in the house. It would be safe in her locker at work.

Carole didn't bother to phone in sick. Both Kristie and her boss tried to reach her, but she didn't respond.

In a quiet moment, before Kristie headed for lunch, Bridget approached her. "What is wrong with Carole? Tried to phone her several times, but she's not replying. I also sent her an email."

"Sorry. I really don't know."

"She's a good, hard worker, and because of this I have been lenient about her recurring behaviour. But this last week, and now today, too, well, that is totally unacceptable.

Unless there is a very good reason for all this, I have no choice but to dismiss her immediately. Of course, she'll have 3 months severance pay, but I just cannot accept this behaviour anymore. The clients, as well as the other employees, have started to complain."

Kristie looked at her boss and slowly nodded several times. "I understand. She brought this on herself."

When Kristie arrived home for lunch, she found Carole scoffing a sizable meal. "You're feeling lots better, by the looks of it."

"Shut the fuck up, bitch!"

Fed up and frustrated by the verbal abuse, Kristie rounded on the woman. "What is wrong with you, Carole? You are in grave danger of losing your job. Doesn't that mean anything to you?"

Carole slammed the fork down on the plate. Chips flew hither and thither. "I told you to shut the fuck up, you miserable rotten bitch!"

"What is wrong with you, Carole? Whatever have I done to you to deserve such treatment?"

"Whine. Whine. Whine," Carole taunted cruelly. Her face was excessively red. There was a mad gleam to her weirdly bulging eyes. "I don't give a fuck about that dead end, dead beat, dead stupid job. Those three bitches can shove their job where the sun don't shine." She threw her plate in the sink where it smashed to pieces. The remains of food went flying.

A moment later the upstairs bedroom door shut with a crashing bang, and in the ensuing silence Kristie heard the lock turn.

"She's mad. She's gone stark raving mad. Oh my God!" With trembling fingers, Kristie collected the shards and placed them in the bin. She cleaned up the mess, as she desperately tried to refrain from breaking down in racking sobs.

The Snow Crystals

That is when she spotted the plastic container at the far end of the kitchen counter. Carole had bought it a few years ago, when they'd had some problems with rodents in their outbuilding. Poison for vermin. They'd not had any mice or rats since then.

And what remained of the deadly poison had been confined to the back of the cupboard under the kitchen sink, forgotten behind the ammonia, bleach, cleaning vinegar, laundry detergent and softener, and other numerous cleaners and polishes.

With growing worry, Kristie eyed the container, and opened it reluctantly. She clearly remembered that she herself had wrapped it in a plastic bag, and placed it in a far out of reach corner under the sink. Two thirds or so had been left over. Now the contents had diminished to less than a third.

Under normal circumstances - *"Whatever normal circumstances ever were?"* - Kristie would have asked Carole about it, but that was now out of the question. What had she needed almost half of a container of rat and mice poison for? What had she done with it?

When had Carole exhumed the container from its hiding place? Some time last night? This morning? She couldn't remember seeing it either yesterday or this morning. *"But then, I wouldn't have,"* Kristie remembered.

Carole had come home yesterday with several bags and plonked them on that section of the kitchen counter. A snarling Carole had ordered her not to touch them. "You touch or move any of that," she'd pointed furiously at the pile littering the counter, "and I'll have your miserable, worthless guts for garters!"

This morning the pile had still been there. And the container could well have been hiding behind it.

Whatever had Carole been up to?

Kristie's hands were shaking as she placed the container in another plastic bag, and once again confined it to a far off corner under the sink.

With this find, the mere thought of sharing the same space, as well as breathing the same air as Carole, let stand eating here, made Kristie feel nauseous.

Unsettled, she fled from the house and bought a takeaway sandwich on the high street.

She was grateful for a pleasantly busy afternoon, and at the end of her working day she was reluctant to go home. She made her way slowly past the brightly lit and decorated shops, intent on absorbing the much-needed positive vibes emanating from each window.

As she walked up to the house, she found it lying in darkness. Perhaps Carole was in her room? She knocked on the door. No answer. No sliver of light beneath the door, either.

Like before, the room was once again securely locked. She crouched down in front of the keyhole. Save for the yellowish gleam of the streetlight, the little she could see of the room lay in darkness. Kristie went out to check if the car was still there, to find that it was gone.

"What are you up to, Carole?" A sick unease filled Kristie. She couldn't put a finger on it, but she knew something was terribly amiss.

CHAPTER THIRTY-FIVE

With a paint brush behind each ear, his specs balancing precariously on the tip of his nose, and a psychedelic array of colours streaked on his face and splattered on his clothes, Donald opened the front door to the urgent knocking.

"Miss Frobisher, hello. How are you?" Donald smiled down at the rotund little woman standing on his doorstep.

He was particularly fond of his gentle, spinster neighbour. Aidan was quite knowledgeable in the horticultural department thanks to his mother, but none was more brilliant and insightful than Daisy Frobisher. As always, Donald could never stop his eyes from wandering down to her enormous bosom. Worse yet, he wished he could forget Aidan's comment after he'd first met the kind-hearted woman. *"She's really sweet, but oh, good God, poor woman, how does she cope with that enormous frontage? You can display an*

The Snow Crystals

entire tea service on there, with room to spare for cake and watercress sandwiches, and then some!"

Donald quickly tore his eyes away from her mammaries, but not before he noticed that the little woman was frantically wringing her hands. "Something the matter, Miss Frobisher?"

It was abundantly obvious that she had disturbed her lovely neighbour as he was working. Normally, she would have giggled or even laughed, and made a comment about his looks. He looked quite comical with a paint brush on either side of his head, and orange, green, blue and yellow smears on his face. But Daisy Frobisher was worried, and laughter couldn't be further from her mind.

"It's Ginger, Mr. MacIntosh. Ginger... my old ginger cat. He'll be 18 next year. I was up early as usual, and he wanted to go out before his breakfast. Unless the weather is foul, he always wants a stroll around the garden, and sometimes, if it is really nice out, he will venture into yours... the unwalled part. He might even go into Mr. and Mrs. Evans' garden. Sooty and Splodge had their breakfast, but Ginger did not appear. Hours later, and he still has not appeared. This is so unlike him, Mr. MacIntosh." She looked up at Donald with pleading eyes. "Have you perhaps seen him?"

Donald had given up assuring her that she could call him Donald. It was to no avail. Oddly, beyond this one formality, none other existed between them. "Have you looked for him, Miss Frobisher?"

"Oh yes! Been around my garden. The Evanses had a look around theirs, too, and together we searched even farther afield."

As she said this, Mr. Evans approached with Wellington, the Evanses' Border Terrier, on the lead. He looked flustered. "Hello, Donald," he called out. "Donald, I just spotted something around the corner, in your garden. Wellington became quite agitated. Miss Frobisher, Donald, could you please come and have a look?"

Oblivious to his clownish looks, Donald followed the sprightly old gentleman. Miss Frobisher tottered in their wake, as fast as her short legs and arthritic knees allowed.

"See, there." Mr. Evans pointed at some shrubs beyond which a short wall of evergreens rose up.

"Yeah, I see it."

Donald recognised the cat immediately. Dear, gentle old Ginger, who visited his garden more often in the summer, and much less so in the winter. Dear sweet, homebody Ginger, whose rather limited territory had shrunk even more as he placidly settled into his dotage.

"I found him. He's alive. But only just!" Donald called out. He gently scooped up the furry body in his arms, and walked back to Miss Frobisher.

She held out her arms, and then dropped them. A sob escaped her lips, as tears sprang to her eyes.

"He's alive," Donald assured the distraught woman, as he continued to hold the shallowly-breathing creature. "He needs to go to the vets immediately."

Donald opened his mouth to offer driving Miss Frobisher to vets, but got no further than "I'll dr...", for Mr. Evans cut him short.

"I'll take you, Miss Frobisher." Mr. Evans tossed the words over his shoulder, as he started off back home, dragging an unwilling Wellington with him. Mere minutes later, with Wellington safely back at home, Mr.

The Snow Crystals

Evans drove alongside the two waiting people. "Get in, Miss Frobisher. Please put Ginger on her lap, Donald. And would you alert the vets that we're on our way?"

An hour later Donald received a phone call from Mr. Evans. Ginger was touch and go. The vets couldn't give any hope... Ginger was an old boy... It appeared that he'd been poisoned!

Donald made himself some coffee, and called Arthur Wright. He had to be advised of this. Someone was going round poisoning the village pets. A sixth sense told Donald who it well could be. He just didn't have any proof!

"Great minds think alike, Donald. I just came off the phone to Aidan, and was about to call you." The story tumbled out of Arthur's mouth. "The Turnbull's cat, Wendy, didn't come home. So unlike her. They found her more dead than alive, hiding in Aidan's garden. The vets say she was poisoned. And I just found out that Miss Frobisher's cat was found poisoned in your garden."

Donald couldn't find the words for a moment. Poisoned pets found in both his and Aidan's gardens! *"How sinister!"* shot through Donald's mind. *"As if we were targeted."* That's when it hit him. It couldn't be otherwise. Both he and Aidan had pets. The poison could well have been meant for their pets. He'd have to go out and check his garden... and Aidan's. Would and could their stalker be so mad as to seek to kill innocent creatures?

"I'm going to check my garden, Arthur. And Aidan's." He felt sick. This was surreal.

"I've already set Ron and his son on searching Aidan's garden and surrounding areas, Donald. Philip will check around your and Miss Frobisher's area. Be extra careful with your ladies, Donald."

"I will, Arthur! I'll go out and have a look around the part of my garden that is accessible from the road."

Shortly after, Donald found something suspicious lying, barely hidden, under the low-lying shrubbery by the path up to his front door. A tiny ball of minced meat with a powdery white substance at its core. Donald did not need confirmation that he'd found death on the same path he walked his dogs up and down several times a day, as he took them for a stroll.

On the other side of the village, Ron's son found something similar on Aidan's property. It, too, was partially hidden by low shrubs along the path leading up to the front door.

A further search brought several more poisonous meatballs to light on both sides of the village. But only in the two men's gardens. No one else's. The little balls were all similar. They'd clearly been made by one person. And Donald knew which person, but he did not have any proof.

By late afternoon, with his planned Monday spent painting on a commission totally gone to pot, Donald cleaned his brushes and put away his work for the day. Since the shocking discoveries of Ginger and Wendy, and the poisoned meatballs in his and Aidan's garden, Donald had lost heart and inspiration. Tomorrow had to be a better day!

Cooking always relaxed him, and Donald was in the process of preparing French Onion Soup, when he received another phone call from Arthur Wright. The Turnbulls' cat might just make it. She was a little fighter. But poor, sweet Ginger was too far gone, and had died. The Evanses were with Ginger's distraught owner.

Like an automaton, Donald finished preparing the

soup, and commenced on the, for him, easily prepared main course. Less than an hour later, having functioned on auto-pilot since his sad find this morning, he finally gave vent to his turbulent emotions.

He angrily wiped away the hot tears he could feel trickling down his cheeks. That could have been one of his girls. Or even both!

He just knew that it was that lunatic of a woman. And it had all started with that eventful Saturday morning. Knowing it was her did not constitute proof. Donald felt like howling. Yes, his girls were safe, and happily and blissfully ignorant of the horror that had been meant for them. Instead of him grieving now, one of the sweetest people he knew, and her beloved pet, had fallen victim. Poor Wendy wasn't out of the woods yet, but there was at least a flicker of hope.

This brought his thoughts back to Aidan, who had been targeted, too. Luckily Tom and Tessa had elevated laziness to a fine art, and preferred an indoor life, or Aidan, too, would be grieving now.

"Even if the police would question the woman, Donald," Arthur had said, "she'd, of course, deny it. Despite all the strange happenings, we have no proof."

Unless she got caught in the act, or someone saw something, they had no proof.

Donald poured himself a stiff drink, and resuming auto-pilot, started to set the table.

CHAPTER THIRTY-SIX

That no one had yet discovered her hiding place, delighted and surprised Carole. "So much for a Neighbourhood Watch Area," she mumbled to herself. She lit another fag, and continued to wait. She'd come well prepared, and she had all the time in the world.

In the dark silence of the car, her snigger sounded like a snort. Neighbourhood Watch? Hah! Things were working out quite well so far. Last night's mission had been a success. With some luck, the result of her actions would filter down to her. Or better yet, she'd soon hear the results for herself. It was bound to be the topic of conversation on Trivia's grapevine, too. But then she remembered that she'd not be there to hear any of it anymore. She shrugged to herself. So what!

Aw! *Snigger!* In her mind's eye, she saw Ponytail all

lost and lonely, walking to the pub on his tod, minus those disgusting mutts. Pity she could not be in two places at once. *"I wonder what he did with them. Bury them in the garden? Euw!"* She did not fancy sitting out on a summer's day, with two rotting canine carcases nearby. Once she'd ensconced herself in the house, she'd dig them up and dispose of them at the tip. Yes, that's what she'd do!

Once again, she thought of Ponytail trudging miserably on his own, minus those horrid hairy extensions on a lead, toward the pub. Aw, the poor dear! No better person than her to console the grieving darling. *Snigger!*

As for Hazel Eyes, he too would be grieving now... but not for long anymore. This night he would join those awful cats of his, on Cloud Nine. She had to stuff her fist in her mouth to keep herself from roaring with laughter. Cloud Nine! A very crowded Cloud Nine. Hazel Eyes... those bitches... those cats... those dogs. Talk about an over-populated cloud! She berated herself, as she really had to contain herself. She'd have a good belly laugh later on, when she was finished. For now, she had to keep silent and her location secret.

Aw! With everyone he'd relied on gone from his life, she'd be ready with arms wide open to receive the grieving Ponytail. With all the roadblocks on her path to everlasting happiness annihilated, Ponytail would be hers. All hers! She wouldn't let him out of her sight!

Shopping... ah, yes, they'd need to eat... and drink. Mustn't forget the drink. Carole wouldn't mind a drink right now. A glass...? No, it would have to be a bottle of that red wine those bitches had at their party on Saturday. Bloody good wine, that! She'd make sure they'd have plenty of that wine in stock in the house. As for food, she'd order online. Good idea! It couldn't get much easier.

She'd make herself indispensable. Once it was abundantly clear that he couldn't do without her anymore, she might award him for being a good boy, and give him some freedom. A hint of leeway. But till that time, she'd keep him under lock and key in every which way. He'd need her for everything! He'd be as dependable on her as a baby is on its mother. *Snigger!*

And then there still was Kristie. Hmmm... Well, tonight was the night. *Snigger!* Carole had already reserved a cloud for her... Cloud Thirteen! Uncontrollable laughter bubbled up, which she gave vent to silently, and stifled once again by stuffing her gloved hand in her mouth.

A car drove into Old Orchard Lane. Carole sat up. The laughter was instantaneously swiped away. Things were happening! She picked up the binoculars, and caught sight of Hazel Eyes struggling out of the car on his crutches. He appeared to be talking to the driver for a few minutes, before he went into the house. Then the car drove away.

The Snow Crystals

Mentally, Carole ticked off Number One.

She didn't have to wait long before another car drove into the lane and stopped on the drive of Orchard House, the Moretons' home. The two women she was expecting got out of the car and went indoors.

Numbers Two and Three. Tick. Tick. All three present and accounted for. Carole smirked.

The binoculars' strength enabled Carole to make out that the curtains were closed first in the women's house. Shortly afterwards, also in Hazel Eyes' cottage. All that could be seen now were the brightly lit Christmas trees in their respective windows. Ponytail neither arrived by car nor by foot to visit either cottage. It looked like the inhabitants of both cottages were in for the night. A satisfied grin crossed Carole's face.

She poured herself some hot coffee, and continued to watch. Still nothing. Absolutely nothing happened. No one left or visited either cottage. The only activity was on the main road, with occasional cars driving through the village, and beyond that nothing else.

Old Orchard Lane lay in perfect peace. The brightly-lit trees and their owners tucked up safely in their homes. Carole hugged herself with glee. It was perfect! It was all going according to plan. She couldn't believe her lucky stars.

Around 10, Carole noted someone walking a dog. Half an hour later, another dog walker roamed about. Some more cars had passed by on the main road.

Beyond that, nothing. A bit later she saw a couple passing by, followed shortly after by the solitary figure of a man. She'd seen them earlier on walking in the direction of the pub. It was paired with a short burst of extra traffic. Pub closing time, Carole concluded. Another dog walker. And then peace returned to the village. Save for the occasional car passing through, all remained quiet.

As she poured herself another coffee, Carole saw the lights go off on Hazel Eyes' indoor tree. A moment later the outdoor decorations were extinguished. The lights in the bitches' house stayed on a bit longer. Carole didn't have to wait long, as soon here, too, the lights were dimmed. Except for the streetlight still casting a yellowish gleam over the three houses, the lane and its occupants slept.

Carole decided the time was right. She had prepared everything meticulously that morning, and rechecked it that afternoon. She removed the bag from the car and placed it on the ground. Cautiously, she approached the road and cast a glance at the neighbouring houses. A light was on in the house with the garden wall, on the left hand corner of the lane. As there was in the house on the right hand side, by which light she and Kristie had found their way into Hazel Eyes' garden, just over a week ago.

With growing satisfaction, Carole noted that sleep prevailed in most neighbouring houses, as they lay in

The Snow Crystals

darkness.

She returned to the car, and with the all-important bag out of the car, she pushed the door to... but didn't close it. The key was in the ignition. When she'd arrived in Woodedge Lane, she'd manoeuvred the car backwards into the hiding place, facing out and away from the village. It had been a bit awkward sitting on the back-seat, keeping an eye on the proceedings in Old Orchard Lane. *"All in aid of a good cause!!"* Carole smiled to herself. *"Mine!"* She complimented herself. All was ready for a quick, easy and, above all, fast departure along the narrow lanes. And then back to Combe-Norton. Everything she needed back home was already set up.

Midnight was approaching fast. It was almost tomorrow. And tomorrow, in mere hours, Ponytail would be hers! Hers! And hers alone! It would be a Tuesday she'd remember for the rest of her life. From tomorrow onwards, she would love Tuesdays. A frisson of sheer delight shot through her.

She picked up the bag, and giving the neighbouring houses another glance, noting the lights continued to be on in those two houses, she scurried across the road, staying close to the shrubs and garden wall on the left side of the lane.

The bitches' house and Hazel Eyes' cottage were both so obviously bedded down for the night. *"Like taking sweets off a baby!"* Carole chuckled. The third cottage in Old Orchard Lane was no concern. She knew it was uninhabited. The estate agent's snub still stung, but beyond that it was no longer of any consequence. She no longer wanted, nor needed The Hollyhocks. Her true goal was within her reach.

She hurried up Orchard House's drive, past the car, to the spot she had chosen. Pity that the car was parked just, but only just, on the drive. Pity it wasn't parked right near the house, or even in the garage.

On the other hand, with the wuss on crutches unable to drive, his car was undoubtedly in the garage. *"All the better. Perfect!"*

She was by the Moretons' garage door, and next to the side window of the office. Hidden amongst shrubs, it was the perfect spot to start. She put down the bag. It was all going exactly to plan. It was all so easy. Almost too easy.

For one last time, she ticked off mentally that which she had found on the internet. How useful Google was! Bless Google! Yes, she owed it all to Google. Tick. Tick. Tick. Yes, she had it all. It was perfect, and she set about her business. Between the suction cup and the glass cutter, the ancient glass window came away easily, leaving a small and impeccable round hole. It was all she needed.

With fascination, she watched the flame. Beautiful! *"From a tiny acorn a mighty oak doth grow,"* flashed through Carole's mind, and she smiled to herself as the following thought hit her, *"From a single flame an inferno is created. How thrilling!"*

It worked like a charm. Silence and stealth were, of course, of the essence, but Carole could not repress the teensiest cry of delight, as one flame became a merrily flickering, warming fire. Which lapped and lapped with eager, hungry tongues... and grew second by second into an all-consuming, destroying conflagration.

Mesmerised, Carole watched. It was beautiful. It was perfect, as she had known it would be.

The heat made her step back some, but she continued to be mesmerised by the dancing flames.

Another step back. The fire was growing. Good!

She picked up the bag, and hurried to the other side of the house. The one nearest Hazel Eyes' cottage. It would be easy to just hop over the wall to his house when she was done with Orchard House. She was relishing the inevitable inferno when she became aware of voices. She quickly lit the prepared device, and within seconds the flames started lapping at the shrubs.

Voices! She heard voices in the distance. Worse yet, the voices came nearer. Became louder. A woman's voice. A man's. They came from behind her. From the main road.

"HEY! WHAT THE HELL...!" Footsteps. Running.

She saw a man come running towards her. She saw a woman with a dog on a lead, standing near the top of the lane.

Where to go? Which way to run? For a fraction of a second she was undecided. The man was closer now, and she could make out that he was not young anymore. That could be used to her advantage.

As he charged for her, she managed to escape over the low wall, and ran to the main road.

A flash blinded her for a nanosecond and threw her off guard. It was the woman. She appeared to be an old woman. And - oh God, no! - she had taken a picture of her. On passing the woman, Carole gave her a shove. She heard the cry, but didn't see the woman fall. The car was mere steps away.

More voices. The alarm had been raised. She heard angry cries, and a stampede of feet.

She hastily slipped behind the wheel, and turned the ready and waiting key in the ignition. The motor purred instantly into life. She closed the door as she drove off at breakneck speed along the narrow lane, away from the village.

CHAPTER THIRTY-SEVEN

Carole drove towards farms and farmland. More narrow lanes criss-crossing each other. Past sleeping hamlets. Lanes of single-car width. She kept up the pace. She had no idea where she was going.

She could see a tiny, sharp sliver of a sickle, the last remnant of the waning moon before New Moon. That teensy sickle moon was her "guiding light". If she followed the moon, she would be travelling away from the village.

She passed another hamlet.

The night was alive. It had started snowing.

"Snow? How can it be snowing? A clear frosty night was forecast."

Snowflakes fluttered and danced about. It could be quite a pretty sight, Carole thought, if snow weren't such a damned inconvenience. She could still easily make out the sickle moon, and the road.

The snow flurry was light, dancing about playfully.

"If it stays like this till I get home, then it's no skin off my nose."

Uphill, downhill. She passed another farm, and yet another. The road bent to the left. The sickle moon hung quietly in the clear sky to the right. By the car's headlights, Carole could see a lane or a road leading off to the right. She'd take that one. Then she'd have full sight of the moon again.

As she turned into this lane, she noted that the moon appeared this time more to the left. She'd decided that she'd take the next turn-off to the left. That didn't take long, and once again the moon hung in the inky sky straight ahead of her. *"Gotta keep that moon in sight."* With the tiny sickle moon in her sight, she was heading farther and farther away from South Woodside. She had no clue where she was, but knew that she'd eventually reach a main road, and then turn right and head for Combe-Norton. Then she could finally finish off her work.

And the snow kept fluttering down, in a lazy dance.

Thinking about what lay ahead of her in Combe-Norton, she remembered the forgotten bag back in South Woodside. *"Darn! But not to worry, I don't need anything from that bag as everything's already set up at home."* Home! She sniggered. After tonight, it wouldn't

The Snow Crystals

be her home anymore. After tonight, her home would be the big rambling house which belonged to Ponytail. It would be hers. As would Ponytail be hers. All hers!

As for the forgotten bag, there was nothing about it that could lead back to her. The bag and contents were from several DIY centres around the wider area. They could be anybody's.

Then she remembered the flash in her face. Oh, blast! That old woman had taken a photo of her as she ran towards her car. With her having been on the run, and with some extra luck, with the photo having been taken by an undoubtedly trembling geriatric hand, all the old bag got was a blur. Carole hoped that would be the case.

The playful fluttering flurry was becoming denser. *"Not good! How could they have gotten the forecast so totally wrong? The idiots!"*

She put on the windscreen wipers. *"That's better."*

Amidst the fluttering white frenzy, she could still make out the sickle moon far off, in the pitch black sky.

It dawned on Carole that it didn't make sense. She could see the moon beyond the snows. It was as if she was caught up in a snow-globe, and someone was wielding it at their behest. Beyond its rounded confines lay the real world, where the frosty, clear-skied night stretched peacefully over the undulating Cotswolds.

How was this possible? *"Madness! Sheer madness!"* She'd stopped believing in fairy tales at six.

Santa Claus was fictional, and the Santa at the Leeds department store was "nowt else than a dirty old man", who got his kicks by sitting little kids on his lap. That's what her mother had told her. And her bubble had shattered. She'd soon gotten over it. Reality made much more sense. Then why was she now caught up in an impossible fairy tale?

Maybe she was asleep, and following the planning and preparation of the last days, and last night's mission, her mind had kept on going as she went to sleep. *"That's it. I'm asleep."* She chuckled to herself. That made sense! The dream indicated the possible pitfalls she had to avoid at all costs, to ensure a satisfactory outcome. *"Dream on."*

With Carole assuming herself caught up in a life-like dream, her mood changed. She could do with a bit of excitement in her hitherto boring life, even if it was a dream.

She no longer cared that the playful fluttering snowflakes had grouped, and were falling faster and denser. After all, it was only a dream!

She could barely make out the moon beyond the onslaught of white. The little that she could see of the sickle appeared more and more to the left. She was sure that she'd come upon a lane or road off to the left soon, and she'd take that. This was a dream, wasn't it?

The snowfall thickened, and she put the windscreen wipers on faster. It was becoming quite difficult to see the road before her through the teeming swirling snows. She put the windscreen wipers on even faster. Snow was starting to gather on the windscreen where the wipers could not reach. Carole was beginning to hope that she'd wake up soon, safe and sound in her bed. This was no longer fun. This was turning into a nightmare!

By the second, the snows grew into an ever more massive army and they staged an angry, white assault on the small car, near on obliterating any view through the windscreen. The windscreen wipers couldn't keep up. Too slow. She put them on faster. Still insufficient. To Carole's dismay, the wipers were on the highest setting, and the snow was obscuring her view more and more with each passing second.

Carole unclamped her left cramped hand off the steering wheel and savagely pinched the other arm. Hard! *"Ouch! Damn it, that hurts."* She'd pinched so hard, she was bound to end up with a bruise. But sod the bruise, this meant that she possibly wasn't dreaming at all. Had it been a dream, that God almighty pinch would have woken her up. Everything was unchanged. The snows were still falling fast and furious.

So, if this wasn't a dream, some wild nightmare, then it was reality. Albeit a nightmarish reality.

With this realisation, icy terror coursed through her veins. Snow had been forecast for later in the week. Not tonight! A clear night with light frost had been forecast.

That is why she chose tonight. Where did this snow come from?

The car was starting to slip and slide.

Where was the moon? The sliver of a sickle was no longer visible through the dense white madness assaulting the car. That perfect little sickle moon had guided her away from the village. Where was it now?

She was caught up in an ever-wilder and denser whirlwind of cold white fury.

Carole's eyes widened in horror as she watched the snowflakes grow in size. They were fat, plump blobs that stuck to everything. The kind of snows that brought entire communities to a standstill. The windscreen wipers were struggling to keep up with the attack. Before, with each swipe she'd seen a hint of road, but it was becoming more and more difficult to see where she was or where she was going.

As, once again, the wipers partially emptied the windscreen, Carole saw the snowflakes slowly changing colour. The white darkened first to palest pink, then to gaudy pink. Still, ever darkening. And the snowflakes were growing larger and larger. The snowflakes were growing into large snow crystals, which soon become huge dark pink crystals which attacked the car.

The noise was deafening. She heard the metal tear and the first crystal got lodged in the roof, right near her head.

Carole screamed.

The Snow Crystals

The crystals darkened even more in colour, still growing in size.

The deafening volume of the crystals' assault overrode Carole's screams.

The crystals were now blood red. A dripping blood red. The crystals shattered the windscreen and the windows. The crystals sliced through the car roof like a knife through butter.

Carole was drowning in a sea of dripping blood-red crystals.

As suddenly as the snow storm had hit, so did it suddenly stop.

A myriad of twinkling stars surrounded the sickle moon, in the peaceful winter night sky.

A barn owl curiously eyed the car as it swooped low past the windscreen. It was the last image Carole saw.

CHAPTER THIRTY-EIGHT

Fourteen Days to Christmas

Aidan dreamt of flashing lights illuminating the night sky, coming nearer and nearer at break-neck speed. And the breathtaking horror of watching the wave of lights atop blood-red fire engines, the white police cars, and the ambulance, all stopping by or turning into Old Orchard Lane. The rumbling noise of the fire engines reverberated rhythmically and madly throughout his dream.

Despite the professional efficiency of the firefighters and police, noise and mayhem prevailed. Holly and Ivy, screaming in desperation the names of their beloved cats, joined the pandemonium. Donald, abandoning his car, the motor running, which merely added to the persistent thumping racket, as he rushed after the two women. Aidan tried to get out of the car...

he couldn't find his crutches... falling...

A sharp pain shocked him awake. And with it, the pain became real. The nightmarish dream had been all too real. As had the thumping cacophony, the resonance of which existed now nowhere but in his memory. For his bedroom was silent. The only sounds came from downstairs. The sound of voices.

He ached. In his panic to follow Donald and the girls, he had been unable to find his crutches. Unaided and unsteady on his feet, and driven by fear for his own home and loved ones, he'd fallen heavily. *"Bruises and a crocky ankle, the way to go, mate... not!"*

He reached for the crutches, thankfully once again within reach, and made his way to his ensuite bathroom.

A bit later, feeling sore, but somewhat more human, he gingerly made his way downstairs. The tantalising smell of coffee drifted welcomingly towards him.

"We're in the kitchen," Holly called out, having heard Aidan coming down the stairs.

"Good morning on this morning after the night before," Aidan intoned heavily, as he made his way into the kitchen. He looked around at the three people sitting at the kitchen table, mugs with coffee at hand. A mug of steaming coffee was awaiting him. Tom and Tessa had put the upheaval of the past night behind them, and lay curled up in their bed by the AGA. It could be such a normal everyday scene. But there was nothing normal about this morning. For one, all looked the worse for wear; Aidan knew he did, too.

"Any news from the vets?" Aidan asked.

"I called as soon as I woke up," Ivy said. "We know that the poor darlings had inhaled smoke. All being well, they can come home this afternoon."

"Home? They have no home to come home to," Holly snapped at her sister, and immediately felt guilty for her reaction. "Sorry. I didn't..."

"I understand, honey!"

"They're welcome to stay in the double guest bedroom. Their litter tray and food can go in the ensuite bathroom," Aidan offered.

"Thank you," both women expressed their gratitude with relieved smiles.

"Did you manage to sleep some?" Donald asked Aidan.

"Eventually. All of an hour or two." Aidan glanced around at his three motley looking friends. "How about you?"

"Not much better," Holly said softly. Ivy confirmed likewise with a shake of her head.

"Same here." Donald yawned. "Sorry."

"Anyone for more coffee? If only to wake up some." With everyone silently nodding, Holly got up and filled up their mugs.

Donald's phone rang. The conversation was short. "That was Arthur. Mrs. Manning will be back home this afternoon. Besides some bruises, she sprained her wrist when she fell. She'll need all the help she can get."

"Thankfully, this is South Woodside, where we can count on our neighbours." Apprehensively, Aidan gave the twins a pleading glance. "Please don't be put off or judge this village by what happened last night."

"Darling..." As Holly said that word, and especially the way she said it, Aidan's heart leapt for joy. "What happened last night has nothing to do with this village. What could have been a disaster for both our houses was averted by quick thinking, and the wonderful community spirit that thrives here."

Ivy nodded in agreement. "It could have been so much worse. I wouldn't know where to start thanking all who rallied around to help us. In the midst of something horrible, there was such bravery, such kindness, such care."

"I just had a horrible thought," Aidan gasped. "Talk about a disaster having been averted! My garage is close to your house. Sparks could have set the thatch alight. The car in the garage has a full tank. My bedroom is on that side of the house... Bloody hell!"

All were silent for a moment as the implications of this sank in.

"Bloody hell, indeed," Donald agreed. "I'd rather not dwell on this."

"I wonder what it's like inside the house. How much damage there is. Besides, everything's bound to stink of smoke..." Holly tried to put on a brave face without much success. "It looked so pretty... The Christmas decorations..." But then her face crumpled, as once again tears came.

Aidan sorely wanted to take her in his arms, but Ivy beat him to it.

Both Aidan's and Donald's, as well as the girls' phones rang several times.

The pub's owner said he'd send over four luncheon meals; anything they wanted. Dinner too, if they wanted it. Or perhaps they wanted to come to the pub? And he was not taking no for an answer; it was on the house. It was the least he could do for his neighbours.

Having rushed Pyewacket and Crystal to the vets in the early hours of the morning, following their rescue by the firefighters, Mr. Turnbull offered to also collect the girls' cats from the vets. It would give him a chance to look in on Wendy, who was not out of the woods yet, but was improving slowly.

Arthur Wright called once again. Mrs. Manning's photo had proved quite useful in identifying the arsonist. The police needed them to see it, to check and perhaps confirm that it was the woman who had been stalking them. They'd be in contact later that morning.

As expected, the police phoned and said that they'd be at The Cottage shortly.

Aidan's secretary called. If he needed any help, everyone was at his disposal.

Bridget phoned for the umpteenth time that morning... she, too, offered help, and informed the twins that there still was no word from Carole.

Holly, desperate to keep busy, took on the role of hostess, and made yet another pot of coffee for the four of them and the two policemen who had just arrived. They were all grouped around the kitchen table.

"Both Ian and Joe were school buddies of ours, and while Aidan continues to regularly consort with the fuzz over a weekly game of squash, I do so over a pint." Far more light-hearted than he could possibly feel, Donald introduced the two policemen to the women.

Without a word, Joe laid a photo in front of Aidan and Donald.

"That's her," Aidan whispered. Donald nodded in agreement.

They handed the photo to Holly and Ivy, who confirmed that they also knew her. "Carole Leach. She works in our gift shop. She didn't show up for work yesterday or today. No reason. No phone call. Yesterday morning, her housemate said that she claimed to be ill."

"Have you found her?" Donald asked.

"Not yet," Ian said. "The same woman who has been stalking you?" With Aidan and Donald nodding simultaneously, Ian carried on talking. "Arthur Wright informed us about everything. We just didn't have any proof. We do now."

"Now we've got to find her," Joe said.

With the mad woman still on the loose, they didn't feel safe. What had started out as a silly game had turned into a fanatical obsession. Carole Leach had proven that she'd not hesitate to stoop to vile murder, be it the murder of a pet or a human. She was a dangerous woman.

"More than likely, she's also behind the hit and run on you, Aidan," Joe said.

"What hit and run?" In shock, Holly looked sharply from Joe to Aidan.

"I was knocked down by someone as Donald and I walked home from the pub last week. The car was long gone by the time we looked up."

"Why didn't you tell me?"

"I wasn't hurt. Just a few scrapes on my hand. Nothing more." Aidan looked into Holly's worried, angry eyes. "I didn't want to worry you."

"I appreciate the sentiment, Aidan, but don't ever do that to me again! If it was her… good God, she could have killed you!"

"But she didn't. I'm still all here."

"Aidan, that's not the point…"

"Excuse me," Joe interrupted. "Can we get back to business? You two can continue your lovers' tiff when we're gone."

Aidan and Holly turned to Joe, their mouths sagging open. Despite the gravity of the situation, Donald, Ivy and Ian did their best to hide their smiles.

"Thank you."

"Joe's got his official cap on. We've gotta shush it!" Aidan quipped, trying to make light of it all, if only for his own sanity.

"Aidan!" Joe glared at his friend. "Going by what we found in the abandoned bag outside Holly and Ivy's house, you should know there's a possibility that both houses were targeted by the arsonist. It was lucky you weren't in."

"All thanks to Donald's culinary exuberance," Aidan said.

"I like to cook. It helps me de-stress. After yesterday's happenings, I desperately needed to relax, and I got rather carried away. I ended up with enough for a battalion, so I invited my cousin and the girls over to help me eat it all."

"For multiple reasons, I was grateful for that invitation. Trust me!" He shot his best friend an apologetic glance. "Between yesterday's miserable happenings and my blasted ankle, I was not particularly looking forward to yet another microwave dinner or eating on my own."

"With Aidan on crutches, Ivy and I wanted to drive, but he stubbornly insisted on us walking over, claiming he needed the exercise, and that the fresh air would do us good." Holly put her arm over Aidan's shoulder, then ruffled his already unruly hair further. "Stubborn and cocky."

"And don't forget lovable!" Aidan grinned at Holly. "We took the garden exit. It's the quickest route to Donald's house, along the back lane. We ran into Arthur

314

talking to some neighbours. In view of what happened, Arthur said everyone was on alert, and keeping an eye out for anything out of the norm."

"Hmmm... wise that. It appears that the arsonist must have thought you were all at home last night, and gone to bed," Ian said.

"I don't know about the girls, but I've got my Christmas tree and outside lights on a timer," Aidan said. "They will have gone off before we left Donald's."

"Ours are on a timer, too," Ivy said.

"So, to all intents and purposes you appeared to be at home." Ian would have said more, but at that moment he received a call, and gave them a sign to be quiet. A moment later he announced gravely, "Well, she's been found." He didn't elaborate. It was enough for his two friends and the women to heave a sigh of relief.

They talked for a few minutes more, then Joe and Ian got up to leave. Donald and Aidan walked them to the door.

"At least you can all sleep easy tonight." Joe smiled at his friends. "As soon as we know more, we'll let you know." He bid them goodbye and followed Ian to the car. He changed his mind about getting in, walked back up the path, and asked Aidan, "Has the date been set?"

"Huh? What date?" Aidan reacted genuinely confused. "What are you on about?"

Donald laughed and placed his arm around Aidan's shoulders. "Aw, bless, let's blame it on his lack of sleep. Yes, Joe, it has. And besides it being as clear as daylight, it's in the stars. But at the rate he's going, he'll be the last to know."

"Like that, eh?" Chuckling, Joe waved at the men, and returned to the car.

"What was all that about?" Aidan asked.

Donald just shook his head, and steered Aidan back into the house, before closing the door.

CHAPTER THIRTY-NINE

Finding neither Carole in her room or in the house, nor the car back in its usual place, or anywhere in the surrounding area, Kristie had gone to work. It appeared that Carole had not been at home that night. Kristie had once again left the light on in the hallway, and it was still on it the morning. Not a sign that Carole had returned home.

The uneasy feeling that had been growing for days worsened when she arrived, just before 9, at work. Bridget greeted her grimly.

"Is Carole still sick?"

"When I got home last night, she and the car were gone. She didn't come home. I don't know what's going on, Bridget. Should I contact the police?"

"Perhaps. If you've not heard or seen anything by lunchtime..." She frowned. "Someone tried to torch Holly and Ivy's house last night."

As Bridget uttered these words, Kristie felt her

knees grow weak. "How awful! They caught the... the..."

"Arsonist? No, not yet. But they apparently have a picture."

"Oh, good!" A growing fear bubbled up. Carole couldn't have been that stupid, that obsessed, that mad, could she now? This was unreal. A little voice at the back of Kristie's mind said *"Yes!"*

Despite the continued worry and unrest nagging her about Carole, Kristie had an enjoyable morning. Lunch at home, or a sandwich from the bakers? Kristie was weighing the options when she was called to Bridget's office. Two police women greeted her sombrely. She was asked to sit down.

"You are Carole Leach's housemate?"

Kristie blinked. She was glad she was sitting, as she felt suddenly weak. "Yes, since we were divorced in our twenties. Carole insisted. She said that we would be able to save money by sharing a house. Cheaper."

"Do you know where she was yesterday?"

"She claimed she was sick and stayed at home. I found her scoffing a huge meal when I went home for lunch. She was in a foul mood." Kristie swallowed, and reminded herself that a lifetime of protecting Carole had come to an abrupt end a week ago. Certainly after all the abuse she had been subjected to. "She's been in a foul mood for the past week, and I've been at the receiving end of it." Kristie tried to steady her hands, which she could feel trembling. She knew more was coming, and feared the worst.

"It's alright, Kristie. We have to ask." The policewoman lay a comforting hand on Kristie's. "I am sorry to tell you that we found Carole dead in her crashed car. She was caught in the act of starting a fire last night, at the house of her employers in South

The Snow Crystals

Woodside. As she fled from the scene, one of the neighbours managed to take a photo of her. The Misses Moreton have already confirmed that it's her in the photo." The woman continued to hold Kristie's trembling hand. "I am sorry, Kristie. A farmer found the car this morning, lodged in a ditch on his land, well away from the nearest road."

That's when the tears started, and they thought she was weeping for the loss of her friend. But she started talking, and it all spilled out. As Kristie came to a semblance of an end, she looked around the room, at the two policewomen, and at Bridget. "I'll give you the key to the house. I don't know what you'll find in Carole's room."

"It's alright. We have the keys she had on her. Officers are at the house now. Her room was the locked one?"

Kristie nodded.

Knowing that the arsonist had been found brought the much-needed peace of mind to the foursome. With her ever-increasing obsessive stalking, Carole had put especially the men through eleven ever-worsening days. Miss Frobisher's Ginger remained the sole fatality, but it still was one too many, and all four were angry on the poor woman's behalf. Donald, who knew Miss Frobisher best, was heartbroken for her. Worse yet, no matter what his friends said, he couldn't dismiss the feeling of guilt to a degree.

Ivy took matters into her hands, and ordered Donald to put on his coat. They took the dogs for a walk. When they returned, Donald was in a much better place.

"We're having dinner at the pub tonight," Aidan announced when Donald and Ivy got back. "I don't know about you, but knowing that mad woman is in police custody, I feel we owe it to ourselves to enjoy a relaxing dinner tonight. Oh, and lunch will be delivered shortly. They're stars, at the pub!"

"Sounds good to me." Donald managed a smile.

During lunch they discussed Orchard House.

"We really need to have a look and see it for ourselves," Ivy said. "The loss adjustor is coming after lunch. Let's have a look then."

"We'll go with you." Donald looked for confirmation to Aidan, who, with his mouth full, grunted assent and nodded emphatically.

"That poor, dear house. It is such a treasure." Tears pooled in Holly's eyes. "Why?"

She'd followed the loss adjuster, her sister and Donald into their home, made it into the hallway, then had barged past Donald and dragged Aidan back out with her. Trembling, she leaned into Aidan, who pulled her close. Together, they stood looking at the chocolate-box facade of Orchard House, with its left and right corners maimed by fire, the shrubs destroyed.

"It will be beautiful again. You'll see. It doesn't even look that bad from the outside." Like he would stroke one of his cats, hoping to console and calm when and if necessary, Aidan stroked Holly's hair.

"No, it doesn't. But still... In the spring I want to plant new shrubs and rampant climbers on both sides. Take away the memory."

Aidan held her closer. "I'll help you."

The Snow Crystals

Together with the adjuster and Donald, Ivy, somewhat braver and more intrepid than her sister, had ventured further into the house. Within minutes she had re-emerged, gagging for much-needed fresh air.

"The house is un-liveable." Ivy's voice quavered.

Donald joined them a bit later. "The stench of the acrid smoke is unbearable, and has seeped into everything." Donald sighed heavily. "As if that horrid burned stench isn't enough, a greasy black film covers the walls, ceilings, floors, and every item in the house. The office took the brunt of the fiery fury, but the smoke has crept everywhere."

They waited for the adjuster to join them, who confirmed what they already knew, that the house would be un-liveable for weeks, if not months.

"Tea or a stiff drink?" Donald asked as soon as they piled back into Aidan's sitting room.

"A stiff drink!" Aidan answered. He gratefully sank into a wingback chair. His ankle ached. His bruises smarted. After dinner at the pub tonight, nothing appealed more than a long soak in a hot tub, and an even longer restful, and above all, safe night.

"For us, too, please." Holly sat down next to Ivy. "I am glad that Bridget sent over some clothes for us."

"Yes, I'll be glad to put on some clean clothes. Anyway, what are we going to do? House-wise, that is."

"I'm sure that we can stay with Bridget, while we look for a temporary place," Holly suggested.

"Sis, her place is a postage stamp. And it is for sale. We'd wreck her chances of selling the place if we clutter it up." Ivy smiled at Aidan. "We're so grateful that our cats can stay with you for the time being. That's a weight off our minds. Anyway, I propose we get ourselves a twin-bedded room at one of the hotels in town, till we find a temporary residence."

"I think I might have a solution." Donald could feel his colour rising. He knew he was blushing, and felt foolish. "Smack me around the head if I am offering this out of turn, but if you want, if you don't find this presumptuous, and I hope I don't offend you, because honestly I never would do that, but if you want..."

"Jesus! Spit it out man!" Aidan exclaimed, laughing.

"Yeah. OK. Deep breath, Donald. I, eh... well, Ivy..."

"Yes?"

"If you want, you can stay with me. That is, if you want. And Holly, you, too, can stay, but I'm guessing you may want to stay with Aidan. We both have room enough, so that should be no problem. I am sorry, mate... Aidan, I shouldn't be organising your life for you. If I spoke out of turn, deck me. I... I just thought that this might be a solution. And..."

"Yes, thank you. I'd love to," Ivy said simply.

"You will?"

"Yes!"

"And that is yes from me, too." Holly looked at an equally red-faced Aidan.

Late afternoon, while they were getting ready to go for dinner at the pub, Aidan's phone rang. It was Joe. Dumbstruck, he listened to Joe's short message, and needed several minutes to let it sink in, before he hollered for his friends.

Donald appeared. "The girls are finishing off settling in their cats. They'll join us in a moment. What's the matter?"

"That was Joe. He couldn't say anything earlier, as they had to find and inform her nearest and dearest first - although for the life of me I cannot imagine her ever having had any nearest and dearest... Anyway, she'd been found dead. She'd crashed the car."

"It's truly over, then!" Donald sighed in relief. "That stupid, silly woman! What was she thinking? You know, in a way I feel sorry for her. What did she think to gain from all this?"

Aidan shrugged. "Who knows? Anyway, Joe said he'd have more news tomorrow. So, all being well, it's over now." He smiled. "I'm hungry. Hope the girls will be done soon."

CHAPTER FORTY

Thirteen Days to Christmas

The police had found all the evidence they needed, as the true obsession and madness of Carole became apparent. If she had not crashed the car, and made it back home, Kristie would now be the one awaiting burial. Carole had planned it all meticulously. Without concern or thought for the neighbours on either side of their Victorian terrace, the police found that Carole had everything ready to start a devastating inferno that would have killed Kristie.

Carole's scathing and premeditated cruelty leapt off the pages of the diaries and notebooks she kept. Kristie might have chosen the numbers, and paid for the winning ticket, but Carole had managed to cajole Kristie into handing over half the winnings. Yet Carole was not satisfied with half. She wanted it all.

The Snow Crystals

That was when the inkling of an idea had been born. She wrote about it in her diary... How was she going to get that other half? That was when she talked Kristie into making a will, naming Carole as her sole heir.

For a few quid extra, in order not to arouse any suspicions, Carole had gone through the same motions. Kristie would inherit everything on Carole's death.

With no plans formulated yet, on how to claim this eventual inheritance, Carole still felt great satisfaction in having initiated this sham. And stupid, ignorant Kristie had fallen hook, line and sinker for it.

Carole had already been counting how much she'd end up with. It was all there, black on white. She knew the amount that had gone into Kristie's bank following the lottery win, but she never knew how much Kristie had managed to squirrel away across the years. When she'd found her bank statements a week earlier, and seen, including the lottery win, how much she was worth, she decided that Kristie had to go. What a wonderful nest egg, and Carole would ensure she'd get it. The how, when and where had been as yet outstanding.

That was until two men chanced into her life... Hazel Eyes and Ponytail. With Carole's sights solely set on Ponytail, she found pairing off Kristie with Hazel Eyes a useful move. That was until Kristie copped out. Furious and annoyed at first, she soon discovered the benefit of Kristie's refusal to participate anymore. It had not merely fast forwarded her, up to that point, as yet unformulated plans for the acquiescence of her eventual inheritance, it had given birth to the how, when and where. The why had been born the day Kristie won the lottery.

If it had not been for that win, Carole would simply

have continued using Kristie under the guise of friendship. Taking, always taking. She was the ultimate manipulator, brainwasher and blackmailer.

Joe closed the notebook and looked at Ian, his friend and partner. "Bloody hell! Phew! That makes for sick reading." He and his partner had been reading the diaries and notebooks, dating back to Carole's teens, which had been found in the dead woman's room.

Ian nodded. "Doesn't it ever? Have a look at this." He handed Joe the last notebook which he'd just finished reading. "It gets worse. Want some coffee?"

"Please."

Joe turned to the first page and entered the account of carefully orchestrated madness. Had he not known Aidan and Donald personally, he would have been horrified. But the mad woman was talking about good friends! Two men whom he had known since they were all young boys together. This made Carole's meticulously extensive and especially horrifically detailed plans for Aidan and Donald all the more sickening.

When he had finished reading, Joe looked at Ian and whispered, "Between you and me, I am glad that she died in that crash." In a normal voice he added, "Was she totally mad, or totally evil? Or both?"

"I think both. Should she have, God forbid, succeeded in killing Aidan, and Holly and Ivy Moreton, and their and Donald's pets, as well as her housemate - mind you, she came close! - in her madness, she totally omitted from the equation that Donald has family and a wide circle of friends. How the hell did she think she'd be able to get away with it?"

"Evil madness, driven by an out-of-control obsession sums Carole Leach up in one, don't you think?" Joe picked up his mug. He'd forgotten to drink his coffee. "Gonna get me some fresh, hot coffee. You?" When he got to the door of their shared office, he turned around and looked at his friend. "Her love slave! Donald would have been her prisoner and love slave. Jesus!"

Joe and Ian decided that, in view of what they'd have to tell Aidan, Donald and the twins, a personal visit would be in order, and made an appointment for late afternoon.

An even greater peace of mind had settled over the men and the twins since they'd heard last night that Carole had not merely been found, but found dead in her crashed car.

Joe and Ian did not reveal the details of Carole's journals to their friends. They revealed just enough for the last pieces of the puzzle to fall into place.

Confirmation that, save for Donald, Aidan, Holly and Ivy, as well as their dogs and cats were meant to die, left the four in a state of shock.

"But not me?" Donald gasped.

"Carole was totally obsessed with you, Donald. She had other, long-term, plans for you."

"What kind of plans?" Donald asked cautiously.

"The long, short and tall of it is that she envisioned that she would spent the rest of her life with you." How could he tell Donald what the mad woman's plans were? Instead, Joe said, "Let's just say that the most frightening thing is that you were the target of meticulously premeditated madness. She was dangerous!"

Nine Days to Christmas

Aidan returned to work on Thursday, while Donald made a renewed attempt at painting.

They spent every evening together, needing each other's company. They dined either at Donald's, at Aidan's or at the pub.

Since that Saturday morning which had started so pleasantly at the garden centre, looking back over the last few weeks, Aidan, as well as Donald, felt like they'd been characters in a terrifying Hitchcock film.

Aidan was grateful for Holly moving in with him, and being the perfect gentleman, he decided not to rush her. His love and adoration of her was like an ache, and as desperately as he wanted her in his life, as well as his bed - which he hoped and dreamed would be of the forever more, for richer and poorer, and till death do us part variety - he all too clearly saw the pain, sadness and the shock she was working through. He recognised her need to cuddle and share her space with her cats. Nights running, she'd fallen asleep in the guest room, cradling in her arms the beloved cats who had come too close to death.

He never pushed or rushed her. She was the woman of his dreams, and he treated her like a princess. Like he swore he'd treat her for the rest of her life... their lives. Their future.

Donald had told him that Ivy was going through something similar. This was their much-loved family home which their grandmother had entrusted to them. And within just over a week of moving in, destruction and death had come knocking at their door in the form of a deluded, deranged woman. A woman who had also been an employee. A woman who had targeted them all. A woman who had murder on her mind.

By Sunday they felt a semblance of normalcy had returned to their lives and, for the first time since the fire, they were able to enjoy themselves. More so, they were able to laugh again.

Six Days to Christmas

It was the week before Christmas, and Aidan felt a wave of loneliness as he waved goodbye to Holly on Monday morning; she and Ivy were leaving for shopping and an auction in London. They'd only be gone for several days - back on Friday - but to Aidan it would feel like forever. Although he knew it was only temporary, the house suddenly felt empty without her. He found solace in her personal possessions, which lay dotted about, and the presence of the twins' elegant feline duo, who had accepted his laidback Brits.

Every evening, during the women's absence, Aidan and Donald had sought out each other's company.

That Wednesday evening Donald was more gregarious and cheerful than usual, and Aidan wished some of that would rub off on him, too. For Donald and Ivy were a definite item now. So definite, in fact, that Donald had been around some jewellers in town, looking at rings.

"And I've found the perfect ring! It's upstairs, ready and waiting."

Donald couldn't look more pleased. They were in Donald's cosy kitchen. With dinner over, they were waiting for the coffee to brew.

"Already?" had been Aidan's surprised reaction.

"I know a good thing when I see it. And Ivy is... well, she is it! And Ivy feels the same about me. How about you?"

"Holly's been quite traumatised by what happened."

"So was Ivy. It hasn't exactly passed us by, either. But, it's over now." Donald got up and poured them each a cup of coffee. "It was obvious how we felt about each other before mayhem exploded in our lives. And the same goes for you and Holly, mate. I know you too well. You desperately want her, but apprehension takes over as you remember your previous faux pas. Well, stop it! You and Holly are made for each other. What's more, Holly knows it, too. So for God's sake, stop prevaricating, and do something about it, man. No time like the present!"

"She's in London," Aidan mumbled.

"No shit, Sherlock! So is Ivy. They're back Friday. You still have tomorrow and most of Friday to get your act together. And don't forget it's the girls' birthday, too, on Friday. So get on with it. Listen to your uncle Donald. You know he's right."

"Quack, quack!" Aidan had laughingly reacted, mimicking Donald Duck.

Five Days to Christmas

With Donald's words ringing in his ears, Aidan went to the jewellers and looked at what they had on offer. He'd come prepared, having taken one of Holly's rings

The Snow Crystals

from her jewellery case. Despite the choice, nothing stood out for him. He wanted something special. Something unique. Something totally different from the standard engagement rings on offer. That was when the jeweller drew his attention to a beautiful Art Deco diamond ring which he had only just acquired.

"That's it!" Aidan whispered. Size-wise he was lucky, too, as the ring was only a fraction bigger than Holly's ring. He left the shop a happy man, and couldn't wait for Holly's return.

CHAPTER FORTY-ONE

Four Days to Christmas

Kristie had adamantly refused to set foot in the house again. She didn't care about anything in the house. All of it was contaminated. All dirty. All vile and evil. Even her clothes. The thought of ever wearing anything that hung in her wardrobe repulsed her. Numbly, she'd scoured several shops, as well as the charity shops, and had found a number of items to tide her over. With the help of a police counsellor, she found temporary accommodation in town, and was given all the support she needed.

It was the week before Christmas, on a suitably miserable grey and bitterly cold early Monday morning, that Carole's body was interred. No one attended. Not even Doris. Least of all Kristie.

She had not merely lost a home. She had lost some

thirty years of her life to a person who had used, abused and manipulated her every breathing moment under the guise of friendship. She was traumatised, but she was free.

On the Friday before Christmas, returning to the small hotel that was her temporary home, she was handed a letter addressed to Ms. Marianne Christina Etherton. It was from the solicitors. Trembling, Kristie read it.

Karma? Justice?

The other half of the lottery win and the contents of Carole's savings and bank account, as well as her meagre possessions, were now Kristie's, as per the will Carole had set up only weeks earlier.

Once again, Kristie burst into tears. But this time, behind the trauma that still had her in its grip, there lay a hint of happiness on her horizon. She was now truly free.

Drying her tears, she touched up her makeup and brushed her hair. Pushing aside the curtain, she noticed that it was snowing. A white fairytale land in the making.

Before she went to the dining room, she lightly touched the solicitor's letter... Carole and Kristie were no more. The Christmas Carolers, as they'd been dubbed many years ago, at the pub Carole favoured, were no more! The pub... another place she would never set foot in again.

Kristie did not exist anymore, either. From this day forward, as per the solicitor's letter, she was reclaiming her own names... Marianne Christina Etherton.

"I am Marianne!" she said out loud, and went down to dinner.

Friday came, and Aidan's excitement grew. Holly would be back later that afternoon. He'd been out the whole morning with Donald on a very successful and satisfying Christmas gift buying spree, followed by an early lunch in a pub.

They'd hurried back to South Woodside afterwards, as Donald had a date with the kitchen. He had a dinner to prepare for four. In between the cooking, he'd be wrapping the last of his gifts, too. Donald had dropped off Aidan and his many shopping bags at The Cottage and rushed home.

Although most of the gifts had already been beautifully wrapped at the shops, Aidan looked with pleasure at his own achievements in gift wrapping, as he placed his latest purchases around the tree. Nothing would delight him more than an ever-growing pile of presents around the tree as the years passed. A daydream of future Christmas mornings floated into his mind. There would be squeals of joy as little hands tore and plucked away the festive paper to reveal Santa's treasures. They'd all be sitting on the floor, he and Holly, and their children... eager, laughing... excited, happy...

The image was so vivid that, when he tore himself away and back to reality, he was rather saddened. If only Holly had shown up sooner in his life... if only. Then he would have been a proud husband with the most beautiful, wonderful wife imaginable, and he could have been a father by now of one, two or even three children.

"Don't get carried away, mate," he muttered to

The Snow Crystals

himself. "You've not even asked her yet. God forbid, she might say no." This thought deflated him totally. His dark musings were interrupted by his phone. A text from Holly, which immediately lifted him up out of the doldrums. She and Ivy would be home soon.

Following their nightmare over the last weeks, Aidan felt he deserved a prolonged seasonal holiday. His employees would be off Christmas Eve until January 2nd. He'd given himself an extended holiday. He couldn't be more looking forward to this Christmas and New Year.

He was sure that Pye and Crystal knew that Holly was on her way back, as the cats were charging about. With their mad-half-hour of the day due, Tom and Tessa had joined in the fun.

Leaving them to their shenanigans, he had gone to his office. The overcast day was already drawing in, and he had to switch on the desk lamp. He looked out the window at the familiar quiet of Old Orchard Lane. To the right, he could see the twins' rambling cottage. The necessary work and repairs would start in the new year. To the left, he could see the usual traffic along the main road.

He had some emails which needed answering and he attended to them quickly. Suddenly, he was overwhelmed by the need to have another look at the crystals which had mystified him for weeks. With all that had happened of late, he had forgotten them.

With the emails done, he retrieved the box from its safe hiding place.

As before, he opened the lid reverently and pushed aside the tissue paper, expecting to see the most beautiful and perfect crystals.

They were gone!

He took out the paper, checked the box. Nothing.

Had he been dreaming all these weeks? Had the gorgeous crystals been a figment of his imagination?

The desk lamp shone down onto the paper where the crystals had lain. That is when he saw it. A faint dust-like residue sparkled clearly as the light caught it.

Was he seeing things? But he had seen the proof that the crystals had been real. They'd disappeared, but he could see the residual glittering dust.

Then, to his dismay, the glittering dust, too, disappeared before his eyes. The box and the tissue paper were empty. It was as if the snow crystals had never been. Gone. All he had left was the memory.

Feeling a great loss, he shut the box with trembling fingers. With the treasure gone, it was no longer necessary to hide the box.

Confused and saddened, he went to the kitchen. Tea. The typical soothing English solution to everything. He'd make himself some tea and wait for Holly. She'd be back soon.

He took his mug with him to the sitting room and languidly started sipping.

Why had the snow crystals disappeared? He looked at the lit tree full of sparkling snow crystals and other baubles. As beautiful as it was, nothing compared to the snow crystals that had floated down before him several weeks ago.

The four cats came bounding into the room. The Brits, unused to so much activity, jumped up on a chair, and curled up to rest and sleep. The white and the black fur balls positioned themselves on the windowsill on either side of a Christmas decoration. They sniffed at it briefly, before aiming their full attention on more interesting matters outside. Tense and still, like statues, neither moved, save for the gentle rise and fall that accompanied their breathing. Like Aidan, they were waiting.

With darkness falling fast now, Aidan was counting the minutes... the seconds.

Tonight was the Carol Service at the church. Neither Aidan nor Donald were religious, but they always enjoyed the traditional seasonal music, and they'd be going tonight with Holly and Ivy, following dinner at Donald's.

This brought Aidan's thoughts to the immense pleasure Donald always got from cooking and entertaining. With his ankle nearly healed, together with Holly, what better time than now to start improving his own meagre cooking skills? *"That is assuming and hoping Holly will be by my side..."* Aidan wished.

With the tea drunk, and restless as he was, he figured that now was as good a time as any for the necessary feline duty.

Before he left for the utility room, he switched on the radio. Christmas music drifted about the house.

He did not hear the cats meowing excitedly. He did not hear the front door opening.

What he did hear was Ding Dong Merrily on High floating into the utility room. It was overridden by a voice calling him. "Aidan? Aidan, darling? I am home. The Christmas season can start."

He hurriedly stumbled into the kitchen, where Holly stood smiling at him. She was still wearing her coat and hat. Snowflakes were scattered over her like a powdery sugar dusting.

Needlessly, she added, "It has started to snow."

Without a word, he took her in his arms and held

her tight for a moment, savouring her nearness.

She'd said that she was back home. She'd called him darling.

"I'm so glad that you are home." Their kiss was like no previous kiss Aidan had ever experienced. Once again, he felt the charge between them. This had never happened to him with any other woman. Donald was right. Holly was it!

As he surfaced for air, he saw it. Why hadn't he seen it before? Or perhaps she'd not worn it before.

"Where did you get that?" He pointed at a pendant hanging around her neck. "It's beautiful."

Holly touched it lightly with her fingers. "Oh, this? Both Ivy and I have one. It was a gift from a great aunt at our birth. It's been in the family since time immemorial. We always wear it."

"What is it made of? It looks like delicate lace, or even carved diamond, because of how it sparkles."

"We tried to find out, but our great aunt never told us. The secret died with her. Jewellers are left baffled. We've given up trying to find out. People who see us wearing it in the summer have jokingly said that it will melt in the sun." Holly laughed. "Hardly. It is truly as hard as diamonds."

Aidan took the snow crystal lying just below Holly's throat in his fingers. It felt so familiar. "And lighter than a feather. It is magical."

"Yes, it is magical."

"Holly, I have something to tell you."

"Can I take my coat and hat off first?"

"How thoughtless of me. Yes. I'll make us some tea in the meantime."

Except for the flickering fire in the wood burner, and the Christmas tree lights, the sitting room lay in

The Snow Crystals

darkness. To Aidan, the room had never looked more magical and romantic.

"Holly, I tried to tell my mother, who accused me of being drunk, but I was stone cold sober. I was leaving work - already dark, and a moonlit, starry, clear evening - when suddenly these snow crystals came drifting down before me. They fluttered down onto the spot where my father died. They were of different sizes. Some small, some quite large. While most lay before me on the ground, a few had fallen onto me, and when I took them in my hands, they stayed intact. The warmth of my hands did not melt them. They enchanted me, so I gathered them all together, and when I got home, I put them safely in a box. The craziest thing of all was that they didn't melt. Ever. They were like the snow crystal you are wearing."

"Icy cold, yet not cold. Soft, feather light, yet unbreakable."

"Yes! Since they didn't melt, I put them in a box in a safe spot in my office..." Aidan looked into Holly's gentle eyes. "An hour or so ago, I discovered that they had disappeared. The powdery, glittery residue they'd left behind disappeared before my eyes." With a trembling voice, he whispered. "You're going to declare me crazy, aren't you?"

"No. Did you tell Donald?"

"Yes, but never had time to show him, with all that's been going on. Call me mad. It is just that the crystal you are wearing reminded me of..."

"Oh, darling, you are not mad. The snow crystals were there for a reason."

"Things did start changing in my life since I found them."

Holly smiled sweetly. "And they guided you to me.

Darling, they disappeared because you don't need them anymore. Their job is done."

Aidan nodded. "Yes, I suppose it is." Holly's explanation felt right. "Is it too early for a Christmas present?" He started blushing fiercely. "I hope I am not being presumptuous." He was grateful for the minimally lit room. "We hardly know each other. We've only just met. Yet I feel as if I've known you forever. It all seems to fall into place. I am..." What if she did not reciprocate his feelings? He'd never be able to look her in the eyes again.

"What are you so afraid of, Aidan?" She took his hands in hers. "Your hands are icy!"

"Yes, I am afraid. That's why I am a pathetic bachelor in my 30s. I've never really been in love." He lowered his eyes, and whispered, "That is, until now. It feels like nothing I've ever felt for anyone. I am in love with you, Holly. Since our hands touched, it felt like I have found my other half. I've felt whole and enlivened. As strange as it sounds, it felt like I've always known you, and was waiting for you to come home. That's why I am now whole. I am in love with you. So much so that I want to spent the rest of my life with you. Since those crystals came into my life, I've been on a journey. One of self discovery, change for the better and, best of all, finding you. I tell you, it's those crystals!" He took something out of his pocket, and held it tightly in his hand. "I got you a Christmas present, but I cannot wait."

Holly sat, outwardly quiet, inwardly heart a-fluttering, listening to his endearing prattle. "I am in love with you, Aidan. From the moment we met. From the moment our hands touched. I knew it from that very moment. Yes, the crystals have something to do with it. Our great aunt said that they were special. That

The Snow Crystals

they would guide our life's path."

Fumbling the box open, Aidan took out the ring. "Will you accept this token of my love, Holly? I want to spend the rest of my life with you."

He could see tears glistening in her eyes. "Yes, I will, Aidan." She held out her left hand, and he slipped the ring on. "It's beautiful. Like you are, my darling."

Then he remembered. "Oh, before I forget..." Holly had pulled him down onto the sofa. "Once again, happy birthday, and I've got a birthday gift for you."

"Another gift? Oh, darling..." she didn't get any further, as Aidan kissed her again.

The two Brits continued sleeping. Pye and Crystal blinked at each other, observed their human severely entangled with who would clearly be their new additional human, blinked once again with mutually shared satisfaction, and turned their eyes to the sparkling snowflakes dancing earthwards.

CHAPTER FORTY-TWO

Donald had dropped all his purchases on the kitchen table, and made himself a mug of tea. Thanks to a useful dog-flap into the walled garden from the utility room, his ladies had been able to stay warmly and safely at home. They looked up with interest at the bags on the table.

"Sorry, girls. Almost forgot. Yes, I bought you some toys!"

In between preparing dinner, he wrapped the last gifts, and placed them under the tree. A text from Ivy that she'd be home soon, lifted his already soaring spirits even higher.

Except for his love life, his life had been pretty good until Ivy appeared. He was a successful artist, but had been noticing more and more, of late, that he needed new inspiration. No one, not even Aidan, was aware of it. People loved his work, and he easily could have continued in the same vein. But deep down,

The Snow Crystals

Donald knew that he needed and wanted to discover new terrain.

And then a gorgeous angel in the form of Ivy, and those beautiful, even magical, snow crystals had fluttered into his life. How, Donald didn't know, but a sixth sense told him that between Ivy and the appearance of the snow crystals there was a mystical connection. For since they both had come into his life, he'd become aware of heightened inspiration. Even the horrible events brought on by that mad woman could not eradicate the new beauty of his creations. With sanity having resumed in his life, he had been going at full speed.

He'd not looked at the snow crystals since before the fire. Overwhelmed by a desire to check if they were still intact and peer at their wondrous beauty, Donald went into his studio and took the box containing the crystals out of a cupboard.

He opened the box, expecting to see a feast of exquisite sparkling beauty. He blinked. Pushed his specs up his nose, and peered with surprise in the box. Except for the remains of one slowly disintegrating crystal, they were all gone. They had not melted. The inside of the box was bone dry.

A noise reached him from the other side of the house.

"I'm home, darling. Donald? Where are you?"

She was home! As he was about to close the box, he saw that the last crystal had also disappeared. All that was left was a glittering residue, which floated out of the box, scattered, sparkling in the light of the lamps, and then dissipated.

"Donald. Ah, there you are!" She rushed toward him.

343

Quickly putting down the small box, Donald enveloped Ivy in a bear-like hug.

"My precious girl. I missed you!"

Eagerly, Donald showed her his latest achievements, and sang her praises as his muse. "I don't want to sound big-headed, for I know I am a good artist. I've got the proof in the pudding. But since you came into my life... just look at it! I've never created anything like this before. I owe it all to you. It's all down to the fact that I am in love with you. So much so that I cannot imagine a life without you." Suddenly, bashfulness took over. "I hope I am not..."

"You know I love you! And I cannot imagine a life without you, either."

"My darling, wonderful, beautiful Ivy, will you do me the honour of marrying me?"

"The honour is all mine, kind sir." She giggled. Then turned serious. "Yes, I will. When shall we set the date?"

Donald pondered for a moment. Shyly, he said, "How about the sooner the better?"

"Oh, yes! Even tomorrow would be perfect."

"You're serious about that? I mean about getting married real soon."

"Yes!"

Donald groaned. "Oh hell, I'd rather be doing something else now, but I've got a dinner to finish off, or we'll be serving the other two lovebirds cold food."

"And we don't want to miss the Carol Service. Come on. There's two of us now... for the rest of our lives."

"I've got a birthday present for you."

"Another one?" Ivy laughed. "It cannot possibly top what you've just given me now."

"A ring..." Donald said shyly. "Wait, I'll go get it."

The Snow Crystals

Ivy clapped her hands in excitement. "In the meantime I'll stir the pans before something burns."

As Donald bounded elated up the stairs to his bedroom, he knew for certain that Ivy and those enigmatical crystals were connected. The crystals had disappeared at the moment that Ivy had come home. Home for good. He couldn't have been happier!

Aidan had just phoned. He and Holly would be with them in minutes. "He said he had some special news for us. He sounded so excited and happy." Donald chuckled. "Bet he popped the question."

"You think?"

"Oh, yes!"

"You've got some inside information? Do tell." She tickled Donald, who squirmed. Ticklishness was his weakness.

"You'll have to wait." He giggled. "Stop it."

Ivy was finishing setting the table, and Donald was manoeuvring a piping hot dish from the oven to the table, when the phone rang again.

"Would you please answer that, darling?" Donald placed the dish in the centre of the table.

"Good evening, the MacIntosh residence," Ivy said. Her words were drowned out, as the dogs started barking excitedly at the loud knocking on the door.

"And thus bedlam erupts." Donald rushed to the door and tore it open. Snow was dreamily floating earthwards around his friends, and turning South Woodside into a Christmas picture postcard. "Sometimes I do wish you'd use your key, mate. Hi, honey." He kissed Holly on the cheek. "Dinner's ready." He returned to the kitchen with Aidan and Holly in tow.

Ivy was still on the phone. "Sorry for the noise. The dogs are excited that our guests have arrived. ... Yes, this is the MacIntosh residence. You have the correct number. ... Yes, Donald MacIntosh's home. ... Hold on, please. Donald, darling, do you have time to come to the phone? It's your mother."

Donald's eyes widened in dismay, and he shook his head.

Thankfully, Ivy understood. "We are at the point of sitting down to dinner... One moment, please. Darling, your mother insists she has to speak to you."

With Aidan and Holly already seated, Donald was pouring wine. He sighed and held out his hand. Ivy gave him the phone.

"Yes, hello Mother. We're starting dinner, and going to the Carol Service in an hour's time. I don't really have time now. ... Oh! Right! ... Yes, I am fine, thank you. And I trust that you are, too. ... You're what? Why?" He gave a sign to his friends to serve themselves, and listened to his mother with mounting disbelief. "I see. Right. ... Sorry, Mum, but the Christmas holidays are fully planned already. ... Yes, with amongst others, Aidan. ... Mother! Please do not start that again, or I will put the phone down."

He still had not shared with Aidan his mother's nasty allegations. Would and could he ever? He listened to his mother droning on for a moment longer. The dinner he had prepared lovingly, and finished off together with Ivy, awaited.

"Mum, we're starting dinner. ... What? ... Who? ... No way, Mum! ... Please do not start that again, Mother!" Donald snarled. "I've warned you before... Mother! ... The answer remains no. Why? ... Because the very soon to be Mrs. Donald MacIntosh might have something to say about that." His statement was met with total silence. "Still there, Mother? ... Thank you, I will. Be talking soon. In fact, I'll call you tomorrow. It's a promise. Give my love to Dad."

Donald looked around the table. "Well, that shut her up! Bon appétit, all. Hope you enjoy."

He smiled with satisfaction. Life was falling into place.

"My parents arrived back home today. Still rattled from a dreadful falling out with my sister and her obnoxious hubby. Feel especially sorry for my dad. Actually, my mum, too. Anyway, I'll call them tomorrow. Unless they manage to find a last minute opening at some country house hotel, it looks like they'll be spending Christmas with us."

He smiled at Ivy. Gave her hand a kiss. Winked at Aidan, and smiled at Holly.

"Tell us your news, Aidan, me mate..." He glanced at Holly's left ring finger, as she held it up for all to see. "That's a double celebration, then!" A big happy grin on his face, Donald also held up Ivy's left hand.

EPILOGUE

CHRISTMAS EVE, ONE YEAR LATER...

Aidan couldn't help constantly staring in total wonderment and adoration at the little girl lying in his arms. She was the most exquisite little person, like his darling Holly. They were two of the most beautiful creatures he had ever seen. And that little beauty was his daughter. Would he ever come down off his cloud of sheerest bliss and happiness?

Mere weeks old, and she had him wrapped around her little finger. He'd do anything to ensure her happiness. He'd protect her with his life. He had only one regret, and that was that he had to wait so long for it all.

"Fatherhood becomes you, then?" Donald chuckled.

"It's magic. She couldn't be a sweeter little lass."

The Snow Crystals

"Little girls grow up, Aidan."

"So do little boys, me mate. Before you know it, your little rascal will be chasing the girls." Aidan grinned.

"I've no intention of informing him about the birds and the bees for a while yet."

"Unless he befriends someone like Archie... what was his last name? T... Tu... oh yeah, Tucker. Archie Tucker. Remember him?"

"He was a right little swine, wasn't he?" Donald laughed loudly. "The shame and bane of the neighbourhood. I remember his poor parents' despairing."

"The Tuckers were good people, but they really should have paid their errant son some more attention."

"Nah, he was a sly little sod. Deceived everyone. No, I'll make sure that my boy will be getting a totally different upbringing."

Ivy caught the last of the conversation as she walked into the room. "Here's your boy, darling. Your turn for doing some upbringing. He's eaten well, so he'll be sleeping like the babe he is through dinner. Not long now." She kissed Donald, smiled lovingly at Aidan. "Susan and Mike will be arriving soon. So, we're all in agreement that we'll ask them to be our babies' godparents?"

Since the babies' births, they'd been beset by the villagers' numerous hints and often, too, quite blatant requests about a possible christening of the two babies, which would be followed by the inevitable celebration. Aidan and Holly, and Donald and Ivy, had only just discussed the matter, and concluded, if only to appease their neighbours, they'd have the children christened.

"The church will be chockers." Aidan had chuckled.

"As will the pub be afterwards," Donald had added, laughing.

"That means, we'll need godparents for them," Ivy had said.

Susan and Mike, if they'd agree to it, were their first choice.

"They were witnesses at both our weddings, so..." Aidan smiled. "None better, if you ask me."

"Let's hope they'll agree." With a final smile at the men, Ivy left the room again.

Donald looked down in adoration at the precious bundle lying on his lap. "Just over a year ago, would you have believed that we'd both be besotted fathers now? We'd both be married to the most amazing and wonderful women? And both have found a happiness far beyond anything imaginable, and that which we talked about often, but always eluded us? Sometimes I have to pinch myself. Is it for real? And then I see Ivy... I touch her, just to make sure she is real... just like this little boy... Aidan, you know I often doubted it would ever happen. But look at us now!" His face shone with contentment.

"Still can't quite believe it myself, either. It all started happening when we found those crystals."

"Crazy how we never got around to talking to each other about our finds."

"Yes. Just like with you, every time I wanted to, or tried, something happened and the moment was lost." Donald glanced at the tree gracing the bay. "I now understand your obsession with snow crystals for your tree. Not quite as beautiful as the real things, but still pretty gorgeous."

"Dinner is almost ready." Ivy came into room,

The Snow Crystals

smiling broadly, wiping her hands on a towel. "Would you two darlings take our precious offspring upstairs, and do the necessary?"

Thoroughly sated, both babies were drowsy, and by all appearances they'd be asleep for several hours.

"Who would have thought that I'd be an ace at nappy changing? The thought occasionally crossed my mind, but look at me now." Aidan chuckled as he and Donald went back downstairs.

"Same here. Just over a year ago, who would have thought we'd be happily married and celebrating Christmas with the loves of our lives, and with our babies? And changing nappies."

"I wouldn't want to change a single thing!"

"Neither would I." Donald suddenly stopped on the stairs, and Aidan bumped into him. "Why have I only now thought of this?"

"What?"

Donald resumed walking down the stairs. "We're cousins. We've always been best friends and soulmates. And now we're brothers, too." He smiled broadly at Aidan.

"So we are! Merry Christmas, brother."

"You too, brother."

As they had done so often before, they embraced, and with their arms around each other went into the dining room, where their beloveds were waiting for them.

Marianne Christina Etherton parked the small, pristine, pale metallic green Clio in a garage located a short walk around the corner from her property. She took the last minute shopping out of the car, and hurried home, her footsteps imprinting in the freshly fallen powdery snow.

The snow glistened and sparkled, and reminded her of other snow crystals. They had long since disappeared. It was today a year ago exactly that she had sought solace in the beauty of the crystals, to find that they were no more. All that had been left behind had been a sprinkling of glittering residue which had disappeared before her eyes. It had been the day that the moneys Carole had so artfully managed to extract from her - under the guise that bosom buddies always shared their good fortune - had been deposited in her bank account by the solicitors.

She did not want to think about Carole anymore, but couldn't help the flashbacks that always hit her at the most unexpected moments. As she walked the short distance to her home with her shopping, the flashback hit and brought tears to her eyes. It went paired with a stab of pain. The rollercoaster of last December was a nightmare she was still recovering from. Had Carole not died in that crash, she would have been the next victim on Carole's mad murderous list.

Although she was never told of the full extent of Carole's madness, Marianne had been informed Carole had left a written legacy which had indicated that there had always been 'something wrong' with her, something that worsened with time. A time bomb waiting to explode.

"Stop it!" Marianne said out loud. It was Christmas Eve. She did not want to think about it anymore. Life had taken an amazing U-turn for her, and she had been granted a chance at happiness.

She loved her job at Trivia, and had been promoted. Life was good now.

Every time the key glided into the door lock, she

The Snow Crystals

was overwhelmed with such pride. This was her home!

It had come onto the market in the early spring, and it had been love at first sight. That love continued to grow.

The first Christmas Eve in her own home. What was not to love about the pretty little old cottage in a backwater area of town? She'd worked hard at doing it up. She'd been able to see the cottage was crying out for TLC, and all the hard work had been therapeutic to her bruised and battered soul. The postage stamp strip of garden running from the front along the side had been full of colour and flowers in the spring and summer. While the minute courtyard at the back, full of flowering potted plants, was a pretty spot to sit on a hot summer's day or evening.

She took off her coat and boots in the small porch, and entered the sitting room. The fire she had lit in the wood burner earlier on was still glowing and spreading a warm ambience. A pure white cat yawned, stretched and got up off the sofa, and came towards her.

"Hello, Snowflake." She cooed and stroked the offered head. The cat had shown up one summer's evening, and had never left again. How had she managed all that time, all those many years, without the unconditional love and companionship of a pet?

Carole had hated animals.

Marianne now knew it had been fear that had driven her to agree with everything Carole wanted. Thankfully, Carole was no more! And because of it, she could finally be who she wanted to be. No one ever called her Kristie again. Kristie had been a creation of Carole's. That was why she had adamantly declared that her name, as per her birth certificate, was Marianne Christina Etherton. And everyone now called her

Marianne. Every time she heard herself being called that, it was like a warm glow lighting up and further healing her scarred soul.

She looked around her sitting room as she had every single day since this pretty cottage had become hers.

As she had promised herself a year ago, she had a small real-life tree with traditional decorations standing by a side window. The room was warm and cosy, and this ambience continued into the kitchen diner, where she unpacked the shopping. One bag, she left unpacked for later. She filled the kettle, switched it on, and went upstairs.

She loved every square inch of her pretty bedroom and bathroom. She changed her clothes, putting on a simple yet chic top and skirt. She touched up her makeup, and brushed her short hair. The bleached, longish hair was long gone. She had a stylish short cut, dyed a muted blonde with silvery highlights. A far cry from the vulgarity Carole had forced her into. She was ready for the evening. A friendly neighbour was coming for Christmas Eve dinner later on.

Back in the kitchen, she switched on the oven where the turkey waited, made tea for herself, and took the bag into the living room.

She took out the snow crystals she had found at Trivia out of the bag, and hung them in the tree.

"Happy Christmas, Marianne! You, too, Snowflake." She hugged her cat. Her heart swelled with happiness.

THE END

Note from the author

Reviews are gold to authors! If you've enjoyed this book, would you consider rating it and reviewing it for me.
Kendra.

Future works

A Victorian Photograph (Michael, antiques dealer and author, is drawn to a woman in a Victorian photo, to discover links to an ancestor of his, which leads him into an adventure with possibly dire consequences.)
Sequels to The Snow Crystals: 1. Living Apart Together (Overcoming the trauma she suffered, Marianne builds up a new life and embraces her newfound happiness.) and 2. The Prodigal Sister (Deidre's return to the UK is hardly welcomed by her family, and least of all by her brother Donald. Would and could she ever be again like

the lovely and loved girl she once was?)

Within the Circle of Protection (The man who has appeared for years in her dreams urgently warns her not to marry Mark, and with days to the wedding Vivian does a runner, to discover that, despite her escape, she continues to be in danger.)

A Coven of Merry Widows (For Esme widowhood brings freedom, the truth and friendships)

For Beyond The Future (In the late 21st century, with too many aspects of life and society having crashed back centuries or more, David, with the help of his extended team, struggles to return a semblance of balance and normalcy, both to his own life and his beloved Britain.)

Escaping the Cult (Remembering how they got there years earlier is the first step which will lead to their escape, and reunion with a world they're not prepared for.)

Because I Am Lonely (Why do family and often friends, too, demand everlasting faithfulness to a deceased partner, thereby condemning the man or woman left behind to a lonely and loveless life?)

The Village Lost in Time (Young Adult novel - En route home, three siblings discover a seemingly uninhabited village which stood still in time, cannot be found on any map… and weirder yet, which they cannot leave.)

CONTACT

Blog: www.thewestcountryishome.wordpress.com/
Email: kendra.hale.author@gmail.com
https://www.facebook.com/kendra.hale.author
(Community page)
https://www.facebook.com/kendra.hale.100

ABOUT THE AUTHOR

For Kendra, who has lived in Canada, the USA and on the European Continent, Great Britain, or the UK, will always be home. Her love for the UK is apparent in The Snow Crystals, and her other/future books, which are all set here. Kendra's knowledge and life-long interest in the world of antiques, collectibles and such, finds its way into her writing. She writes fiction in different genres.

Paradox Book Cover Design
Patti Roberts.
E: pattiroberts7@gmail.com

Printed in Great Britain
by Amazon.co.uk, Ltd.,
Marston Gate.